LOST BOYS

Book Two of the American Nomads

N.L. MCLAUGHLIN

Printed by: Twisted Sky, LLC ISBN: 978-1-7367059-4-0

Proofreading provided by the Hyper-Speller at https://www.wordrefiner.com

Cover art provided by Meagan McLaughlin MeaganEMcLaughlin@gmail.com

Contents

To all who wander

"I went on 'The Road' because I couldn't keep away from it;
    because I hadn't the price of the railroad fare in my jeans;
    because I was so made that I couldn't work all my life on
"one same shift';
    because—well, just because it was easier to than not to."

Jack London

"Don't touch me, I'm full of snakes."

Jack Kerouac

Chapter 1

"Momma, Momma! Look at all the ants!" the blond toddler shouted, as he crouched at the edge of the narrow driveway. He picked up a stick and poked the mound.

"Colter, don't mess with those," the beautiful, young mother warned. "They bite. You'll get hurt."

Taking hold of the toddler's hand, she led him to the minivan and watched as he clambered up into his car seat. As soon as he settled, she buckled him in.

"Let's go, Dex!" she called toward the house.

A young boy of roughly eight years, same blond hair as the mom and the toddler, dashed outside. Backpack dangling off one shoulder, sneakers untied, a half-eaten wedge of toast hanging from his mouth, he skidded to a halt beside his mother, then tossed his backpack inside. With a lighthearted grin, he vaulted into the van and fastened his seatbelt.

A nostalgic smile spread across Daniel's face as he sat in an old, black Jeep, camouflaged by the vehicles that were parked along the charming, suburban street. Birds chirped in the trees while squirrels romped about, carrying nuts from one lawn to another. The delicate perfume of flowers wafted on the morning breeze.

Watching the pretty mom and her two, young children brought back a wave of recollections, of a life that now was nothing more than a dream. A time when he was the young dad leaving for work, his lovely wife accompanying him to his truck while his young son hopped about at her heels, happily chasing the squirrels who ran up and down the oak tree in the front yard. Daniel couldn't remember how many times he had to pull Finn from that tree and hand him off to Tricia.

He remembered pulling into the same driveway after a long shift at the firehouse, greeted by a somewhat older boy; still fairly young, riding his bike. At first sight of the truck, the boy beamed up at him, flashing one of the most genuine smiles Daniel had ever witnessed. There were no words to describe how much Daniel loved seeing that smile. Jumping out of the truck, he would scoop Finn up in his arms, breathing in the earthy scent of soil and that floral fabric softener Tricia loved so much. He loved that boy with every fiber of his being.

The smile faded from Daniel's face, turning into a contemptuous sneer. *Lies.*

He took another drag from his smoke, observing the minivan pull out of the driveway and roll down the street. As it passed him by, the toddler smiled and waved at Daniel, both the boy's mother and older brother, oblivious to the stranger who watched as they drove away.

Daniel had been spying on the house for the past two weeks, studying the routines of the new occupants of the home he once shared with his own family. *A lifetime ago.* He learned their routine. Every morning, the tall, athletic dad left for work. The absence of a uniform left Daniel to believe he was some sort of office hack. He cared little for those types. They were always so weak and boring.

The pretty mom, with her long, blonde hair always tied up in a messy bun, reminded him of his wife, Tricia, when she was younger. The resemblance ended with the hairstyle. Truth was, Tricia was nothing like this woman. She had no heart or soul. What she had was a darkness that consumed everything she touched. It grew inside her like a fungus, with an insatiable hunger for pain and strife.

It wasn't always that way, or at least she was much better at hiding it in the early days. Sometimes when the mood struck him, Daniel would focus real hard, and like a dream, random memories of a happier time long ago would materialize through the haze of hate and pain. A time when a young firefighter was full of hope and promise, his pretty wife seemed happy and his son was the most precious thing in the entire world.

Bullshit.

Daniel climbed out of the Jeep and leaned against the door. He took one final drag from his cigarette, then tossed it on the ground, extinguishing it with the toe of his black boot. One last glance around the street confirmed there was no one about. Setting his focus on the house, he made his way around to the side yard.

When he owned the house, the window to the laundry room was a constant on his list of things to repair. Never able to lock, Daniel tried a few remedies, but none ever worked well enough. The only way to fix the issue would have been to replace the window. He never got around to that. Standing in front of it now, he could see that the new home-owner hadn't either. He slid the window open, then slipped inside.

It being Tuesday, Daniel knew he had the house to himself until noon. The mom would drop Dex, the older boy, at school, then take Colter to his gymnastics class. After that, they would go to the park for an hour so the little guy could climb the rock wall. They would come back around noon for lunch, then the pretty mom would put the little boy down for a nap.

With plenty of time to burn, Daniel decided he would check out the home and see what the new residents had done to the place.

The scent of fabric softener and a delicate, floral perfume hung heavy in the air. The door to the laundry room opened with a resounding, sustained creak as it swung on its hinges. That was another one of those things that required fixing, but since it didn't bother him unless he was dealing with it at that moment—he never got around to it. Too easy to forget about.

The kitchen looked the same as always. Not much different. Same white cabinets. Same old, tile flooring, same old drawer pulls. *At least they changed the curtains.*

He rounded the corner into the living room. Shiny hardwood floors had replaced the old carpet. A nice upgrade for sure. Daniel stood in the center of the room and swiped his boot across the floor. This was the spot where he almost ended Tricia's wretched existence for once and for all. Just a few more seconds and he would have been free of her; but then the kid had to interfere. Daniel shoved his rage down, inhaling and exhaling until calm washed over him. Yes, replacing the old, smelly carpet with wood floors was an excellent choice. He turned and wandered down the hall toward the bedrooms.

The new owners decorated the first room with dinosaurs. A perfect setting to inspire the imagination of a young boy. When he owned this home, the original intent was that this room would belong to the second child that he and Tricia were planning to have. That never came to be, so the room turned into a catch-all for everything they accumulated over the years that they never could quite find a place for. It was good to see it being used for its initial purpose. He wondered what it would have been like if they had had a second child. Would it have changed anything? Would that second child have looked like him? Shaking his head to oust the thought, he strolled down the hall.

Running his hand along the smooth drywall, he marveled at the seamless repair. The memory of that night came rushing back. Tricia's confession that over the years, she aborted not one, but two, unborn babies, all because she would sooner die than see him happy. The rage arising from all the years of pent-up hate for the way his life turned out; for all the shattered ambitions and lies. He flexed his hand. He could almost feel the warmth of Finn's head in the palm of his hand as he smashed it into the drywall. A malevolent smirk crossed his face. *They certainly did a superb job on the repair.*

A hand-drawn warning on red construction paper hung askew on the next door "Do Not Enter" it cautioned. Daniel chuckled, then turned the doorknob and stepped inside.

The room smelled of fresh laundry with a modest hint of soil. He wondered if that was the standard scent of all little boys. Sports posters hung on the walls. Models of rockets and aircraft sat proudly on display. Honestly, the only actual difference was the color scheme. He stood in silence; waiting, for what? He didn't know. Sadness, anger, bitterness; an emotion of some sort? The days of feeling bad over everything he lost were long over. All the normal emotions had burned through him one at a time, leaving nothing more than the charred remains of hollow memories and a solemn vow for vengeance.

He spun around and stalked across the hall to the master bedroom.

The fragrant perfume of fresh blossoms in the spring hovered around the threshold. He inhaled. Such a pleasant smell. Tricia never used perfume, it made her sneeze. No, when they lived in this house, the air smelled of pine cleaner, fabric softener and whatever food she was cooking up for dinner.

The bedroom walls were a soft gray. That too was an improvement over the pale tan Tricia insisted on painting every wall in the house.

Daniel climbed on top of the bench at the foot of the bed and separated the ceiling fan from the mount. Holding the fixture with one hand, he groped around in the ceiling, searching for a cache of money he hid there. Gone. *Of course, she would remember that hiding place.* After placing the fan back in place, he climbed down, taking care to straighten the comforter. He didn't want to leave any trace he had been there. No sense in destroying the pretty mom's sense of safety and comfort in her own home.

It was safe to assume that Tricia emptied all the hiding places she knew about. Key point; the ones she knew about. He smirked and stormed back to the laundry room.

About a year before everything came crashing down, the washing machine sprung a massive leak. Water spewed out and flooded the entire room, destroying the drywall. The entire room needed to be restored. Of course, the first thing Daniel discovered when he began the demo was a small rag stuffed inside the drainage hose. Right away, he knew who was responsible, so he found his son and made sure the boy understood the error of his ways. To his credit, Finn never whined or complained. He took his beating like a man, then went right to work on the demolition of the room. He didn't even ask for any protective gear from the drywall dust. It was for the better, anyway. There was no way Daniel would have given him any.

Thinking back on it, Daniel still had to admit a small amount of respect for the kid. When confronted, Finn held his ground. He didn't cower, or run, or even lie. No, the boy stood strong and seldom ever flinched. Say what you want about the kid, he had serious backbone.

It took a full month to complete the renovations of the room. Since Daniel did all the restoration work himself, he installed an extra hiding place. One that only he would know about.

Standing in the laundry room now, Daniel pulled the washing machine away from the wall, took out his knife, and chipped away at the grout around the tiles. It came away easily. Next, he lifted four of the tiles, exposing a piece of concrete backer board. He leaned that against the wall and peered down at the metal safe tucked away inside the hole, precisely how he left it. It was a large one, with a dial combination lock. Daniel blew the dust aside, then quickly unlocked the door.

Come to papa baby. Stashed inside were all the things he would require in the event of an emergency. Five thousand dollars in cash, a fake ID and passport, a set of keys to a storage locker at the other end of town, two boxes of ammo and, the best item of all, a shiny, black revolver still wrapped in muslin cloth.

In the safe, a lone photo rested on the metal floor. Two people beamed up at him, suspended forever in time. One a young, handsome father; the other, a boy around five years old, holding up a huge catfish, flashing a toothless grin. The cheerful man in the picture was no longer recognizable to Daniel. It was as though he were staring at someone else—a stranger who only looked like him.

His hand trembled as he stared down at the image. A kaleidoscope of emotions whirled around inside. He snorted, crushed the photo into a ball, tossed it into the safe, then slammed the door shut.

After taking particular care to put the tiles back into place, Daniel slid the washer against the wall, cleaned up his mess, and made one more cursory check of the home. Once he was certain everything was exactly the way he found it, he climbed out the window and sauntered back to the old Jeep.

The next stop was a run by the storage facility to pick up the gear he had tucked away. If his memory served him correctly, the locker contained camping gear, freeze-dried food, and extra clothing. There should be at least another two thousand dollars as well. It was time for a road trip to visit Tricia. She was going to be thrilled to see Daniel. He could hardly wait to see the look on her face.

///

Chapter 2

A DELICATE SCENT OF PINE PERMEATED THE CRISP, COOL, MOUNTAIN air. Beth drew a deep breath, filling her lungs. The sound of flowing water surrounded her, creating a backdrop of white noise against the birds chirping in the treetops. She wiggled her toes in the plush carpet of grass, basking in the sensation of the cool blades against her skin. Such a gorgeous day. Standing on the edge of the forest, taking in her surroundings, Beth felt as though she and her friends were the only people on earth.

River called her over to a large, decayed tree covered in verdant, green moss.

"What am I looking for?" asked Beth.

"Porcini mushrooms," replied River. "They look like this." She handed a reddish-brown mushroom to Beth, who spun it around in her fingers, examining the details.

"You wanna make sure it's firm and not rotted," explained River. "No black spots. You also wanna make sure the underside is yellow-brown, not green. That means it's past the "eat by" date." She smiled.

Beth poked the top with her finger, feeling the slight stickiness of the cap. She was never a mushroom person; they always seemed peculiar to her.

"I don't know," she said. "What if I accidentally pick one that's poison or something?"

"You'll be okay." River patted her on the shoulder. "Just look for this type." She held up the mushroom. "And stay away from the ones with red caps and white dots. Those are poisonous."

"They are?" responded Beth. She shook her head. "You see, that's why I stay away from mushrooms."

River chuckled. "There's nothin' to worry about. These are all fine." She moved around the base of the hollowed-out tree. "Here's a few!"

Beth was more than happy to help River gather mushrooms, but she had no intention of eating any of them. Just the thought of eating the horrible things made her stomach turn.

A few yards away, Cash shouted, "Huckleberries! A whole bunch of them."

Now that sounded like something Beth would like. She and River ran over to Cash, who was kneeling in front of a small bush. He held up a hand full of purple berries.

"They look like tiny blueberries," said Beth.

"Kinda," replied Cash, as he popped one into his mouth. He offered them to her. "Go ahead; they're delicious."

Beth took one and apprehensively popped it into her mouth. The sweet flavor exploded on her tongue. "I could totally eat these all day long," she sighed.

"Well," warned River, "let's save some for dinner."

After collecting as many as her hands could carry, Beth placed her haul with the rest of the food they gathered so far. She dumped the berries in a large container, then brushed her hands on her thighs, wiping away the purple juice.

In the river, Finn and Teague stood on slippery rocks. The cold water swirled and churned as it rushed past them, spilling down the waterfall to the pristine lake below.

"Hold it steady!" shouted Teague. He wrapped the net around his arm, closing the distance between himself and Finn. The mesh spasmed and twisted in their grasp as a fish attempted to break free.

"This one's gotta be big," said Teague.

"It is! I can see it!" exclaimed Finn. The net jerked, causing him to slip off the rock. "Now hurry and get it before it works its way loose."

After a moment of struggling, Teague reached into the water and pulled out a two-foot-long rainbow trout. He held it by the gills and raised it high above his head.

"Yeah!" he shouted. "Now that's what I'm talkin' about!"

Finn let out a low whistle. "Holy shit, that's huge!"

Teague kissed the fish and tossed it to shore, where it landed at Beth's feet.

"It's so pretty," she said, peering down at the pearly scales shimmering like rainbow glitter. "It's almost too beautiful to eat." She flashed a sly smirk at Finn. "But it's gonna look even better all grilled up and on my plate."

Finn responded with an enthusiastic thumbs up.

"That's my girl," quipped Zac, as he looked down at the thrashing fish, its mouth opening and closing as it struggled to breathe. "Man, we are gonna eat good tonight. I can already taste it."

Beth pulled out her phone and focused the camera on herself, then she hit record.

"So here we are on this gorgeous morning in the mountains, catching our food for the day," she declared, smiling as she panned around the area to show off the items they gathered. She aimed the camera at the water and focused on Finn and Teague.

"How's the water boys?"

"It ain't warm," replied Finn.

"It's cold, cold," said Teague.

Beth zoomed. "What do you think the temperature is?"

Teague shrugged and glanced at Finn. "I don't know. What do you think?"

"Why the fuck you askin' me?" asked Finn, then he smirked and replied, "I'm gonna guess it's probably around forty-five degrees, give or take."

Still recording, Beth leaned over and stuck her hand in the water. "Brrr, yeah, it's pretty cold."

She focused on the duo, wrapping the net around their arms. They plunged it down into the water.

"Saving that tennis net from the trash was a pretty cool idea, Finn," said Beth. "In fact, it's one of the few ideas you've had that didn't end up nearly killin' someone." She giggled.

"Hur der hur," responded Finn sarcastically, raising a middle finger in the air.

A moment later, Finn held up another large trout, its wet scales glinting in the afternoon sunlight. "One more for the feast," he announced, as he tossed it aground.

"I think we're good," said Zac, peering down at the catch.

"Nah," replied Finn, "One more. That way there's one for each of us," he said, as he repaired a break in the net.

"You're just having fun doin' this," said Teague, grinning at him.

Finn smiled and nodded in agreement. "Nothin' like the fresh, mountain air and cool, clean water to rejuvenate the soul."

Teague chuckled. "Or freeze your balls off. Speaking of which, let's wrap this up." He smirked. "The boys are gettin' a little too cold for comfort."

The net spasmed; another large catch.

"Heads up! Incoming!" shouted Teague, as he tossed another fish onto the riverbank. It flew past Beth, scarcely missing her head.

"Hey!" she exclaimed.

"Beth, can you bring that over here?" asked Zac, from a few feet away.

Not wishing to pause recording, Beth scanned the area for some place to put her phone. She settled on a cluster of rocks near Zac, just far enough back to take in the whole meadow and record everyone. She propped the phone up on a small boulder, using smaller rocks for support, then walked back to get the fish.

The fish was still flopping around uncontrollably. As she reached out, it lurched and thrashed wildly, making Beth jump backward and squeal.

"Come on, Beth, don't be a pussy. Pick up the fish," prodded Finn.

"Just shove your thumb in its mouth and grip it by the gills," added Teague.

"But its mouth is opening and closing," she protested. Not wishing to do what Teague suggested, she attempted to lift the fish off the ground with both her hands holding onto its body. The fish thrashed violently in her hands, wiggling free and dropping to the ground, nearly landing in the water.

"If that fish gets away," warned Finn, "you're standing in this ice bath until you catch another one to replace it."

"Come on, Beth, you got this," encouraged Zac.

Beth reached down again and, this time, did precisely as Teague suggested. She made certain she had a firm grip on the fish before lifting it off the ground. Holding the fish high, she turned to Finn and stuck out her tongue.

He responded with silent applause.

Careful to maintain her grip, Beth carried it over to Zac and gently set it on the ground, where it remained quietly opening and closing its mouth.

"And with that, it looks like we got all we need," said Teague. He turned to Finn. "Let's get out of this cold water."

Finn took a step to the side and stumbled. Losing his balance, he lost his grasp on the net, dropping it into the water. The current carried it across the river, coming to rest among a thick cluster of reeds.

Reluctantly, both Finn and Teague waded knee-deep, through the icy water, to recover the net.

"Woo, that's cold," said Teague, shivering.

Finn grinned impishly. "Got some shrinkage goin' on there?"

"Mais la!" replied Teague. "My legs are so chilled right now, I'm afraid to look and see the effect it's havin' on all my extremities."

Finn laughed.

"Y'all hear that?" called Zac.

Beth perked up her ears. She heard nothing but the white noise of the river flowing.

"I don't—," said Cash.

Zac placed a finger to his lips. "Shhh."

Beth thought she heard a faint rustling of leaves deep in the wood, but she couldn't see what was making the noise. The sound grew louder as it seemed to get closer.

A twig snapped, followed by more rustling. She stared into the woods, this time certain of the direction the sound emanated from. A black shadow moved among the brush. Branches swayed back and forth as the mysterious animal crept closer.

What is it? Beth squinted her eyes.

A small, furry head peeped out from a shrub.

Beth could barely contain herself. "Aw, look! It's a baby bear!" she whispered.

Ignoring the humans, the baby bear waddled into the clearing.

"Look at how cute he is," exclaimed Beth. To her bewilderment, none of the others seemed to notice the cub. Instead, they all remained still, staring into the forest, listening for something.

"What are y'all doing?" she asked.

Zac held up his hand. "That cub's too young to be out alone."

The cub let out the most adorable attempt at a roar Beth had ever heard as it stood up on its hind legs and smelled the air. She giggled. It went down on all fours, then waded across the river and ambled over to the pile of fresh fish lying exposed on the ground.

"Hey! Pshh!" cried Finn, "Get away from there! Go on! Get out!" He splashed through the water toward the little bear, swinging his arms to scare it away.

Undaunted, the cub buried its fuzzy little face into the pile of fish.

"Dammit!" Finn ran up behind the cub and kicked, landing a blow on its hind end. The little bear gave out a yelp and skidded to the side.

As if on cue, something big crashed through the forest, heading in their direction. Beth stood frozen in place as a giant black bear burst into the clearing.

"Finn, get back!" shouted Teague.

The mama bear ran to her cub. After a brief inspection, she stood up on her haunches and gave out a mighty roar.

Beth's heart was about to pound right out of her chest. A mere fifteen feet separated her from the beast. The bear took no heed of her;

instead, it dropped on all fours and charged straight for the two humans who were closest to her—Finn and Teague.

"Shit!" shouted someone.

Beth watched them wade back across the water and scramble up the nearest tree. The trunk moved and swayed from their weight as they climbed. More than once, a branch snapped off in their hands. She wanted to scream, but her throat constricted, rendering her mute. She could scarcely catch her breath. Her feet were like two blocks of concrete, cementing her to the spot.

Somewhere behind her, Cash hollered, "Get up! Get into the trees now!"

She didn't even hear him approach, but suddenly, Zac took hold of her arm and dragged her over to a thick, tall tree. He got down on one knee and cupped his hands.

"Climb! Now!" he ordered.

Beth stepped in his hand and pulled herself up on the first branch. Chest heaving with the exertion, she paused only to be prodded along by Zac, who was climbing close behind. She reached up and grabbed the next limb, struggling to lift herself, quickly realizing her arms were not strong enough. Panic rose up from her belly. Zac's hand pressed against her bottom, lifting her high enough to wrap her legs around the branch.

He went up past her to the next row of branches, then reached down. "Come on."

Beth took his hand, and once again, he lifted her to safety on a branch just opposite him. Able to breathe again, she glanced around the clearing.

River and Cash sat high in a tree not too far from the edge of the waterfall.

Across the stream, Finn and Teague clung precariously to the thin trunk of the young tree. Below them, the mama bear paced, occasionally rearing up on her hind legs and pushing the tree with the full force of all her massive weight.

Finn swung a dead branch at the mama. "Get away!" he shouted. The stick connected with the bear's head. This only enraged the animal.

She roared and shoved harder, causing the tree to rock violently back and forth.

Undaunted, Finn jabbed the branch toward the head of the bear. His stab landed right in the bear's left eye, causing her to drop to the ground, shaking her head. A moment later, she gave out one angry roar and pounced upon the tree with more conviction than before.

With each thrust, the sound of splintering wood resonated over the din. The roots of the tree pulled up from the earth. Finn and Teague scrambled farther up the trunk. Weakening under their combined weight, the tree leaned toward the ground.

The bear shoved—the sound of cracking wood punctuated her growls. The tree was falling.

A great snap reverberated throughout the clearing. The tree had finally buckled under the weight of the mama bear. As it fell on its side, the duo let themselves drop.

Beth held back a scream as she watched the bear charge at her friends. Finn and Teague ran full force to the edge of the waterfall, and without hesitation, they launched themselves into the air. Arms and legs bicycling, they disappeared from view.

The giant creature stopped and bellowed angrily as she bounced up and down on the rocky cliff.

Zac called out, "Talk to me, Cash! Do you see them?"

Cash climbed high enough to peer over the edge of the waterfall. He shook his head. "Nothing yet. There're two spots in the water where they went in, but so far, nothing. They haven't come up yet."

Her quarry now completely out of her grasp, the mama bear turned and ran toward a new target.

Clinging to the tree trunk, Beth stared in horror as the giant beast splashed across the water, heading right for Cash and River.

Too busy fretting about the fate of Finn and Teague, none of the others noticed.

Cash held up his hand. "Hold on!" he called out. "I see Finn!"

"Teague?" asked Zac. The worry in his voice punctuated Beth's fear.

Cash shook his head. "Finn just dove under. I think he's looking for him."

The mama bear hit the tree. It was much too big for her to knock down, so after a moment of standing on her haunches, she went down on all fours and paced, stopping off and on to let out a fierce roar of rage.

"He's got him!" shouted Cash, startling not only Beth and the others, but the bear as well. "Finn's dragging him to shore now."

"How bad does he look?" asked Zac, more nervous than ever.

The more concerned he sounded, the more anxious Beth became. She wanted to cry.

"I can't tell from here," replied Cash. "He's not moving, and it looks like there's blood on his head."

The bear roared, raised up on her hind legs, and began furiously pushing on the tree. Cash and River held tight to the trunk.

"Beth," said Zac, his voice emitting a level of calm that Beth did not possess.

Unable to force any words from her lips, she stared back at him.

"Listen to me," he continued. "I need to distract the bear."

Tears welling up in her eyes, she opened her mouth to speak.

"Shh, shh, listen. I'm gonna be the decoy and lead the bear away. As soon as we're out of sight, I want you to hit the ground and run toward Cash and River. Can you do that?"

Beth nodded, trembling so hard her lips quivered.

"Good. Stay with them. As soon as I can, I'll backtrack and meet up with everyone at the camp. You got it?"

Tears spilled down her cheeks.

Zac smiled. "You got this," he reassured. He placed a hand to the side of his mouth and called out, "Cash! I'm gonna play decoy!"

"The hell you are!" shouted River in response.

Zac shook his head. "We got no other choice."

A round of heated chatter emanated from the other tree. Beth could not make out what they were talking about, but River didn't like any of it.

Cash shouted back, "What's your plan?"

"I'll run into the woods and get the mama bear to follow me!" replied Zac.

River's response came quickly, "That's a dumb idea."

"We ain't got another option," responded Zac. "If I don't do this, y'all could be next. Not to mention whatever help Teague needs right now."

More heated discussion ended with River turning her face away.

Cash called over, "What do you need us to do?"

"Just get down there and help them. I'll meet y'all back at the camp!" Zac turned to Beth. "You ready?"

"Uh, huh."

"All right, I'm gonna count to three, then go for it!" he said loud enough so everyone could hear. "Wish me luck."

Zac took a couple of deep breaths, then dropped softly to the ground. He bounced on the balls of his feet and waved his arms above his head. "Yo mama bear, come and get me!" He whistled and hurled rocks.

The bear bellowed, then charged.

Kicking up bits of grass, Zac peeled off, running straight into the woods, taking both bears with him.

Chapter 3

"Finn, get back!" shouted Teague, fear resonated in his tone.

The giant black bear burst forth from the woods, rearing up on two legs. She let out a thunderous roar, then went down on all fours and ran over to her cub, who was pawing indignantly at the air. She nudged him gently, sniffing and examining the baby. Satisfied with the condition of her cub, she turned and charged at Finn.

Finn glanced around. The only place to go was up and the only tree close enough was on the other side of the river. Void of options, both he and Teague scrambled through the water and up the slender trunk. He reached out and grabbed hold of a branch, only to have it snap off in his hand. Tossing that aside, he reached for a second. The tree swayed with their movement, so much so that he feared the whole thing would tilt sideways.

Across the meadow, the others were shouting incoherently.

A branch broke off in Teague's hands. Luckily, Finn was close enough to catch hold of his arm and keep him from falling.

On the ground below, the mama bear bellowed as she paced around the tree. She let out one more roar, then planted her giant paws against the trunk and gave a massive shove; then another and another. With each thrust, the entire tree quivered and shook, threatening to snap and toss both Finn and Teague onto the ground.

Finn knew the tree was short-lived under these circumstances. They had to do something. He broke off another dead branch and swung it hard, hoping to at least get her to stop shaking the tree.

"Stop it!" shouted Teague. "She's just getting more pissed."

Undaunted, Finn continued to swing, occasionally hitting; sometimes missing. The sole constant was that with each swing, the bear became more enraged. The tree continued to shake and tremble.

"Drop the damn branch!" ordered Teague.

Finn ignored him. He held the branch like a spear and jabbed, aiming for the bear's eye. *Got it!* The bear dropped to the ground and swung her head from side to side. She gave out a bloodcurdling roar that made the tiny hairs on the back of Finn's neck stand on end. His heart thumped against his rib cage.

The enraged bear stood on her hind legs and, with the full weight of her massive body, she shoved the tree. The sound of splintering wood resonated over the noise, accompanied by a vibration deep inside the trunk.

Both Finn and Teague scrambled higher. The ground below moved and swelled with each powerful thrust as the roots broke free from the soil.

"This is bad, bad!" said Teague.

"We gotta jump!"

Teague glanced over at the edge of the waterfall. "Looks like we have no other choice than to go for a swim."

The tree buckled and swayed. A hollow snap erupted from inside the trunk.

The bear shoved with more vigor, seemingly aware that she was winning.

Finn clung tight to the trunk as the tree made its final plunge toward the ground. Legs dangling, he dropped onto the soft grass and charged for the edge of the cliff, then launched himself over, vaguely aware of Teague in his periphery.

For a moment he was flying, cool air flowing through his sweat-soaked hair, then his feet hit the water. The ice-cold liquid swallowed him whole, wrapping him in a chilly blanket from head to toe. The entire world disappeared, the only sound was that of his heart beating in his chest. Finn turned his face up toward the light and swam, breaching the surface.

Surrounded by calm water, Finn spun around in search of Teague— there was no sign of him, anywhere.

"Teague!" he called out. The only response was the sound of the waterfall. Panic took hold. He inhaled, held his breath and dove, swimming deep into the icy abyss.

Eyes open wide, he swam in the direction he believed Teague would be. A faint yellowish glow, surrounded by a crimson cloud, came into view. He reached out, grasping handfuls of water, pulling himself closer until finally, he could get hold of Teague's arm. A moment later, he breached the surface, an unconscious Teague in tow.

Finn checked for a pulse; it was faint but at least there was one.

As soon as he reached shore, Finn took hold of Teague under the arms and dragged him out of the water onto the soft sand.

"Come on, open your eyes," he begged, gently tapping Teague's face.

Nothing. Time stood still as panic swelled deep inside him. He rolled Teague to his side and watched as water poured from his mouth. So much water.

Please be okay. Please, be okay.

Fighting back tears, Finn lay Teague on his back and gently breathed into his mouth.

Come on, come on.

A violent cough caused Teague's entire body to spasm. He turned to his side and purged even more water from his lungs. Climbing up on all fours, a trickle of blood streamed across his face. He heaved and gagged as his lungs gasped for air.

Relief washed over Finn.

"Hoo lawd!" gasped Teague. "That was a close one."

Words remained trapped in Finn's throat. Unable to respond, he merely nodded.

Teague smiled. "Let's not do something like that again. Sound good?"

Finn chuckled, his heart finally feeling light again. He leaned close and kissed Teague on the side of his head.

The sound of snapping twigs drew their attention to the hillside. Fearful that the mama bear followed them, Finn stood up, ready for another confrontation. Grabbing a fallen tree limb, he stepped closer to the trees, squinting his eyes to see what was barreling toward him at such a rapid pace. His pulse calmed as soon as he realized it was Cash and the others.

"You okay?" asked Cash.

Finn nodded.

"Good. Good," said Cash, "you had me worried there." He nodded toward Teague. "He okay?"

"Yeah," replied Finn. "He's good."

"Good, good," replied Cash. He clasped a hand on Finn's shoulder and leaned close. "How about next time you leave the damn bear alone," he hissed. "Think you can do that?"

Finn glanced over at Teague and nodded, then he looked around, noting the others. "Where's Zac?" he asked.

"Probably still running through the woods with that bear on his ass," replied Cash. "He got the unfortunate task of playing decoy. We're supposed to meet him at the campsite."

"Oh shit," said Finn.

"You get to take the heat for that one, my brother," replied Cash. "That shit show is all yours."

Finn nodded. "Hopefully he'll be all worn out by the time he gets back."

Cash chuckled. "Never underestimate Zac's desire to beat someone's ass when they do something stupid." He glanced over at Teague, then back at Finn. "If you both are okay, let's get back to camp."

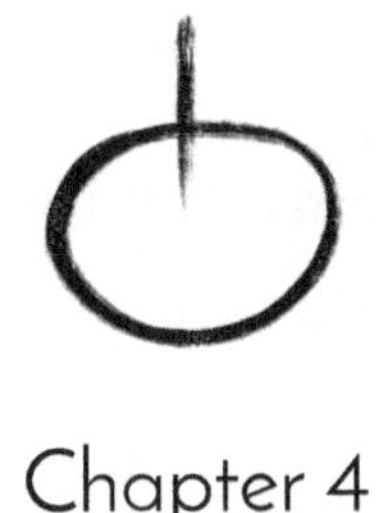

Chapter 4

Twigs snapping underfoot, Zac ran through the woods. Behind him; the persistent pounding of the bear's loping gait prodded him to keep moving. Careful to avoid stumbling on a hidden log or falling into a random hole, he plowed through the brush. Saplings reached out with their wispy tendrils, slapping him in the face. The earthy perfume of decaying pine needles burst from the soil with each stride.

How long is she going to chase after me? He must have run three miles already; surely, she was tiring.

Zac was physically fit, and he could hold his own when he needed to run, but long distance was not his thing. His legs grew tired, and his lungs burned; he wasn't certain how much longer he could run, but he knew he had no intention of going out by a bear attack.

The crashing noise was closer now; the mama bear was advancing on him. Poor judgment overtook him, and he glanced back, just long enough to lose sight of the ground in front of him. His foot snagged on a lichen-covered log buried among rotting leaves. The next thing he knew, he was plunging down a steep incline, rolling over tiny seedlings and soft ferns, kicking up a cloud of fresh dirt.

He came to a stop at the edge of a rocky creek bed, banging his skull against a large rock. Adrenaline forced him back to his feet and into the ankle-deep water. He splashed across to the other side and listened.

Birds chirped, wind rustled through the trees, the water gurgled at his feet—no sign of the bear. He peered up at the top of the hill. The bear stood, sniffing the ground, seemingly reluctant to make the trek down the hillside in pursuit of her quarry. She huffed and bellowed as she pawed at the soil, then turned and retreated, leaving behind the peaceful sounds of the forest.

"WOO! Hell yeah!" shouted Zac, his voice reverberating off the hillside.

Once his heart settled down in his chest, he knelt down by the water and washed the dirt and forest debris from his face. Hair-thin scrapes stung when his salty fingers swept over them. A thin tear spread across his jeans just above the kneecap, red blood stained the denim; he could feel the sticky, cool sensation of it running down his calf. It wasn't too bad. Painful, yes—debilitating, no. He'd be able to make it back to camp, though he was going to have to take it a little slow.

The physical exertion, coupled with the sudden crash of adrenaline, was taking its toll on him. He leaned back onto the spongy, forest floor and looked up at the pale, blue sky through the trees. Zac closed his eyes and let the gurgling sound of the water lull him into a light nap.

He awakened to the sound of gently rustling leaves. Something furry brushed against his hand. Startled, Zac bolted up only to find a large marmot staring up at him. The little creature rose on its haunches and smelled the air. It waddled closer, sniffing and prodding the ground, climbing right up on his lap.

"I got nothing to share with ya, little guy," said Zac, holding out his hands. He watched as the little animal sniffed around, then clambered down and disappeared into the forest.

Alone again, Zac peered up through the trees; the sky had a rosy glow. The sun would set soon; if he had any hope of getting back to camp before sundown, he had better get started.

When he set off running from the bear, he made it a point to head straight west, knowing that their camp was east of their position. If he remained true to his bearings, all he had to do was head east, and he would come to the river; from there, it would only be another quarter mile to the camp. The problem was when he fell down the hill; he lost all sense of direction. He peered up at the sky, hoping to see even the slightest variation in color; a darker shade would give him a sense of the sun's position. There wasn't much to go by, but he thought the sky was a little redder toward the hill. He examined the base of the trees, hoping the adage was true that moss only grew on the northern side of trees.

Zac looked up at the hillside. It was going to be a steep climb back up to the top. *It's a damn miracle I didn't bust nothing on my way down.*

He wiped his palms on his thighs and began his ascent.

Soft soil crumbled in his grasp, cascading down along the hillside, creating tiny rockslides. The only substance that Zac could take hold of was the millions of roots sticking out like cat whiskers. Pulling and climbing, he silently willed the roots to hold; he didn't want to fall down the hill again.

When he arrived at the top, he allowed himself a celebratory break. His knee throbbed, probably from the soil and debris that was no doubt buried deep inside the wound. The gritty dirt had rubbed his fingertips raw. Zac chuckled to himself as he took stock of his current situation.

Time was not on his side. The sun would not wait for him to get back to his friends. On the upside, all he had to do was follow the wide swath of destruction made by himself and the bear earlier. He found a sturdy branch for both a weapon and a hiking stick, then began the slow, arduous trek back through the woods.

The welcome scent of fire wafted through the trees; he was close. The sky above had gone completely dark, littered with a blanket of tiny, white lights. The light of the moon helped Zac keep true to his path.

Up ahead, through the forest, a slight, red-orange glow flickered; he made it.

River was the first to reach him. Wrapping her gentle arms around his neck, she hugged him tightly. "Boy, if you ever pull something like that again, I will end you." She stepped back to look him in the eyes for emphasis.

Zac laughed. "Don't worry, I have no intention of ever doin' anything like that again."

"Come here," said Cash, as he pulled Zac close and hugged him. "You had us worried."

"Had to run a little longer than I originally thought I'd need to," replied Zac, with a wry smile. "That mama bear wasn't too happy. She did not wanna give up." He nodded toward Teague. "How're you? Last I heard, you went down and didn't come back up."

Teague smiled. "It's all good. I'm still breathin'."

Zac stopped in front of Finn. "How about you? You okay" he asked.

Finn nodded and said, "Yeah, I'm fi—"

Mid-sentence, Zac hauled off and punched Finn in his abdomen, causing him to lurch forward, one hand holding his stomach, the other holding his knee for support as he gasped for air.

Zac leaned close and whispered, "That's for messin' with that goddamn bear." He knelt down on his undamaged knee so he could be eye level with Finn. "If you ever do something stupid like that again, something that could hurt any of the others—I will beat your ass into next year. We clear?"

Finn nodded.

"Good." Zac smiled and patted Finn on the shoulder. He stood up and glanced over at the fire. "What's for dinner? I'm starving."

Chapter 5

THE MID-MORNING SUN RADIATED WARMTH UPON HER SKIN, CREATING A delightful contrast to the brisk mountain air that billowed through the woods. Beth breathed in then exhaled slowly; fall was on its way; it was good that they were heading south. She took in the forest's beauty all around her; never in a million years would she have imagined she would love being in the backcountry so much.

So many changes had taken place in her life in such a brief time. Since leaving home several months ago, Beth had become accustomed to the rigors of nomad-style travel; by no means a pro, she could certainly hold her own. All the hiking had pushed her body to develop lean muscle, so carrying her backpack for great distances was no longer a challenge.

Gone forever was the timid, teenage girl, in her place a bold and competent, young woman. Everything was so much better for Beth. Even her online following had increased well beyond anything she could have ever imagined. People from all over the world followed her. They shared her images and videos, extending her reach even further every day. In the eyes of many, she was a trailblazer, someone they praised and wished they could be like. They told her this regularly.

Beth delighted in their praise. She was more popular than in her wildest dreams.

Stepping through the tree line, she entered an immense green meadow where tall grass swayed to the cadence of the breeze. A musical giggle carried on the wind from River and Cash, who were walking several yards ahead. They had such a natural vibe between them. Beth wondered if there would ever come a time when they would be honest about their true feelings for one another.

Way up in front, practically out of sight, Finn and Teague trudged along; always in their own world, they seldom ever hiked with the rest of the group.

Beth slowed her pace, waiting for Zac to come up alongside her.

"How much farther do you think?" she asked.

Zac peered up at the sky as though it provided some clue to answer her question. "I'm gonna guess another five miles or so." He plucked a long stalk of grass and popped the end into his mouth, letting the rest dangle from his lips.

"After that?" Beth prompted.

"Once we get to Grand Junction, we'll catch a ride to Denver, then head south thru Pueblo. Not sure exactly, but I think we're set to meet up with Bells, D.B., and Max in Trinidad. The goal from there is to work our way south and west toward Phoenix."

Since the memorial, Beth had spoken little with Bells, D.B., and Max. Of course, she interacted with them on the server periodically, but nothing memorable. Max was always so lighthearted, whereas Bells was a more sarcastic version of that. D.B. seemed moody, as though he cared little for greenies. Insecurity reared its ugly head. Would they hate her or like her? Was she going to say or do something that would embarrass her in front of them? For all she knew, they could be laughing at her already. She sincerely hoped that this little meetup would not end up being another occasion where she felt out of place— like an intruder at a family reunion.

"Don't sweat it," said Zac. "They're all great folks. You'll get along with 'em just fine."

His statement stunned Beth. "U-um," she sputtered, at a complete loss for words.

Zac chuckled, then removed the grass stalk from his mouth. "Well, it's clear you're worried. And I'm tellin' you there's no need. You're gonna love them, and they'll adore you. Trust me." He winked, popped the stalk back in, and chewed.

"How do you know what I was thinking?" Beth demanded, her tone far more petulant than she wanted. She secretly hoped he didn't pick up on that—but she knew better. One thing Zac was excellent at was reading between the lines. He knew what you were thinking without you even needing to say a word. Sometimes it was cool, while other times, infuriating. At that moment, it was embarrassing. She waited for his response.

He snickered and sighed as he peered up to the sky with that southern boy "lawd, help me" expression of his. "Everybody has some sort of tell," he explained. "Something that gives away what's goin' on in their heads. Some are easier to read than others." He grinned at her. "When you get worried, your forehead gets all wrinkly, and you get this little line right between your eyebrows." He tossed the piece of grass and snatched another one. "I also know you. I know you fret a lot about what other people think of you. You want them to like you." He shrugged. "So, it only stands to assume that what would worry you would be the prospect of meeting up with new people and what their judgment of you would be." He paused, then flashed an amused smirk. "So, did I nail it? Or what?"

Beth shoved him. It was like pushing against a stone wall. "No," she declared flatly. "Well, maybe, but not exactly," she confessed.

He laughed and nudged her playfully with his shoulder. "Beth, you got nothing to worry about."

Zac was perhaps the most authentic person of anyone Beth had ever met. If he declared it was going to be okay, then it would be fine. She chuckled, willing herself to relax, letting her thoughts wander as she imagined how much fun Phoenix was going to be.

A sharp whistle called out from up ahead; Beth and Zac caught up with the others at the edge of a serpentine road that snaked its way down the mountain. Across the pavement, a startled doe loped into the wood, her two fawns in tow. A group of motorcycles rolled by, followed by a large white truck. Beth and the others waited for the vehicles to pass, then they made their descent, following the road into town.

The town was a picture-perfect postcard. Shops lined both sides of the street, providing an extensive array of t-shirts, nick-knacks, patches, and trinkets. Tourists bustled about on the sidewalks, hopping from shop to shop, carrying sacks filled with all the goodies they found.

The mouth-watering aroma of cinnamon wafted heavily in the air. Beth inhaled, her belly rumbled. She searched around for the source of the enticing scent. "Who wants to come in with me?" she asked loudly as she nodded toward a small pastry shop.

"I was just thinking the same thing," said River. "Anyone else interested?"

Teague pointed across the street to a wooden bench sitting under a tall Aspen tree. "We'll let y'all choose something for us. We're claiming that bench." Without another word, he and Finn crossed the road.

"Get somethin' for me," said Zac. "I need to find a knife. I'll meet up with y'all when I'm done." He turned and strolled down the side-walk, disappearing inside a hardware store.

"Looks like that leaves us," said Cash, grinning. He stepped between River and Beth, holding his arms out. The trio hooked arms and sauntered into the shop.

A tiny bell atop the antique, wooden door announced their entry. As it closed behind them, the little bell rang a second time. A large, middle-aged woman rose behind the counter. Her smile was radiant and friendly. "Good afternoon. You're just in time; we close in about ten minutes. That means whatever you choose will be 50 percent off."

The sweet aroma of sugar blended with cinnamon, and chocolate permeated the air. The old wood floor creaked under her feet with each step. Beth approached the counter. "Why is that?" she inquired.

"We make our goodies fresh every morning," replied the woman.

"Some, we sell to local shops, the rest we sell here. At the end of each day, whatever remains, we send over to the food pantry in town."

"That's super sweet of you," said River.

The woman flashed a prideful smile. "A community can only thrive if we all work together, helping one another out when needed." She held out a wicker tray loaded with samples of various baked goods. "Go on, try some samples before you decide."

The hungry trio dove right in. Rich chocolate cake smothered in decadent chocolate icing. Cinnamon buns with smooth cream cheese icing. Carrot cake with tiny slivers of fresh carrot covered in a sweet cream cheese frosting. It was all so tasty. Beth had a hard time figuring out which one she preferred most. Based on the reactions of Cash and River, they were suffering the same issue.

In the end, they opted for a mixed box of samples of every delicacy the shop offered.

Across the street, Finn and Teague sat perched atop the back of the bench, heads together, deep in conversation.

Having had her fill in the shop, Beth left her friends under the aspen tree, and wandered off toward the bookshop nearby. Paperbacks and hardcovers from authors she had never heard of adorned the display in the giant window. A lead sculpture of a giant bullfrog propped open the heavy, wood door. A unique bouquet of new books and sage wafted out onto the sidewalk, enticing her to come in.

She sauntered inside, then down the travel aisle, past books about exotic locales from Belize to Thailand. Around the corner, she found history books and biographies. These never appealed to her; she scrunched her nose and turned down another aisle. After strolling down each row, perusing a book here and there, Beth made her way back to the front of the store and out onto the street. The others were still busy at the bench—Zac was nowhere in sight. Not quite ready to join the group, she strolled farther down the street.

Every shop she passed contained variations of the same items. T-shirts, shot glasses, magnets, postcards, and posters. Tourists milled around, sifting through the offerings, all seeking a special item to remind them of their trip.

Beth recalled a vacation her family took to Port Aransas when she was younger. A giant shark sculpture adorned the entrance to a surf shop. As her parents entered through the front door, both she and Tomas giggled and ran up the ramp that led through the mouth of the shark. Entering the store, a blast of cool air greeted them. It was a significant change from the hot sun outside. Beach music played out from the speakers on the wall. Her mom helped her pick out a T-shirt while Tomas opted for a boogie board. She smiled as she recalled how she and Tomas posed inside the gaping mouth of the shark, both children pretending to be scared as their parents laughed and took a picture.

As soon as they got home, Beth's mom put that silly photograph in a frame adorned with mermaids and seashells. She placed it on the mantel, where it stayed for years until the night Tomas flew into a rage and hurled it across the room, where it crashed into the wall and shattered into hundreds of pieces.

Beth remembered her mom weeping as she knelt on the floor, picking up the broken pieces.

A pang of regret stabbed at her heart. She hadn't thought about her parents in a long while. Beth wondered how they were doing. Were they happy? Were they angry at her for leaving? Had she broken their hearts the way Tomas had? All these thoughts made her sad. That was the last thing she wanted to feel. Sweeping aside her sadness, she opened her phone and skimmed through the new comments on her posts. Soon after, taking advantage of the free Wi-Fi, she uploaded her latest video. She could hardly wait to see what her followers thought.

Chapter 6

THE PALE, BLUE COTTAGE SAT IN THE CENTER OF THE STREET, surrounded by a rainbow of identical, pastel-colored homes. Palm trees lined the sidewalk, each house adorned with similar flowering shrubs. Such a picturesque neighborhood. Tricia always said she wanted to live on the coast one day.

Daniel sat in his Jeep, smoking a cigarette and sipping lukewarm coffee while poring over the contents of a large manila envelope on his lap. It cost him a good sum of money and a lot more time than he wanted, but his guy was finally able to locate Tricia. All in all, it was money and time well spent. Looking over the contents of the report, Daniel had to hand it to the detective. He did his job well, leaving no stone unturned. Say what you will; no one can sleuth better than ex-cops—especially crooked ex-cops.

When he first got out of prison, Daniel hit a roadblock in his search for his ex-wife. After exhausting all his options, he wasn't sure he could find her. The woman had disappeared like a ghost; she just ceased to exist one day, leaving behind no trail to follow. He had to hand it to her; she did an exceptional job covering her tracks. However, his connections paid off. *Who knew spending time in prison could be a positive thing?* His former cellmate hooked him up with an ex-cop he knew, and sure enough, the detective found her. No longer, Tricia, she had changed her name to Melody. That she chose that name, of the millions of other options possible, only spoke to how wicked she was. She even had a new last name, Rivas, the name of her new husband.

Daniel stared down at the black-and-white photo of the new husband. This Rivas fellow wasn't bad looking. Poor bastard. He wondered how much Jorje Rivas knew about his new wife of four months. It was a fair bet, not much. A scowl crept across Daniel's face as his mind scrolled through the memories of all the years he and Tricia spent together. An icy cold sensation coursed through his veins. Oh, how he loathed that woman.

The front door to the bungalow opened, and Mr. Rivas stepped outside. Smiling and dressed impressively in his uniform, he turned and faced the person inside. Daniel watched with smoldering anger as the handsome man gave his new wife a peck on the cheek.

Tricia always had a thing for firefighters. Daniel wasn't surprised that she married another one. He almost felt bad for the man; the poor, dumb bastard didn't know the monster he let into his life. Oh well, it was fortuitous for him that Daniel was around to save the day.

Daniel watched as Jorje drove past in his shiny, black truck.

Poor dumb bastard thinks he got the entire world in his hands right now.

The truck disappeared around the corner. Daniel waited several minutes, watching the street through his rearview mirror. Once he was sure Mr. Rivas would not come back, he climbed out of the Jeep, stomped his cigarette out on the sidewalk, and headed toward the tiny, blue home. Careful to avoid being seen by Tricia, he slithered down the side of the home and into the backyard. The white vinyl fencing provided sufficient cover from the neighbors. He crept up onto the back porch and peeped inside. No sign of her.

Quietly, he turned the doorknob. Unlocked. Of course, it was. After everything Tricia went through to bury her past, she was probably sure there was no way he would ever find her. Chalk that up to one of her fatal flaws—her oversized ego. He shook his head. Never underestimate Daniel's desire for retribution against the people who ruined his life.

The kitchen was vacant. Dirty dishes rested in the sink; otherwise, the room was clean and organized. He tiptoed into the living room, then down the hall toward the bedrooms, taking time to examine the photographs that hung on the pale, gray wall. On a boat or at the beach, the happy couple smiled or kissed in each one. A picture of their wedding. Her in a billowy, white dress; him in a dark, blue suit, both standing in front of the courthouse, holding their marriage license.

He entered the master bedroom; an airy, floral dress lay across the top of the bed, waiting for its owner. The bathroom door was closed, muffling the sound of the shower. Clouds of steam escaped through the seams around the door. He stood in silence, breathing in the delicate, floral bouquet of soap, mulling over whether he should storm into the room and rip her out by her wet, soapy hair or wait patiently on the end of the bed until she came out.

He tapped his chin. Which facial expression did he want to see? Each one had its own appeal.

In the end, he opted for sheer terror.

With a malevolent grin, he flung open the bathroom door, reached inside the shower and grabbed a fist full of hair, then pulled her against him. Feet slipping on the wet tile, she attempted to regain her footing —to no avail.

"Don't scream." He hissed in her ear.

Trembling, she nodded.

He dragged her into the bedroom and hurled her down on the floor where she cowered; naked, wet, and positively terrified. Daniel grinned and knelt down beside her.

"Hey baby, long time no see," he said. "I bet you thought you'd never see this handsome face again. Well, lucky you, I took the time to track you down. I really, wanted to see you again." He swept a soaking wet strand of hair away from her eyes. Her face was red and blotchy from sobbing, snot running from her nose. He was reveling in this. "Oh, yeah." He snapped his fingers. "I also want my money. All of it." His words dripped with red-hot hate.

"Daniel," she sputtered, "I-I…."

"I-I what?" he jeered.

"I-I'm so sorry," she pleaded, "Please, please don't do this."

"Don't do what?" he demanded. "What exactly do you think is gonna happen here?"

She wept uncontrollably.

"Get up!" he hollered.

She didn't move.

"Get the hell up and put some clothes on. Now!"

She bolted to her feet and dressed quickly. As soon as she finished, Daniel zip-tied her hands together, pulling the strands so tight the plastic cut into her wrists. He shoved her down on the edge of the bed.

He glared down at her for a good long while, basking in her fear. When he finally broke the silence, she flinched. "Melody?" he scoffed. "That's sick—even for you."

She didn't respond.

"Does the new hubby know what a piece of shit you are? Who you are? Or all the crap you've pulled? I assume not," he sighed, "Maybe we should stick around so we can tell Jorje all about you when he gets home."

Her eyes grew wide as she panicked and shook her head back and forth.

He snapped his fingers. "Oh wait, he's a firefighter. That means he won't be back for at least twenty-four hours." He rubbed his chin. "Darn, it looks like it's just you and me, baby. And I wanted to meet him. I bet he's a great guy. Probably a fool, though. I mean… he fell for you." He eyed her up and down and sneered.

"W-what do you want?" she begged, through sobs.

"W-what do I want?" he mocked. "I want what's mine. What you took from me." He paused and stared down at the floor. "Well, at least the money you stole, I'll never get the important things back. You made certain of that." He glared at her. "I want all the money you took."

She shook her head. "I have nothing—,"

Before she could finish, he backhanded her so hard she tumbled to the floor. "Stop fucking lying!" he boomed. "Jesus! You just can't help yourself. Can you?"

Crouching on one knee, he leaned close. "Do you honestly think that I didn't do all my research? I know you have a nice, plump bank account stocked full of cash. I even know the balance. Should I tell you?"

"All right," she stated, "I'll give you the money. All of it. Just please don't do anything."

A malevolent sneer spread over his face. "That's what I wanna hear. Cooperation." He jumped to his feet and paced around the room. This was going much better than he imagined; he actually expected more of a fight from her. Apparently, the years had softened her up. Daniel was almost disappointed.

He stood in front of her. "We're gonna go for a drive. Get up."

She remained still, weeping.

"I said, get up!" he ordered. "Now!"

Daniel left her hands tied to ensure she tried nothing foolish. As they left the house, he draped a sweater over them to hide the restraints, quietly reveling in the purple and blue hue of her fingers.

Outside, he wrapped his arm around Tricia's shoulder and guided her toward the Jeep. As far as Daniel could tell, they were the only two people around; there was no sign of anyone; no neighbors, landscapers, or delivery people. Great for him—bad for her. He opened the passenger door and shoved her inside, then slammed the door closed. The sound of her tugging on the door handle as he walked around to the driver's side made him smile. Did she seriously think he wouldn't have disabled the passenger door handle before picking her up?

Stupid woman.

The day prior, Daniel secured a room in a shabby motel two cities over. Surrounded by truck stops and stripper bars, it was the kind of place that made your skin itch just looking at it. The motel sign was rusted and missing some letters where the paint had chipped off; just below that, the neon "vacancy" sign flashed along with the message "hourly rates available." The desk clerk had an air of "don't give a shit," which was perfect for Daniel's purpose. He wasn't there to make friends.

He guided Tricia into the room and pushed her down onto a stained, floral chair. Tiny bits of dust burst into the air, floating in the slivers of sunshine that beamed through the curtains. Not being one to take risks, Daniel tied her ankles to the chair's legs.

"I thought we were going to the bank?" she asked, glancing around nervously at the grimy hotel room, struggling to mask her revulsion.

Daniel laughed. "We're just gonna hang out here for a bit. We'll get to the money soon enough. In the meantime," he plunked himself down on the bed. The mattress reeked of sex and cigarettes. "We're gonna watch some TV and take a break from the heat of the day." He aimed the remote at the old television in the corner and turned it on.

They sat in silence as he flipped from one channel to another.

Admittedly, Daniel could have taken care of the money at any time, but money wasn't the only thing he was after. He wanted to inflict maximum terror on Tricia. Her fear and anxiety fed his hate. As he casually flipped through the channels, he watched her from the corner of his eye, growing more and more anxious with each passing hour.

It was dark when he finally turned off the TV. "Okay, sweetheart, time to make a transfer." He pulled out a brand-new laptop and fired it up.

Her face was a mask of confusion.

"Oh, allow me to explain," he said. "We're not going to the bank. There's no need. We're gonna do a bank transfer right here." He tapped the laptop. "Ain't modern technology great? All we need is for you to log in." He sauntered across the room and placed the computer on her lap.

She peered up at him with big, round eyes.

"Go on, log into your account."

Using one bluish/purple finger, she carefully typed in the account number and the password then hit enter. The screen changed, revealing the account with a balance of two hundred and fifty thousand dollars.

Daniel whistled. "It's a good thing for me you kept this hoard hidden from your new hubby. Let me guess, this is the back door. Your escape route in case things go south."

She didn't answer. She didn't have to.

Daniel started a transfer of all the funds to an untraceable international account. "I'd thank you for your contribution, but we both know this money is mine, anyway." Transfer complete, he switched over to his account to confirm the transaction was complete. Satisfied with the results, he logged out and closed the laptop.

"Well, that's it," he announced, as he hopped to his feet. "Time to take another ride."

Tricia shook her head. "You can just leave me here. I won't tell anyone about this."

He leaned against the door, watching her plead. She had to know her efforts were futile. There was no way in hell Daniel was going to leave her sitting in this motel room. When she finally stopped prattling on, he cut the ties around her ankles, then ushered her back out to the Jeep.

They traveled south, through several small towns, eventually coming to a stop at an old picnic area on the side of the highway. It was a typical roadside rest stop, trash cans overflowing with garbage and graffiti spray-painted all over the concrete picnic tables—yet the grass was neatly trimmed. Typical of a government-run facility—half-ass. He surveyed the area, making sure they were alone, then Daniel climbed out of the vehicle, taking the keys with him.

After stretching his legs and relieving himself, he strolled up to the passenger side and opened the door. "All right, Princess, come on out."

Tricia looked around nervously. "What are we doing here?"

"This is the end of the line. Where we part ways." He reached in and dragged her out into the humid night air.

She searched the darkness. "How am I supposed to get home?"

Daniel snickered. "So, what part of 'this is the end of the line' did you not understand?" he asked.

She stared at him blankly, trying to process what exactly he was getting at.

Once again, Daniel stood patiently waiting for the spark of understanding to ignite on her stupid face. Her eyes grew wide. There it is. The look of panic as she finally understood what he meant was pure joy to witness. He gave out a loud chuckle.

She broke down again. "Please, let me go. I won't say anything to anyone. You can go your way, and I'll go mine. I'll never say a word to anyone. Promise."

"After everything you've done. Do you seriously think I would ever trust you? Do you honestly believe you deserve to go free?"

"Please," she whimpered. "I mean it this time—"

"I mean it this time," he mocked. He stared at Tricia with disgust. Not just for her, but for himself as well. He hated himself for being so stupid all those years ago. For falling for all her lies. For sticking around even when he knew he should have left. He loathed her with every fiber of his being for giving him a son, then ripping him away.

"You're full of shit," he said flatly. "Lying is as natural as breathing for you. You've told so many, you don't even know the difference anymore."

He glared directly into her eyes. "No, Melody," he said, his words dripping with disdain. "You're a parasite with a long history of destroying other people's lives."

She broke down into uncontrollable sobs.

Daniel's anger gave way to quiet resolve. He pulled his hunting knife from its sheath, and with one sweep, he put an end to this chapter of his life.

Chapter 7

THE DENVER SKYLINE LOOMED LARGE ON THE HORIZON AS THE TRAIN rolled into the rail yard. Overhead, the evening sky paled ever so slightly with the first signs of dawn. Cash checked the time on his phone; it was six a.m.; they were rolling in at the perfect time. The night crew would be tired; the last hours of the shift were always the worst, Cash imagined that would be the case, no matter what the job. With any luck, the crew would all be sitting around the office, stooped over mugs of hot coffee instead of out making rounds.

The train slowed and pulled inline between two other trains. As soon as it came to a halt, they hopped off. With Cash in the lead and Teague bringing up the rear, they crept between the cars, stealing across the tracks, through an adjacent copse of trees, then out onto the street.

Denver was far too big of a city to catch on during the day; the yard would be teeming with workers soon. When dealing with larger cities, it was best to sneak in and out during the hours between dusk and dawn. According to Porter, their next ride out would be at nine o'clock, which meant they had the entire day to do whatever they desired. As it turned out, they wanted showers and sleep.

The ride in was less than desirable, Cash was never a fan of riding in coal-filled gondolas, but they had to take what they could get. Fine, black dust filled the creases of his skin. He could feel it in his pores. A long, hot shower and some good, solid rest on something softer than a pile of rocks were exactly what he needed. Judging by the looks on everyone's faces, they were all on the same page. If his map was correct, a small motel was just a few blocks away. Cash was sure it would be a dump, but as long as it had hot, running water, he didn't care.

An eighteen-wheeler rolled by, producing a blast of warm, diesel-scented air that kicked up a cloud of debris; the sound of the air brakes echoed off the metal buildings. It turned slowly, receding down a side street, leaving behind a plume of black smoke in its wake.

Streetlights buzzed and flickered, then turned off, as the pale, gray sky gave way to the vibrant yellows and oranges of the rising sun.

A loud crash erupted in the alley, followed by a hiss and growl from a cat, yet unseen. Cash leaped back just in time to sidestep a giant rat running toward the street, a massive black cat close behind. The rat hopped off the sidewalk and sprinted toward the gutter; safety was a few feet away. The cat launched itself into the air, landing on top of the rat, snapping the smaller creature's neck in its powerful jaws.

Cash shrugged. *Cat's* gotta eat. He continued down the street, past warehouse after warehouse. Industrial areas like this were always so bleak. No trees, no shops, no cheerful chatter, just concrete, bricks, and the distinct smell of trash and oil.

He rounded the corner and came to an abrupt stop; across the street stood the motel. It was everything Cash had imagined. Yep, I can smell it from here.

A single-story, U-shaped, mini compound with the office sitting at the edge of the sidewalk. Broken glass shards dangled precariously from the sign where the letter "M" used to be; the remaining letters flashed off and on "otel."

"Is this… Is this where we're staying?" asked Beth.

"Try not to show so much excitement," admonished Cash. "It's here, and it's cheap. And seriously, the only thing I care about is whether the shower has hot water."

"Ooh! A hot shower!" said Beth. "That'll be wonderful." She rubbed her hands up and down her arms in anticipation.

"Don't get your hopes up too high," warned Teague, as he counted their money. "A place like this—" He nodded toward the motel. "We might be lucky to have lukewarm water."

Teague handed the money to Cash. "You're up. Go get us a deal on a room."

Cash spun around to face the others. "Anyone else have any requests?"

"Hot water!" exclaimed Beth.

Cash nodded. "Duly noted, ma'am." He tipped an imaginary hat toward her. "And you, Madam?" he asked River.

She smiled and replied, "Well, fine sir, I would very much prefer a room with a magnificent view."

"Ah, my lady," he responded, "I shall do my best to procure the room with the best view of a run-down warehouse as possible." He turned with a flourish and strolled into the office.

The rickety, wooden door gave out a painful creak as he entered the dank office, screaming out once more as it closed behind him.

The air had a dingy hue; tiny dust particles floated about in the rays of sunshine that made it through the nicotine-coated window blinds. In the corner, an automatic air freshener released a pathetic plume of vapor. The smell of cheap weed permeated the entire space. Candy wrappers and empty, fast-food containers littered the desk.

Cash pushed the small button atop the desktop bell. Ding, ding.

The door behind the desk flew wide, releasing a puff of smoke, followed by a pot-bellied man with dark, brown hair, thick glasses, and a scruffy beard. He took a hit from the joint in his hand, paused momentarily, then exhaled. "What can I do for you?" he asked.

Cash put on his most genuine smile. "I need a room."

The man looked Cash up and down, then past him to the ragtag group outside. "Just you or the entire group?" He took another hit from the joint.

"All of us," replied Cash.

The man nodded and shuffled the rubbish on the table in search of something. He felt around his pockets, then finally shook his head. "I swear if my head wasn't attached…" he quipped. He handed the joint to Cash. "Here, hold on to this for me," he said, "while I go find where I put the key to the lockbox." He turned to wander back inside the room. "You can take a hit if you want," he called, over his shoulder.

Cash did not have to be told twice. He took a hit—the room might have reeked of cheap weed, but the joint was anything but.

The man returned from the room carrying a bronze key. "The room's fifty-five dollars for the night. We don't take credit cards," he declared.

Cash grinned. "How about thirty dollars for a few hours?"

The man took another hit from the joint and exhaled. "I can let you have the room on the far end for thirty-five. But you have to be out by midnight."

"You have yourself a deal," said Cash, as he counted out the money.

The room reeked of old carpet, stale cigarettes, and alcohol. Two, queen-sized beds sat in the center of the room opposite a TV stand. A threadbare and stained love seat sat against the wall.

"You think they were going for dingy yellow, or are the walls just coated in nicotine?" asked Cash, as he entered the room.

Finn lifted a painting from the wall, uncovering a perfect square of floral wallpaper with a white background.

"Well, that answers that question," quipped Cash.

"Maybe a little air will help," said Teague.

He twisted the knob on the air conditioning unit below the window. It clicked and thudded to life, then erupted in a loud rattle—reminiscent of a fan belt on its last leg. Instinctively, Teague and Cash took a couple of steps back, not sure whether it would explode into flames. The rattling gave way to a low, persistent hum, and cool air rushed from the vent.

Finn hopped on the bed nearest the bathroom. A cloud of dust plumed around his body. "Dibs!" he declared, and he bounced on the mattress, kicking up even more dust.

"Beth and I will take this one," said River, and she plunked down on the edge of the bed.

"Hey, hold on," protested Cash, "You guys always get the bed, leaving Zac and me to sleep on the floor or the nasty, fold-out sofa." He glanced over at the worn-out loveseat and cringed.

"I could sleep on the love seat," offered Beth. "That way, you could share the bed with River."

"Works for me," said River.

"Sounds like a fair offer," said Teague.

Cash shook his head. "Nah, River does that snoring thing."

"What snoring thing?" she demanded.

"It's a half whistle, half snore," replied Cash.

"I do not."

"Yeah, you do," interjected Beth.

River placed her hands on her hips. "Oh yeah? How come this is the first time I'm hearing anything about this?"

"Because," replied Cash, "it's one of those things that's both annoying and very cute."

Everyone nodded in agreement.

River huffed and folded her arms in mock disapproval.

"But, I wasn't talking about them," said Cash. "How come you two always get the second bed?" He pointed at Finn and Teague.

"Two bodies per bed," replied Teague.

"You two gonna share?" asked Finn, smirking.

"I'm in," said Zac. He leaned his head on Cash's shoulder. "It's been a while since I got to snuggle up to someone during the night."

Cash shoved him away as the others laughed.

"Yuck it up, assholes," he scoffed. "Fine. I'm calling the shower first."

He strolled into the bathroom and turned on the faucet. The pipes rattled and moaned, followed by a high-pitched whine. Teague and Finn appeared in the doorway, their eyes following the progression of sound as the water traveled through the pipes in the wall.

The rattling and whining became knocking and clanging. Cash stepped back toward the door jamb. A loud bang reverberated in the walls, then thick, brown water sputtered and spewed out into the tub. The putrid stench of sulfur permeated the air.

"You have fun with that," said Finn, as he patted Cash on the shoulder, then hurried away.

"It's getting lighter," said Teague, pointing to the rancid water pouring from the spout.

Cash watched as the water became rusty red, then orange, and finally, it ran clear. He breathed a sigh of relief.

He waited long enough to ensure the water remained clear and for the stink of sulfur to dissipate, then stripped down and climbed in.

The warm water washed over his body, rinsing away a week's worth of grime; at his feet, black coal dust swirled in the puddle around his feet. He closed his eyes and tilted his head up under the steady flow of warm water, and lost all track of time.

Shortly after sunset, clean and rested, they caught their ride out of Denver. Unlike the previous ride, this train was hauling empty gondolas, which made for a much more relaxing trip, considering that the weather cooperated and the sky was clear.

Cash was the first to lower himself into the metal car. A fine, chalky residue clung to every surface. He clapped his hands together, creating a faint puff of dust. His hands were still coated, so he wiped them off on his thighs. While his hands were no longer an issue, his pants had white chalk all over them. He sighed and swatted away as much powder as possible. At least it wasn't a pile of coal.

"This is gonna be a dusty ride," quipped Zac, as he slapped a hand on Cash's back, leaving a chalky handprint.

Beth and River landed next, followed by Teague and finally Finn. Each came to terms with the fine dust in their own way as they found a spot to settle in.

Beth ran her hand across the floor of the car, leaving a distinct line in the chalky grit. She studied the dust on her hand, then squealed and hopped to her feet. "Give me a hand!" she shouted at River.

"With what exactly?" she asked.

Beth giggled. "This dust is like chalk."

"Uh, huh?"

"Help me clean some away."

River pulled out a cloth and helped Beth sweep an area clean. "Now what?"

Beth got down on her hands and knees. "Now," she said, as she picked up a rock the size of her palm, "We're gonna play hopscotch." Using the rock, she drew the outline, then broke it down into squares. "Ta-da…"

"I haven't done this since I was little," said River.

"Me too," replied Beth.

The train car jerked, causing them both to stagger before regaining their balance.

"This is gonna be interesting," said River. She reached her hand out to Cash. "Come on, you gotta play too."

Cash shook his head. "I sucked at this on the playground. I'm pretty sure I'd suck even worse now."

"Doesn't matter." She pulled him with her. "We're all gonna suck at it this time."

"Come on, Zac," pleaded Beth, "you too."

Beth stood with her back to the outline and tossed her rock behind her. It landed four squares up. "Wish me luck." Standing on one foot, she hopped to the first square. "One…" the car swayed, knocking her off balance. She fell into River's arms. "This is not gonna be easy," she stated, with a smile.

It was now River's turn. She stood with her back to the outline and tossed the rock, then spun around. The rock landed one square away. "Well, at least I got a chance of makin' it." She shrugged.

"Better do it quick," chided Cash.

River blew him a kiss then hopped on one foot to the designated square. Struggling to move with the sway of the train, she leaned down and picked up her stone.

"Woo! Come on, River!" cheered Beth.

River jumped and spun around, pinwheeling her arms to maintain her balance. She hopped twice, landing safely off the board. Raising her hands in triumph, she took a low bow as the others clapped. She held her hand out for Zac.

"I suck at this game," he stated. He tossed his rock and turned around.

"Not bad," said Cash. "You only have to make two jumps. You got this," he said, though honestly, Cash didn't think he did. Zac was fit and muscular, but he was not exactly known for agility—except the one time he was being chased by a guard dog in the middle of a shipping yard. He was incredibly agile then. Cash smirked at the memory.

River and Beth chanted, "Zac, Zac, Zac."

Cash joined in.

Zac made it to the square, then slowly bent down. The train jerked hard, nearly knocking the others off their feet. Cash caught himself just in time to see Zac topple over.

"I almost believed you had it, man," said Cash, as he reached out a hand to help Zac to his feet.

Zac flashed a sheepish grin and brushed himself off, sending fine plumes in the surrounding air.

"All right, Cash," said Beth, "you're up."

"This'll be a breeze," he stated, with a grin. He tossed his stone over his shoulder, then turned to see where it landed—four squares up in the middle of the outline.

"What was that you said?" teased River. "A breeze? Care to rethink that?"

Cash shook his head. "Piece of cake, baby. Piece of cake."

He rubbed his hands together and stretched. "Now, allow me to show you how it's done."

The train weaved and bobbed. Closing his eyes, he focused on the sway of the car. After a deep breath, he stood on one foot and hopped. One, two, three—one more. Struggling to maintain his balance, he jumped just as the car jerked left, nearly knocking him off his feet. After a moment's struggle, he regained his balance.

"Almost," taunted River.

"Come on, Cash," prodded Zac. "You can do this, man. Don't let River stay in the lead."

River shoved Zac playfully.

Cash inhaled, then released his breath. He let his body move with the sway of the car and gently lowered himself down to pick up his rock. Standing upright, he lifted the rock in the air and grinned triumphantly. Now to just get back.

"Woo-hoo, Cash!" shouted Beth. "Come on."

"Don't cheer him on," admonished River. "He's the enemy."

Beth nodded in agreement. "Oh, right." She promptly shouted, "Give it up, Cash, you're not gonna make it!"

At that moment, Cash knew there was no way he was going to let himself lose. He winked at River, then hopped three times quickly. Making the last jump off the board with ease, he finished with a low bow. "What was that?" he asked, cupping a hand to his ear as he leaned close to River. "Go ahead, say it."

She put a hand against his chest, holding him at bay. "Say what?"

He grinned and pushed closer. "Tell me how great I am."

River chuckled, letting her hand drop to her side. She stared up at him with a wide-eyed, innocent stare, then said, "For me to say that it would have to be true." She flashed a big smile. "However," she continued, "I will say I am impressed."

"I'll take that," responded Cash. He turned toward the other end of the car, where Finn and Teague lounged against their packs. "You're up. Which one of you is going next?" he asked.

Finn didn't look up from the book he was reading by flashlight.

Teague shook his head. "I'm gonna pass. It's way more fun watching y'all make fools of yourselves."

River gently shoved Cash aside. "Okay, Beth, looks like you're up again."

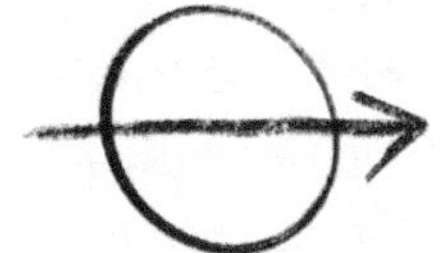

Chapter 8

The train rolled uninterrupted along the tracks for hours. Overhead, the sky paled, signaling daybreak. Teague had made this trek before, and he couldn't recall the ride from Denver to Trinidad being so long. In fact, he had no recollection of rolling through Pueblo. Something was off. He took out his phone to look at the map—dead.

"Mais la," he muttered. He shoved Finn, who was sleeping. "You got your phone?"

Finn rummaged through his pack. After pulling out virtually all the contents, he finally handed over his phone.

Of course, it too was dead.

Teague turned his attention to the others. Beth was awake and busy playing with her phone; for once, he was glad to see her with the device in her hands.

"Beth," he called out, "can we use your phone to look at the map?"

She glanced up, surprised. "Uh, yeah. Sure," she replied.

"Something up?" asked Zac, stretching and yawning.

Teague shook his head. "Not sure," he responded, "I just wanna see where we are."

Finn hopped to his feet and peered out over the lip of the gondola. "No mountains," he declared over his shoulder.

"Oakley," announced Beth, "Kansas."

"Get the hell out," cursed Cash, as he pulled out his phone. By the time he opened up the map, Teague was by his side.

"Well shit," sighed Zac. "How did we catch the wrong train?"

Teague took the phone from Cash and proceeded to pinch and pull the map to better understand their predicament.

"What does this mean?" asked Beth.

"That we're going on a brief side trip," replied River. "We'll figure it out and be back on track soon enough."

Everyone waited quietly for Teague to complete his calculations.

"Okay," he said, "looks like there's a decent-sized yard in Abilene. We can get off there, then catch another ride south through Wichita." He zoomed in on the screen. "From there, we'll catch a ride heading west toward Amarillo."

"Weren't we supposed to meet up with Max and the others?" asked Beth.

Cash took his phone back. "I'll let them know we're on a detour."

"Let 'em know it's probably gonna be a day or two," said Teague. "And send Porter a note asking which trains are going our way."

Rolling into the Abilene yard, the train slowed and blew its whistle, signaling their arrival. According to Porter, their next ride would roll through in a little over an hour. Catching on during the day was always tricky, let alone in the middle of a rail yard. Things could go wrong real fast. Everyone was going to have to keep up and stay hidden.

Crouching low, Teague followed the others, weaving his way between cars and over tracks, coming to rest safely concealed behind the dense brush along the edge of the yard. From there, they could see all the trains coming and going. A perfect spot to guarantee they would not miss their ride out.

"Any changes on the server?" Teague asked Cash.

Cash shook his head. "Nope, just a whole lot of shit talking about our fuck up." He handed the phone to Teague, who scanned the thread.

```
Cash: Porter, we need times for a ride from
Abilene, KS to Wichita.
```

Max: Kansas. The fuck you doin' in Kansas? Aren't we supposed to meet up in Trinidad?

Cash: We had a setback.

Gunner: What kind of setback?

Bella: Anyone hurt?

Tripp: Haha, dumbasses caught on the wrong ride. Didn't you?

Cash: No one is hurt.

Gunner: Good to know.

Bella: That's a relief.

Cash posted a middle finger emoji in response to Tripp.

Max: So how did you end up going from Denver to Kansas instead of straight south to Trinidad?

Tripp: Come clean. Inquiring minds wanna know.

Cash: We accidentally hopped the wrong train.

Ben: LMFAO, you dumbasses.

Tripp: Bahahahaha. I knew it.

Max posted a meme of a man laughing and pointing.

Ben posted a meme of a lost and confused man.

Tripp: Sam wants you to know he's laughing his ass off.

Cash posted a GIF of a person holding up their middle finger in return.

Porter: You threw me off when you said you ended up in KS. I had to double-check the messages. Thought I sent you the wrong way. I'll get the info on a ride from Wichita for you.

Cash: Thanks, man.

Gunner: Since everyone is good, I'm out. Later.

Bella: That's my cue. Be safe. Spinner says hello.

Max: So, what's the plan now?

Cash: Not sure just yet. The plan is to get to

Wichita, then catch on to Amarillo. After that,
we can head west toward Albuquerque.
Max: Bells and D.B. wanna know if we could just
meet up with y'all in Amarillo.
Cash: Sounds good. Might take a couple of days,
though.
Max: No worries. I ran into some locals who
invited us to party. We'll just burn some time
here in Trinidad, then hop to Amarillo and wait
to meet up.
Cash posted a thumbs-up emoji.

At the bottom of the thread, Porter came back with the information they required. Teague snapped a screenshot, then gave the phone back to Cash.

The Abilene yard was bustling with activity. Workers milled around on the tracks, checking the connections between the cars.

"This has got to be one of the busiest small yards I've seen," said Teague.

"We're gonna have to split into groups of two," replied Finn.

Teague turned to the others. "Zac, you and Beth go first. River and Cash second, and we'll go last."

With little discussion, Zac and Beth disappeared between a couple of oil tankers. A subtle bird whistle signaled they were settled, so Cash and River took off. Teague watched anxiously as they disappeared between the two, black tankers. He strained his ears, listening for shouts from the workers or Zac's bird call. This was taking forever.

At last, a melodic whistle sounded out. It was time to go. Not a moment too soon, the train began to move.

Teague and Finn crept out of their hiding spot and crawled over the coupling between the two tankers. Once on the other side, they bent low and peered through the underbelly of the second train.

Finn went first, climbing between two boxcars. He peeked around the corner and quickly slammed back against the wall, placing his arm against Teague. He pressed his finger to his lips. "Shhh."

The sound of footsteps on gravel drew near. One track over, their train was picking up speed. The probability that they would miss this ride was turning into more of a reality with every moment that passed. Teague's phone was dead—Finn's also; if they missed this ride, they would have to go into town, find a library and contact Porter via computer to figure out a new hop.

The footsteps drew closer. Crunch, crunch, crunch.

Holding his breath, Teague pressed his back against the wall, adrenaline coursing through his body; he struggled to control his breathing.

Crunch, crunch, crunch.

If he and Finn were to jump off at that moment, they would be seen —no matter how fast they ran. The only thing to do was stay put and hope the man turned around or something distracted him.

Meanwhile, the train the others were already on continued to creep forward.

A radio squawked. "George, come in."

The footsteps stopped. "George here."

"Get back up here. Alan needs your help with a tank."

"On my way."

One final beep of the radio and the footsteps quickly moved away from the area where Finn and Teague hid. Realizing they dodged a potential disaster, they breathed a sigh of relief.

A sharp whistle interrupted their celebration. The last four cars of their train were in sight; they had to catch one or be left behind. Shooting out from their hiding place, Finn and Teague ran alongside the moving cars. The train was gaining speed, making it harder to keep pace. Finn took hold of a ladder at the rear end of a grainer, heaving himself up on the porch. He reached out and grasped hands with Teague, then helped pull him aboard.

As soon as they cleared the train yard, Teague peered out between the cars. Up ahead, Zac leaned out from between two grainers. He shook his head and flashed a thumb's up.

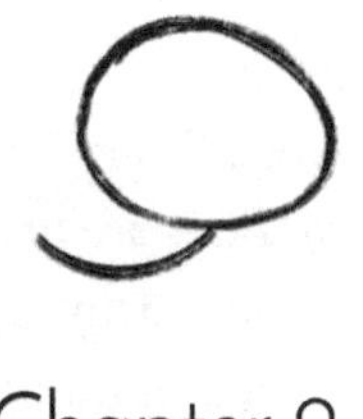

Chapter 9

ACCORDING TO PORTER, THE TRAIN WAS SLATED TO PASS THROUGH Wichita, then on to Wellington. From there, they would catch another ride west. Enjoying the scenery, as well as the downtime, Finn rested his head against the metal wall, allowing the vibration of the rolling train to course throughout his entire body. Like a physical form of white noise, nothing else mattered; there was nothing else to feel. He breathed in—how he loved the scent of grease and metal. He lived for this.

Beside him, Teague stared out at the scrolling scenery. A serene smile on his face as the wind whipped through his hair. He glanced over at Finn and smiled a perfect smile. No words were necessary between them. Hands entwined, they sat in blissful silence, savoring the moment of perfection.

Finn wished it could always be like this. He wondered what it would be like if it were just the two of them. No other people to worry about or listen to. He and Teague could go anywhere, do anything and never have to explain anything to anyone.

It was mid-afternoon when the train rolled into Wellington. Finn climbed off the car, pausing for a moment to wait for Teague. They joined the others in a secluded spot, camouflaged among shrubs and tall trees. According to Porter, their ride out should be ready in approximately thirty minutes.

This was a much smaller yard; sometimes that was a good thing; other times—not so much. If the area was too small for an entire crew of workers, they would have an easier go of sneaking onto a train. However, if the modest-sized yard had a full team, that would complicate things. More men with a smaller area to monitor meant a heightened risk of being caught.

"I'm gonna go scout the yard," said Finn, to no one in particular, "I wanna see how many workers there are around."

He crept away from the group. Staying behind the shroud of trees, he skirted down toward the office building. Several trucks sat lined up in the lot out back; that was not a good sign. More vehicles meant more people.

The office doors swung open and several men wearing yellow vests strolled out, heading toward the tracks, inspecting the cars as they passed by.

Much to Finn's dismay, three of the men were heading right toward the copse of trees where the others were hiding. Finn glanced around, trying to figure out a way to get back to the others without being spotted. The quickest route was along the tracks, but that was where the men were walking, which meant his only option was to run into the woods and circle back around. He would have to run fast because the men were already uncomfortably close.

Head down, Finn took off into the woods, doing his best to keep the yard in his periphery while also taking care not to step into a hole and bust his ankle. He stormed into the clearing, nearly stumbling over Zac. Teague, Cash, and River were peering through the brush, watching the workers slowly work their way closer.

Finn crouched down beside Teague. "The yard is crawling with workers."

"How many of them are there?" asked Teague.

"Maybe eight." Finn shrugged. "Least, that's how many I counted."

Teague rubbed his chin. "If we're catchin' that train, we're gonna have to be careful."

Cash nodded. "Looks like we split up again."

"The good news is," continued Finn, "our ride is sittin' on the tracks." He pointed. "Right there."

"As long as we keep our heads down," said Teague, "and stay hidden, we should have no trouble getting out of here."

The others nodded.

Zac handed his phone to Teague. "Take this," he said. "That way, if we get separated, you can at least message, and we can work it out from there."

Teague tucked the device into the front pocket of his pants, then readied his gear.

The train engine thundered to life; it was time to go. Finn and Teague went first this time. Staying close to the cars, they crept alongside several double stacks, climbing aboard the first gondola they came across. Unfortunately, it was half-filled with coal; this was going to be a messy ride. Just before he dropped inside, Finn glanced back to see River disappear between two cars. Things were going smoothly.

The whistle blasted, followed by an abrupt jerk. At first, slow and bumpy, the giant picked up speed, jolting them around as it stretched out along the tracks. Hoods pulled up over their heads, bandannas over their faces, and glasses covering their eyes; Finn and Teague lay close against the coal. As the train left the yard behind, they shared a triumphant high five.

Their muted celebration ended with the unexpected sound of Zac's phone buzzing.

Teague pulled it from his pocket and opened up the screen. "Mais la!" he yelled. "They're not on!"

"Bullshit, I saw them get on," replied Finn.

Teague shook his head. "The cars weren't hooked up. When the train pulled away, it left them sitting right there."

Finn took the phone and read the message. He peered up over the lip of the gondola. Sure enough, only two of the double stacks were in tow behind the one they were on. "Dammit," he cursed.

Teague played with the map, moving and expanding the screen, trying to work out what they would do next. "Okay," he said, "looks like Alva is where we're gonna get off and wait for them to catch up."

Finn nodded. *If it was just the two of us, we wouldn't be dealing with this right now.*

Teague messaged back and forth with the others, letting them know the plan. Once everything was worked out, he sighed and opened the server app.

Finn leaned close, reading along as Teague typed.

```
Teague: Porter, we're gonna need another train
from Wellington.
Tripp: Did you seriously fuck up again?
Max posted a meme of a man with his hands on his
hips.
Max: I'm starting to think you don't wanna
meet up.
Teague: The train wasn't connected. Me & Finn are
heading toward Alva. The others are still in
Wellington.
Ben posted a GIF of a man laughing.
Max posted a GIF of a boy, shaking his head
disapprovingly.
Cash posted a middle finger emoji.
Tripp posted a GIF of a woman blowing a kiss.
Porter: I'm on it. Be back with the info.
Teague: Thanks, man. Oh, and while you're at it,
can you give us another hop from Alva?
Porter posted a thumb's up emoji.
Bella: You kids are batting a thousand on this
trip.
Cash: It's just one of those days, I suppose.
Max: We're still heading for Amarillo. See you
when you get there.
Cash posted a thumbs-up emoji.
Teague: See you there.
```

Porter came back on with the train info. After taking a screenshot, Teague put the phone away. They could do nothing more. With several miles left to go; they settled down and waited till they arrived at their destination.

When they entered Alva, they hopped off at the train yard outside of the city. According to Porter, it would be at least four hours before the others caught up with them. Hungry and bored, the duo made the relatively long walk into town to find some grub.

"Should we try to hitch a ride?" asked Finn, standing on the edge of the road.

"I'd say yeah," replied Teague, "if one comes along."

Teague stuck his thumb out at a red sedan. The car sped by.

"Must not be her type," quipped Finn.

Teague gave him a playful nudge. "This one might be the one. Get ready."

A beat-up, white dually hauling an empty cattle trailer rolled toward them. Walking backward, Finn stuck his thumb in the air. Upon spying him, the white-bearded driver slowed his truck, coming to a complete stop alongside him.

"Y'all want a ride into town?" asked the old man.

Finn nodded gleefully.

"Then hop on in," replied the old man. He reached over and popped open the passenger door.

The cab of the truck smelled of sour whiskey. Finn leaned almost half his body out the window in a weak attempt to escape as much of the noxious air as possible. Behind him, sitting in the back seat, Teague was doing the same. Making eye contact through the side-view mirror, they shared a conspiratorial smile.

"My name's Abner," said the old man, holding his hand out.

Finn shook hands. "Finn." He pointed to the back seat. "That's Teague."

Abner glanced at Teague in the rearview mirror and nodded. "Haven't seen you two around; y'all must be passing through."

"We're waiting for friends," replied Finn.

"How long are you fixin' to be in town?"

Finn shrugged.

"Think you'd be up for taking on a minor job for me?"

Finn glanced back at Teague. "Maybe. Depends on what it is and how much it pays."

Abner smiled. "Might be a bit tricky, but I can promise you it'll pay real good."

"Tricky as in difficult," asked Finn, "or tricky as in illegal?"

The old man chortled. "Both."

Finn was intrigued. "We're all ears, Abner."

"Tell you what," said the old man. "You boys hungry?"

"Always," replied Finn.

The old man grinned. "How about I take you, boys, to lunch at the diner in town? We can cover all the details over a nice hot meal."

Chapter 10

"IT'S CALLED CATTLE RUSTLIN'," SAID ZAC.

"Cattle what?" asked Cash.

"Rustling," replied River. "They want to steal somebody's cows."

"It's not really stealin'," interjected Finn.

Zac stood firm with his arms folded across his chest. "The hell it ain't," he responded. "You takin' someone else's cattle without permission?"

"Sorta," replied Finn.

Zac shook his head. "Sorta," he mimicked. "You know in some states, cattle rustlin' is a crime punishable by death."

"Hold on," Cash raised his hand. "Death?"

"In Texas for sure," said Zac.

"Then I guess it's a good thing we're in Oklahoma," countered Finn.

Cash turned to Zac. "What's the law in Oklahoma?"

"How the hell do I know?"

"Now hold up," interjected Teague, "Just hear us out."

Zac shook his head. "I cannot believe you're on board with this."

Teague stepped forward. "It's not as bad as it sounds."

Zac leaned against the door of the white truck. "I'm listenin'."

"We're not stealing cows," explained Finn. "We're returning them."

"How's that?"

"The old man, Abner, had his cows stolen by this other rancher a couple of weeks ago. We're just gonna reclaim what's rightfully his."

Zac could hardly believe his ears. He also couldn't believe he was contemplating going along with it. He stood silent, waiting to hear more.

Finn continued, "According to Abner, this other rancher paid some guys to sneak up on his property and steal six of his cows. He just wants us to get six cows back."

Zac tapped the hood of the truck. "Abner. That's who owns this truck. Is that right?"

Finn and Teague nodded.

He walked down along the body of the truck to the trailer. There were a few rusted spots here and there, along with several dents, but overall, the trailer was in better condition than the truck. They were definitely farm vehicles. There was no doubt they were used to doing some hard work. He stepped back over to the others. "What do you know about cows?"

Teague shook his head.

Finn grinned. "We don't have to know anything. We got you."

Zac nodded skeptically.

"Wait," said Cash, "we're not seriously considering this. Are we?" He glanced hopefully between Zac and Teague.

"How much is he paying?" asked Zac.

Finn's face lit up. "A hundred per cow."

Zac let the total roll around in his head. If they pulled this off, they would walk away with six hundred dollars. He couldn't recall the last time they had that much money at one time. No doubt it would come in handy. "You got a map to where we need to go?" he asked.

Teague pulled a folded piece of paper from his back pocket. He pressed it out on the hood of the truck while everyone clustered around. Pointing to one location, he said, "This is where we are." He moved his finger over. "This is the ranch where we get the cows." He slid his finger across the surface. "This is where we deliver them and get paid."

Zac studied the map while pondering over the idea. All in all, it didn't seem too hard. He already could see how they could pull it off quickly. "If I agree to do this—" He stared at Finn. "You absolutely have to listen to me and do what I say."

Finn smiled and placed his hand on his heart. "Absolutely."

Zac opened the door to the cab of the truck. He climbed into the driver's seat, then leaned out the door. "What are y'all waitin' on? Get in. Let's do this before I change my mind."

Following the map drawn by Abner, Zac drove to a derelict stretch of land on the outskirts of town. A thick growth of trees and shrubs lined the side of the road, creating a canopy that swallowed the blacktop as far as the eye could see. Driving down the shadowy road, Zac nearly missed the gate. He pulled into the driveway and surveyed the area. Rusted T-posts and rotting branches held up the old barbed wire fence. It was a miracle the cows even stayed in the pasture.

Finn jumped out and swung open the gate; it creaked so loud, Zac was sure it could be heard miles away. The cows in the field hardly even took notice as the vehicle backed in.

Zac threw the truck in park, and everyone hopped out. He breathed in deep. "Ah, smells like country." Smells like home. He dug around in the toolbox for some leather gloves, noting any items that might come in handy.

The cows were now fully aware of the intruders. They moved closer but still maintained a healthy distance.

"Aww, look, Beth!" shouted River. "A baby cow!" She held her hand out to a brown and white calf. "Guys, look at this cute, baby cow."

"It's a calf," replied Zac.

"Baby cow," she rebutted.

"Calf is a better word," he countered, "calling it a baby just fosters feelings toward it."

River shrugged. "Call it what you want. I'm callin' it a baby cow."

She held her hand out and clucked her tongue. "Here, baby, come on over. I'm not gonna hurt you."

The calf moved close enough for Beth and River to rub its head.

"I've never touched a cow before," said Beth. "It's a lot softer than I thought it would be."

"I know, right?" replied River. "Who's the cute baby cow?" She rubbed the calf behind its ears.

Beth giggled. "He looks like a Toby to me."

"That's an adorable name," replied River. "Hey there, Toby. Do you like that name?"

"Do not name the damn calf," admonished Zac.

"Why not?" demanded Beth.

"Because you don't name your dinner." He smirked. "Makes it harder to eat."

"Hey, Cash," River called over her shoulder, "come on over and meet Toby. He's sweet."

"Well, go on, Cash, your girlfriend's callin'," teased Zac.

"Do they bite?" asked Cash.

Zac chuckled. "Pretty sure the blonde will."

"I heard that!" shouted River. "And he's right, I do bite."

Cash approached apprehensively, reaching out his hand. The calf leaned into him, wiping milk and saliva from its mouth all over his arm. "What the hell?" he exclaimed, barely able to mask his disgust. "What's all over its face?"

River chuckled. "Milk," she replied between fits of laughter. "He must have just nursed."

Cash extended his arm away from him as though he were willing it to no longer be a part of his body.

"Come on, Cash," teased Zac, "It's only milk. You like ice cream and cheese. Where did you think it came from?"

"I know where it comes from," scoffed Cash. "I just never wanted to get this close to its origins." He wiped his arm off on his thigh.

A deep bellow erupted from some place off in the darkness.

"What the hell was that?" asked Cash.

Zac searched the field. "That's a bull," he responded. "I don't see him anywhere."

"Maybe he's in another pasture," replied Teague.

Finn wandered toward the noise.

"Let's hope so," replied Zac. He concentrated on the task at hand; it was time to get serious. The last thing he wanted was a run-in with an angry bull.

Cash approached, still holding his arm away from his body. "So, what's the plan?"

"Just workin' that out now," replied Teague.

"Is there a call or something?" asked Cash.

Zac scoffed but said nothing.

Cash continued, "Do we tie a rope around their necks and guide them in?"

With that one, Zac shot an amused glance at Teague, who appeared to be holding back laughter.

Cash stepped away and held his arms out on both sides. "Maybe a couple of us can get behind one of them and sort of push them along into the trailer." He gestured with his hands.

As entertaining as it was listening to Cash give his input, Zac wanted to get this done and over with, though a part of him could have listened to Cash's ideas on cattle loading for hours. He opened the gate to the trailer and climbed inside. "You two stand there and help guide the cows." He called out to River and Beth. "You two, step to the side and try not to get stomped on. If any mamas with calves come up, try to keep them away. We don't want the babies or their mamas."

He lifted a sack of protein cubes and shook it. The sound was enough to excite the cows and get the herd to move closer.

Zac stepped back and emptied the bag on the floor of the trailer, then skirted along the side wall, doing his best to stay out of the way. The first two cows climbed up in search of a tasty treat. Two more sauntered in; they were almost there. Zac stood by the tailgate. A quick count told him they had exactly six cows.

"Shut the gate," he shouted.

Teague and Cash slammed the tailgate closed with a loud clang.

The cows in the field, having a sense they were not getting any treats, moved closer.

Zac searched around for the bull. No sign of him—that was good. They needed to get going. "River," he called out, "You're driving. Hop in the truck and get ready to pull out."

River, followed by Beth, hopped the fence and ran up to the truck's cab, then climbed in.

Zac struggled to secure the latch; the combination of rust and dents made it challenging. Flecks of rust and old paint fell away as he banged away at the metal, trying to force the peg in place.

"Do you feel that?" asked Cash.

"Feel what?" asked Teague.

"The ground."

Zac paused and listened. The earth below his feet rumbled, slight and distant at first, then heavy and closer.

A great bellow erupted. Zac turned around just in time to see Finn running, a giant, angry bull close on his heels. "Climb!" he shouted.

Faster than he had seen them move in a long time, Teague and Cash followed Zac's command.

The ground trembled as Finn and the bull rushed past. The giant beast was so fixated on Finn, he didn't pause or even note the three men atop the trailer. Beneath them, the cows called out, stepping around restlessly, making the entire trailer move.

In the field, Finn zig zagged, keeping just out of the bull's reach.

Clinging to the roof of the trailer, Zac and Cash looked at Teague.

"Don't put his on me," he protested. "This is all Finn."

"Ain't it always?" asked Zac.

Finn cut left and darted up a giant oak tree; below him, the bull paced and pawed at the ground, bellowing in rage.

"That boy sure can climb fast," said Zac, genuinely impressed with Finn's agility.

Teague scoffed. "You would, too, if you had a bull on your ass."

The trio shared a chuckle.

"So, what are we gonna do now?" asked Cash.

Zac sighed. "First, we gotta get the truck out and close the gates."

"And what about Finn?" asked Teague.

"We'll get his dumbass once we have the load secured on the other side of the fence. He can stay in the tree 'till then. Maybe while he's up there, he can think about why he's in that predicament." Zac slid across the roof toward the front of the truck, leaning over as close as possible; he said, "River, give us to the count of ten, then pull the truck forward, past the gate. We'll close it behind you."

River nodded and flashed a thumbs-up.

Zac jumped down, landing quietly on the ground alongside Teague and Cash. Careful to make as little commotion as possible, he crept around the back to inspect the latch one last time; it was secure. The truck pulled forward. As soon as it passed the gate, Teague and Cash swung it closed. The cows and the trailer were safe. Standing along the fence, the trio watched the bull pace, huff, and bellow beneath the tree.

"Damn," said Zac, "I was sure the sound of that gate closing would be enough to get his attention."

"He really wants a piece of Finn," said Cash.

Teague stepped up to the fence. "I'll create a diversion."

"No, you're not." Zac grabbed hold of Teague's shirt and pulled him back. "I'll do it."

Teague opened his mouth to protest.

"No, you're not either," interjected Cash. He pointed to Zac. "You had the bear." He faced Teague. "You also had a run-in with the same bear. It's my turn to save Finn's ass."

"I'm faster," argued Zac.

Another bellow from the bull echoed across the pasture.

Cash nodded. "Probably, but I don't have to be faster than you." He smiled. "I just gotta outrun the bull."

"If he catches up with you, your ass is toast," warned Zac.

"That's exactly why he won't."

Zac agreed. "Don't underestimate the speed of that thing. And don't forget for one second how pissed off he is."

Cash flashed a crooked grin. "Don't underestimate my desire to avoid being crushed by a rampaging bull." He climbed the fence and stepped forward seven paces, then gave out a sharp whistle and waved his arms over his head as he called out, "Come on, you big bastard." He whistled again. "Come and get me."

The bull pounded the earth and bellowed. Without another thought toward the human in the tree, he took off toward Cash.

"Run, Cash!" shouted River.

The moon hid behind a group of clouds, making it hopeless to see much beyond a few yards. Zac could hear the bull from where he stood, but he could see neither Cash nor the bull. The ground beneath his feet rumbled; he cursed the clouds.

The others called to Finn.

Cash's silhouette materialized through the darkness; the bull fast on his heels. He vaulted over the fence, soaring for a moment, then Zac caught him before he could crash to the ground, softening the fall.

The bull crashed into the gate head first, causing it to rattle and shake on its hinges, while Finn and Teague leaned against the metal frame to help it remain in place. The bull backed up and bellowed. It stood still, panting, staring at the humans on the other side of the barbed wire.

"That was close," said Zac.

Finn grinned sheepishly. "It worked, though."

Zac sighed and shook his head. "Let's go get paid so I can pretend like this was all worth it."

Chapter 11

CHEWING HER LIP WHILE TUGGING ON A LOCK OF HAIR, RIVER WATCHED anxiously as the scene unfolded in the side-view mirror. She breathed a sigh of relief when Cash flew over the fence, landing safely in Zac's arms. Seeing the guys share a laugh over the whole affair set her tension at ease. She looked over at Beth just in time to see her hold up her phone and make a silly face.

"Rustling cows," giggled Beth, as she typed.

"What are you doing?"

"What does it look like? I posted a story."

Annoyance welled up inside River. "You did not just post a picture telling the world we're rustling cows. Did you?"

Beth gave a nonchalant shrug. "It's no big deal; it's not like anyone is out there searching for people who are stealing cows from some old man's pasture."

River shoved Beth's phone down, away from her face, so Beth would have to look at her. "What have I told you about posting? What has everyone told you about posting?"

Beth rolled her eyes. "Don't be so paranoid. It's not like anyone online knows where we are. I'm not telling them our location."

River fought back the impulse to yell at her. "Beth, some of us don't want to be a part of your show. We don't want a bunch of random weirdos online knowing everything we do. It's creepy."

"My fans aren't weirdos," argued Beth, "They're all very cool."

My fans. Something about Beth's choice of words did not bode well in River's gut. Her stomach felt as though it were full of lead.

The front passenger door opened, followed by both back doors. Zac climbed up, causing Beth to scooch over to the center of the seat. Finn, Teague, and Cash filled up the back seat.

"All right, River," said Teague, "Let's bring these ladies back home."

Following his directions, River navigated the dark, tree-lined road. The trailer, loaded down with its living cargo, weighed heavily on the truck. Each time she hit the brakes or rounded a corner, she glimpsed at the side-view mirror, worried about causing any harm to the cows in the back. The mood in the cab was light. The others didn't seem to share her worries at all. As far as she was concerned, this drive couldn't be over soon enough.

"Take the next right," directed Teague.

River slowed, watching the trailer as she veered around the corner. Less than twenty yards up the road, a set of blue lights flashed behind them, followed by a loud blip-blip as the police cruiser signaled for them to pull over.

"Shit!" exclaimed River. She turned on her hazards and pulled over.

"Just stay calm," said Zac.

Inside her chest, River's heart raced. Her entire body tensed. Behind them, the officer climbed out of his patrol car and approached the truck.

The flashlight beam stung her eyes, blinding her momentarily. River squinted and held up her arm to shield some of the glare. "How's it going, officer?" she said, doing her best to sound light-hearted and casual.

"Evenin'," replied the officer. He shined his flashlight around the inside of the truck, pausing on each face.

"What seems to be the problem, sir?" asked Zac.

The officer aimed his beam in Zac's face. "Well, I'll tell ya," responded the officer, "but first, I'm gonna need y'all to step out of the vehicle and line up along the side here."

River struggled to contain her breathing. Fear coursed through her body. She climbed out of the truck and took her place in line. The others seemed to take it all in stride—except Beth, whose face was ghost white. River was sure that any moment Beth would break down into tears. The officer took turns patting each one of them down, inspecting their IDs, pausing for a moment as he studied Cash's—a vague smirk on his face.

"Y'all are from all over, I see," he stated. He relaxed his posture and rested his hands on his belt buckle.

No one responded.

The officer scrutinized the group, resting his gaze on each of them one at a time. "Y'all can relax a little. I won't keep you too long; I know Abner's waitin' on ya," he said. "I just want to make sure the ladies in the back are all secure. Wouldn't want any of them to get hurt."

He shined his flashlight inside the trailer as he walked around to the back. After a few bangs on the gate, he returned.

"Looks like everyone's secure back there," he said, "Y'all did a better job than the last group."

"Come again?" asked Cash.

The officer grinned. "You kids don't think this is a one-off, do you?" He chortled and leaned back on his heels. "Nah, this happens just about every couple of weeks around here."

"This?" asked River, still trying to maintain an air of innocence.

"Stealin' these cows," replied the cop. "This has been goin' on since I was a rookie. Abner and Amon are brothers. Been fightin' for well over a couple of decades, from what I can tell. Not sure what kicked it off. I've given up trying to figure it out."

A shocked silence hovered over the group. River had questions, lots of questions. But she didn't want to fall for any sort of trap. So, she listened.

The cop turned off his flashlight. "I can't stop the antics. Believe me, I tried. So did my predecessor." He stared down the length of the trailer. "Things were wild before they settled on passing cows back and forth. Used to blow shit up on one another's property." He whistled. "I'm not sad they stopped doin' that. Those damn explosions freaked people out; some of them were so big, you could feel the ground rumble from a mile away." He shook his head. "Like a damn earthquake."

River held back a giggle. The officer seemed nice enough, but she didn't want to push her luck.

"They always hire drifters who wander through town," continued the officer. He examined the group one more time. "Don't worry, they'll pay. One thing those old boys do is pay their debts. Got more money than god, though you wouldn't know it seeing how they live. Their family used to own most of the land around these parts."

The radio on his chest squawked. "Glen, come in," said a female voice.

The officer pressed the button and tilted his head toward the radio. "Glen here. What's up, Sophie?"

"Just got a call from Lucy Garcia," replied the woman over the radio. "A couple of kids are racing on Shipley Road again. I'll bet you a steak dinner that it's the Staley boy and the Colter kid."

Officer Glen grinned. "Well, that's a losin' bet. You and I both know the Colter kid was grounded for two weeks after the last stunt he pulled in the Johnson's sorghum field."

"It's been three weeks," countered the woman.

"Well, damn." The officer shook his head. "Okay, I'm just wrappin' up here with another episode of Amon and Abner's shenanigans. I'll be over there in a few minutes."

Officer Glen looked directly at River. "You drive carefully and make sure these ladies get to their destination safely."

Unable to utter a single word, River nodded.

"The rest of y'all," said the officer, "stay safe and keep out of trouble while you're here." With that, he turned on his heels and walked away. A moment later, the blue lights turned off. There was one final bleep, bleep from the cruiser, then he drove away.

Still in shock, no one moved or spoke a word as they watched the taillights of the police car recede into the darkness. Just like that, they were standing on the dark country road in silence.

"Someone wanna tell me what the hell just happened?" asked Cash.

Everyone broke into laughter.

"At least he was nice," said Beth.

Zac chuckled. "Leave it to you two to get us wrapped up with more weird shit. I sure hope the old man pays."

"He will," replied Finn. "You heard Officer Glen. The old men are loaded."

"Wait 'till you see the house," said Teague.

"What's up with his house?" asked River, genuinely curious.

Finn snickered.

"Let's just say the old man's a little eccentric," replied Teague.

River turned to face Teague. "How so?"

"He lives in a houseboat."

"That's not weird."

Teague grinned. "It's a giant beast of a boat sitting in a tiny water pond. The boat barely fits. It looks like a kid's toy in a bathtub."

"He's got a crow's nest too," interjected Finn, "with a rifle and a scope on a tripod."

"The whole thing sits in the middle of a big, old cow pasture on top of a hill," said Teague.

River burst out laughing. "Now I have to see this old man." She hopped up into the driver's seat. "Let's drop these girls off."

Chapter 12

"HERE'S YOUR ROOM KEY," SAID ABNER. STANDING IN THE MASSIVE parking lot of the casino, he passed the card to Cash. "Room 512 is all yours for the night. Two beds and one pull-out sofa, just like you requested."

"Thanks for the room," said River.

Abner waved his hand. "No worries. Y'all deserve it." He smiled. "The room's a comp room, anyway. They send me those just about every month."

The old man climbed into his truck, then leaned out the window. "Try not to lose all your money in there. But if you do, I got more work if you want it."

The group stepped back away from the truck as the old man drove away. He hit the horn twice on his way out of the parking lot, then disappeared down the highway.

"That has to be up there for the most bizarre chain of events so far," said Cash, as he remained staring down the road.

"Nah," argued Zac, "The entire fiasco in Jacksonville is still number one."

Cash chuckled and nodded his head. "Ah yes, Jacksonville. You might have a point there."

"It might not have been so bad if you two hadn't hooked up with those weird girls," said River.

"If I recall correctly," replied Cash, "and might I add, my memory of the whole cluster fuck is murky, those weird girls helped us get out of it."

River scoffed. "Remember the boyfriend?"

"Alligator dude," said Cash, with a chuckle. "Who could forget him? In my defense, I didn't know she had a boyfriend."

"Don't forget the rest of the family—" Teague whistled as he shook his head.

"But the blonde was hot," chimed Zac, with a faint smile on his face.

"This is true," agreed Cash.

"All right, enough reminiscing," interrupted Finn. "Let's go check out our room."

A blast of cold air greeted them as they entered the casino. Bells and sound effects echoed from every direction while happy pop music played in the background, barely detectable through the din. Under the watchful gaze of two security guards, the group made their way to the elevators, where Teague pushed the button.

On the fifth floor, they shushed one another as they walked down the corridor toward their room. Cash pushed the card into the reader, then swung the door wide and gestured to River. "Your room is ready, Madam," he said, as he gave a bow.

River chuckled and sashayed in. "Why, thank you, fine sir," she said, waving her hand in the air.

"I hope it doesn't smell like the last room," whined Beth.

The room opened to a narrow hall with the bathroom on one side and a small kitchenette on the other. Beyond that stood two, queen-sized beds covered in fluffy comforters, multiple soft pillows, and crisp white sheets.

Zac turned immediately into the bathroom. "Aw yeah! This is what I'm talkin' about!" he exclaimed.

Beth and River hopped on the first bed. "Dibs!" shouted Beth.

Cash sat on the edge of the remaining bed. "This one's mine. I'm getting a bed this time. I don't even care if I have to share it with one of you." He pointed at Finn and Teague.

The bathroom door banged shut, followed soon after by the sound of running water.

Teague stood before the sofa bed. "We can make this work."

"I think we can," replied Finn.

They pulled off the cushions, tossing them aside on the floor, and opened the bed. "Yeah, this'll work." Finn plopped himself down on the pure-white bedding, causing a loud squeak to erupt from below the bed.

Teague laughed and bounced onto the bed, making the same sound. Every time they moved, the bed protested noisily. They shared an impish laugh. Then, like toddlers in a bounce house, they hopped and moved, creating a sound reminiscent of a large brood of angry rodents.

"You two are gonna have to sleep dead still," said Cash.

Teague rested his head against the cushions. "What's the plan?"

"We're gonna win some money," replied Cash.

"Cards?" asked Teague.

"Hell yeah!" Zac shouted, from the bathroom. "There's a bunch of different settings on the showerhead!"

Cash nodded, ignoring the bathroom outburst. "Of course."

"What are we gonna do?" asked Beth.

"This one's like a soaker hose!" shouted Zac. "What's that called? Like a rain shower or something?" Zac paused as though waiting for an answer. "There's also a mist setting. Kinda dumb if you ask me. But, whatever."

River chuckled. "We'll explore the casino," she told Beth.

Beth smiled. "Sounds cool. I've never been to a casino before."

"Your job," Cash pointed at Teague. "Is to keep him from getting arrested or thrown out." He pointed at Finn, who opened his mouth to protest.

Cash waved his hand dismissively. "Don't. Remember Reno?" He paused briefly but didn't wait for a reply. "Well, I do."

"That was not my fault," protested Finn.

Teague nodded in agreement. "Finn's right, I was there. It—"

"Not important," argued Cash. "It happened. And now, you two are banned from ever entering that casino for life."

"Wait," said Beth, "I wanna hear what happened."

The bathroom door burst open, spilling a plume of floral-scented steam. Zac strolled into the room, wearing boxer shorts, a fluffy white towel wrapped around his head. "I, for one, feel thoroughly refreshed."

"On a scale of one to ten, how great was it?" asked River.

"Ten out of ten."

River jumped to her feet. "That's all I need to hear." She took hold of her bag and traipsed into the bathroom. "I'm gonna be awhile," she said, with a flourish and closed the door behind her.

"How's the sofa bed?" asked Zac.

"A little noisy," replied Cash.

Zac sat heavily on the edge of the sofa mattress. A loud squeal erupted from beneath the bed. He roared, then bounced up and down. "I've heard rusty springs on old trucks make less noise than this."

"You done?" asked Cash, sounding an awful lot like the lone adult in the room.

"We should leave at least two hundred in the safe," said Teague, "just to be sure we still have at least that much."

"Oh ye, of little faith," replied Cash.

"Faith's got nothin' to do with money," replied Teague, as he punched their shared code into the hotel safe and placed the money inside.

From the bathroom, River called out, "Whoo! Zac, you were right. The soaker setting is amazing! I feel like I'm standing in the middle of a warm rain shower."

Zac pulled his shirt over his head. "Looks like I'm with you," he said to Cash.

Cash sighed. "Just follow my lead. When I signal you to fold —fold."

"Aye, aye captain," replied Zac, as he brandished a mock salute.

"This shower gel smells amazing!" shouted River. "For the record, you were right, Zac, the mist thing is stupid."

Chapter 13

THE ELEVATOR CHIMED, AND THE DOOR WHOOSHED OPEN TO THE electronic cacophony of hundreds of slot machines. Cold air circulated around the cavernous room, faintly scented with a hint of air freshener and the occasional waft of cigarette smoke. River and Beth stepped into the brightly lit room and promptly turned down one of the many rows of slots.

A cursory scan of the screens told River whether the last person to play left behind credit. She identified four that did. After hitting the cash-out button, she collected the tickets and moved on to the next row.

This time, Beth followed River's lead and checked all the machines on the opposite side. Several aisles later, the two had amassed five dollars' worth of tickets.

"What are we gonna do now?" asked Beth.

"We're gonna make this grow." River wiggled the tickets in her hand. She looked around for a suitable machine. "Come on," she said, taking hold of Beth's hand. "Let's go over here."

They skirted past a group of young men on their way to the next row. As they passed by, two of the men couldn't help but take notice of the attractive duo in their midst. River flashed a flirtatious smile and winked at the tall one with dark hair. His face turned red, then he glanced away.

"Let's try this one!" exclaimed Beth.

River figured it was as good as any, so she inserted the tickets into the slot. She crossed her fingers. "Come on. Momma wants a new pair of boots," she chuckled, then hit the button.

Beth giggled and crossed her fingers, too.

The electronic reels spun. Music and sound effects emanated from the flashing screen. Then—nothing.

River glanced over at Beth. "One more time?"

Beth nodded enthusiastically.

"Here goes."

The machine lit up with the same sound and lighting effects as before. River stood close to Beth, watching the display with anticipation. Lights flashed, music played, and the screen exploded with a rainbow of colorful gemstones and gold coins. The words "Big Win!" lit up the screen.

"What's happening?" asked Beth.

"I think we just won!"

"Woo-hoo! What did we win?"

River stared at the screen, trying to make sense of all the code flashing by as the machine showed each winning line. A small group of people crowded around, all watching the animated display.

"How long's it gonna go on for?" asked Beth.

River shrugged. "The longer, the better for us!"

A banner appeared on the screen displaying a dollar amount of one hundred and fifty dollars.

"Woo-hoo!" the two girls exclaimed, in unison, as they high-fived one another.

After cashing out, River turned to Beth. "Okay, little sister, do your magic one more time. Pick another winning machine."

They passed the bar and wandered by a glass dividing wall. The sign over the entrance said, "Poker." Peering through the glass, they found Cash and Zac seated at a table in the far-left corner. Both had serious expressions on their faces as they studied the cards in their hands.

"They don't look like they're doing too well," declared Beth.

River smirked. "Nah, Cash is doin' just fine." To the untrained eye, Cash appeared detached, but River knew him well and could tell when he was misleading or playing someone. "If you look close enough, you'll see the corner of his mouth is curling up—ever so slightly. You see?"

Beth squinted her eyes. "No, I don't. I think you're seeing things."

"It's impossible to miss." River leaned closer to the glass. "Whenever he knows he's winning, Cash gets that silly, little, crooked smirk. You had to have noticed."

Beth shook her head. "I don't usually spend a lot of time studying Cash's facial expressions. However, you seem to have dedicated a lot of time to staring at his face," she teased.

River blushed. "It ain't like that."

In the room, Zac sighed and tossed his cards on the table. He was out. Three of the other players followed suit shortly after. This left only Cash and one player wearing dark sunglasses and a black hoodie.

"See?" said River, "I told you. He's doing just fine."

"Uh, huh," snickered Beth.

"Stop." River gave Beth a slight jab. "I know my boys. That's all."

"Right," Beth responded. "So, what sort of facial ticks does Finn have? Any smirks or subtle tells?"

"That's not the point."

"So, what you're saying is that you don't know any," prodded Beth.

"That is not what I'm saying at all!"

"Okay, then tell me one."

River attempted to come up with one just to prove Beth wrong. Unable to think of anything, she could merely shrug.

Beth laughed. "I bet Teague can describe a few."

"What's that got to do with any of this? He loves Finn. Of course, Teague would know all of his quirks and tells." As soon as the words came out of her mouth, River wanted to take them back. A soft groan escaped her lips.

"You just made my point," announced Beth, smirking from ear to ear.

"I did no such thing."

"You know, it's okay if you like him; it's not like it's any sort of big deal or anything."

River sighed. "I'm not saying I like him. I like him—like a brother. The same way I care about the others. Brothers are special. Lovers are a dime a dozen."

"And soul mates are one in a million, just sayin'," responded Beth.

River peered through the glass as both Cash and the hooded stranger added to the pot. Pshh, soul mates. There's no such thing. It was time for the two players to display their hands and see who won. Hoodie man went first, sitting up straight; he spread out his cards while flashing a confident grin.

Come on. Willed River, studying Cash's reaction. Holding her breath, she watched as he coolly placed his cards on the table in front of him, all the while brandishing his cocky grin.

River couldn't help but smile. She loved seeing that crooked smirk. It was the most Cash thing ever.

"Tell me you didn't see that," she said to Beth.

Beth shook her head. "Of course, I saw that. He just won. Who wouldn't be smiling?"

Hoodie man reared back in his seat and crossed his arms while the table burst into laughter and congratulations. After a high five with Zac, Cash leaned forward and raked in the pile of chips.

River peered over and found Beth smirking with her arms crossed. "Stop it," said River, as she spun Beth around, facing away from the poker room. "Let's go find another game to play."

Chapter 14

The elevator chimed each time it passed a floor. Teague dug around in his pockets, pulling out a few dollar bills. "Looks like twenty."

Finn shook his head. "That ain't shit. We need to get some more. I know I'm hungrier than twenty dollars' worth."

Teague nodded in accord.

The elevator halted, and a computer-generated woman's voice declared, "main floor." As the doors slid open, a blast of cool air burst all around them; the clamor of several hundred electronic slot machines assaulted their ears.

"Then we best get lucky," said Teague, as he stepped out onto the casino floor.

Lights flashed all around while animated figures danced on every screen. The air smelled of a blend of bad cigars, air freshener, and the slightly familiar scent of waffles. The sound and lights were disorienting. It was almost too much for Teague; he could only imagine how Finn was handling the stimuli overload. Everywhere he looked, people of all ages and persuasions sat gawking at flashing screens. Their eyes unblinking as they sipped drinks, smoked cigarettes, or sucked on vapes.

Teague paused and faced Finn, who was looking overwhelmed. "Where you wanna go first?"

"You choose." He shook his head. "I can't."

Teague vacillated between freezing in place exactly where he stood, dashing for the door or spinning around and retreating to the comfort and quiet of the hotel room. Maybe they could find a sandwich or something and take it back upstairs.

Not that he was unfamiliar with casinos or disliked them; they had been in such places before. Mostly, he enjoyed them. It was more a matter of being eased into the experience. After spending the past couple of weeks in the tranquility of the mountains, the casino's artificial atmosphere was overwhelming his senses. He would have preferred to spend a couple of days in a city where he could get used to the sound, activity, and all the people first.

He swept his hand against Finn's arm. "Come on, let's go this way."

Avoiding the center rows, they skirted along the exterior wall, zigzagging through a never-ending throng of people. It's like swimming with salmon in the river, thought Teague, as he dodged out of the way just in time to evade being run over by an old man riding a motorized chair. Hunched over and yelling for people to move, the old man sped along as fast as the machine would carry him—which was more of a vigorous walking pace. Following close behind, a young security guard walked. He gave a sharp nod to Teague, then shook his head over the foolishness of the whole thing.

The more they roamed, the more Teague felt at ease. He still wasn't ready to saunter down any crowded rows, but overall, his anxiety dissipated.

They came upon the poker room. "Cash and Zac must be in here," said Teague, peering through the large window.

"You see 'em?" asked Finn, as he, too, leaned against the glass, scanning the room.

Teague slapped his arm. "Right there. The table in the corner." He studied the players at the table. As usual, Cash remained indecipherable. Zac had an enormous grin on his face. No doubt, he had a good hand. Teague chuckled; Zac was one of those people who was honest to a fault. Usually, this was a good thing; however, with poker, the capacity to lie or at least hide your feelings was imperative. Teague studied the faces of the other players around the table. Nothing. The man wearing the hoodie seemed pretentious, but otherwise, Teague could discern nothing about how the hand was going.

"Cash's got a pretty impressive stack of chips," he told Finn.

"That's good. 'Cause Zac looks like he'll be out in another hand or two."

Teague laughed. "That it does. Though, he seems pretty confident that he's gonna win this round."

"Yeah, but that giant smile on his face is gonna tell the other players they should fold before the pot gets big enough."

Finn was right. It was best to keep your opponents guessing, especially if you held a good hand.

As fun as it was to stand there and critique their friends' play from a distance, Teague was ready to do some playing of his own. He looked around the area, noting the craps tables that stood several yards away. "Come on, let's go over there."

The noise level around the table was even louder than the slot machines, though it was a more natural noise; the sound of people laughing, cheering, and talking. Small crowds encircled each table, overseen and encouraged by a team of dealers. Luckily for Teague, he was taller than most of the people; therefore, he could see what was going on with ease. He saw the bets being placed; they were far too rich for their budget. His stomach growled. If he was feeling this hungry, he could only imagine how starved Finn must be.

He turned to Finn. "Let's go see if we can't find some cheap food."

Once again, they were weaving their way through the human river, only this time, they were going against the swarm. A variety of scents accosted his senses. It was almost impossible to distinguish between cigars, cigarettes, artificial air freshener, perfume, and aftershave. Cheerful faces, angry faces, and distraught—the whole gamut of emotions passed by in an endless parade. A gray-haired woman wearing brilliant red lipstick pushed a stroller with a mesh cover.

Teague leaned over to peep inside; a tiny, tan dog shivered against a fluffy blanket. Eyes darting left and right, the dog's body jumped every time someone hollered.

More bells and music—more howling and cheers. The entire place was full of excitement.

Finn took hold of his arm and pulled him out of the throng toward the wall, halting at the entrance to a sandwich shop. "Here we go, let's eat," he said.

Unfortunately, their twenty dollars did not go very far. Even after ordering a cup of water, they could only manage one sandwich and some chips. They found a secluded spot near a gaudy water fountain.

The sound of cascading water was an unusual addition to the chaos all around them. Cheers, shouts, laughter, clicks, dings, and music—all the while, lights flashed, words scrolled by on digital screens, and cartoonish characters danced and performed.

Teague wasn't in the mood for all this activity. He hoped Finn wasn't, either. "What do you say we finish up, then head back to the room?"

Finn smiled and nodded. "Maybe we can find the hot tub," he suggested. "Being outside sounds good right now."

The horde of people was even thicker than before—if that was even possible. Passing by a row of slot machines, Teague thought he glimpsed River among a cluster of people. The group was too thick to be sure, so he didn't bother to stop.

As they cut through another row of machines, Teague accidentally crashed into a small, elderly Japanese woman, practically knocking her over.

"Oh! I'm so sorry!" shouted Teague over the din. He held her arm as she steadied herself.

"No worries," the old woman replied, "I'm not that weak." She brushed him away.

Teague leaned down and picked up her sweater. As he handed it to her, the machine she was playing lit up. Flowers, coins, and gems cascaded down from the top of the screen while the words "Major award" flashed in brilliant, gold letters.

"You see that?" said the old woman, as she took hold of Teague's arm. "You bring me luck."

Teague nodded and smiled politely as he attempted to free his arm. The old woman held tight. He shot a bemused glance backward at Finn, who stood by, smirking.

"My name is Yukuko," she said.

"Teague."

"Nice to meet you, Teague," she flashed a pleasant smile. "I've put lots of money into this machine, and only after you banged into me did it pay anything back. Stay here and let me see if I can hit again."

Slightly confused and unable to go anywhere with Yukuko holding his arm, Teague agreed to stay put.

She hit the button. The machine spun, then rang out again. This time even louder than before.

"Woo!" shouted Yukuko. The little woman grabbed hold of Teague's face and planted an excited kiss on his lips, then jumped backward. "Yes! Another jackpot! You are my lucky charm."

Teague stood suspended in place. A bewildered look on his face, not sure what to do.

Unable to hold back any longer, Finn busted out laughing. "Congratulations," he said to Yukuko. "Hear that, Teague? You're her lucky charm."

Teague glared back at him.

Yukuko let go of Teague's arm. "You stick around. You owe me that much after almost running me over." Her face softened. "At least a couple more hits."

Irritation welled up inside Teague, but he didn't want to hurt Yukuko's feelings.

"Are you hungry?" the old woman inquired. "I will buy you dinner at the buffet around the corner if you stay for three more spins."

At the mere mention of food, Teague's stomach grumbled. He looked at Finn, who nodded. Looks like I'm here for the duration. He sighed. "All right," he replied. "Three more spins. After that, you owe us dinner."

Yukuko's eyes lit up. She flashed a big smile. "Agreed!"

An hour later, they stood in a vast buffet room. Ornate fixtures hung from the ceiling. Heavy wood tables and chairs filled the center of the room. Waitstaff, wearing white shirts and black trousers, hustled about removing plates and pouring drinks. A savory blend of enticing aromas floated through the air.

True to her word, Yukuko paid for their dinner, though honestly, Teague was not expecting something so grand. Stainless steel counters lined the walls, each presenting different cuisine, all ready for the taking. Roasts, pasta, seafood, and salad—the options were far beyond anything he had imagined. He grabbed two plates and filled them to near overflowing.

Chapter 15

"WHAT'S THE TAKEAWAY?" ASKED ZAC.

Fresh from the cashier's cage, Cash was busy counting their winnings. "Four fifty," he replied. "It ain't great."

"But it's more than we started with," interjected Zac.

"Fifty bucks," agreed Cash. "Not gonna lie, we should've done a lot better."

Zac nodded. "Hoodie dude was a lot better than I would have guessed. I should've dropped the last two hands."

Cash nodded. It was hard to disagree with that statement. He put the money in his wallet and looked around. "Let's find the others. I'm hungry, and I'm gonna bet Finn's about ready to eat a small child."

Zac chuckled. "Hell, that was me an hour ago."

"Me too."

"So," said Zac, as he took stock of the immediate area. "Any idea where to start?"

As if on cue, a loud ruckus exploded around the corner. Someone was winning and having a great time while doing so.

"Let's see what's going on here first," said Cash.

The row of craps tables fanned out before them; each crowded with people—all having a great time. The table on the left was the rowdiest.

It also had the biggest collection of men and women. Based on all the hooting and cheering, someone was doing a lot of winning. Cash and Zac weaved their way over.

The sheer volume of people clustered around the table made it impossible to get close enough to see what was happening. Frustration rose inside Cash. He wanted to know what all the commotion was about. Meanwhile, behind him, somewhere among the slot machines, more shouts burst forth.

Zac wandered off toward the cheers and laughter around the slots.

Cash remained by the craps table, striving to get closer to no avail. Finally, he gave up and backed away. Whatever was going on was not meant for him to see. He sighed, then spun around to follow Zac.

The crowd around the slot machine was considerably smaller than the craps table. A welcome change for Cash. This time, he could get close enough to see what was going on. A woman with dark hair and black eyeliner sat in the chair, surrounded by several men and women —all holding drinks, all cheering.

Cash watched the screen as the woman pulled the crank arm on the side of the machine. The reels spun, then lit up and flashed. The device went red, and the reels turned again—then again, followed by yet another spin. Each time they came to a stop, the winning amount increased. First one hundred, then two-fifty, followed by five hundred. With each roll, the crowd cheered louder. The woman wriggled in her seat, turning around to slap a high five with the gray-haired woman on her immediate right. The machine whirred; another red spin. The pot was now at nine hundred. One more spin. Bells chimed and music played. The screen froze, and the word "jackpot" appeared on a white background. Eighteen hundred dollars. The crowd roared and clapped as they celebrated the win.

Cash glanced at Zac, who was watching from the other side; they shared a sigh of awe. What he wouldn't do for that kind of win.

An attendant appeared carrying her tablet. Cash stepped aside so she could get to the machine. As the crowd continued to celebrate, he slipped between the devices and into the next row. He sauntered down the aisle and came out beside yet another row of slot machines, where he met up with Zac, who slapped him on the arm and nodded toward another cluster of people. It was a small group, not as animated or excited as the last group. They were younger and all men, with two familiar young women standing in the center of them all.

Cash casually strolled up and stood just outside the circle. As usual, River was stealing the show. Her casual nature, coupled with her big, green eyes and beautiful smile, melted many hearts, his own included. He studied the two men on either side of her, both of them vying for her undivided attention. Both failing. He almost pitied them.

His gaze drifted back to River, only to find her smiling and staring directly at him. Such a beautiful smile. She stepped through the mob and wrapped her arm around his. The faces of the two men melted from hopeful to dismayed to sneering.

Unaware of this, River spun around to the group, waved goodbye, and then tugged Cash away.

"How did you do?" she inquired.

"Not as good as I would have liked."

Zac sauntered up with Beth in tow. "But not too bad. At least we're up; a little."

"How about you?" Cash asked River. They paused in front of an elegant buffet restaurant.

She thrust out her chin. "We got up to three hundred dollars," she proclaimed proudly.

"Sweet! Add that to our haul, and we did pretty well."

River shrugged and looked apologetic. "Unfortunately, we didn't keep it all."

"That's okay. How much did you keep?" asked Cash.

River smiled innocently. "None of it."

"You gave it all back?"

"I couldn't stop pushing the buttons," she offered. Then she flashed an innocent smile.

"Your killin' me, woman," sighed Cash. "Oh well, at least it didn't really cost us anything."

"I'm hungry," interjected Beth.

The savory scent of beef wafted through the air, making Cash's mouth water. "Yeah, we all are," he responded. "Let's find Finn and Teague and get some food."

"Any idea where to look?" asked River, as she glanced around the immediate area.

Cash shook his head. "I suppose it's a good thing we have no clue where to start. It means they haven't gotten into trouble."

"Found 'em!" shouted Beth, pointing inside the restaurant.

Seated at a table in the corner, nearly hidden by a stack of dirty dinner plates, sat Finn and Teague. Busy focusing on the food they were devouring, they didn't even notice their friends waving their hands to get their attention.

"Come on," said River, taking hold of Cash's arm and tugging him along behind her.

A stout man stopped them in their tracks at the entrance. "Pay line is over there," he said, pointing at the cashier who stood nearby.

"We just wanna go chat with our friends," said Cash.

The stocky man moved his head slowly from side to side. "No pay; no entry."

Okay then.

Cash realized there would be no working around this one. He sighed, then replied, "I guess we'll just go pay then." The man nodded in reply.

Cash turned to the cashier. "How much is it?" he asked, pulling out his wallet.

"Thirty dollars," replied the cashier.

He counted thirty dollars and handed it over.

She blinked up at him and shook her head. "Each."

"Each?" asked Cash, eyes wide. He glanced at the others, then back at the lady. "Like, thirty dollars times four?"

The cashier nodded.

"That's a buck twenty!" Cash blurted, incredulous.

The lady nodded yet again.

He turned to the others. "That's a lot more than I wanna pay. How about you guys?"

"I'm hungry," whimpered Beth.

Zac shrugged. "The food must be good."

Cash looked at River. "I'm gonna hate myself for this," he declared.

She beamed back at him. "Ah yes, but your belly will be full of amazing food."

"It better be amazing."

Begrudgingly, he paid the full fee. They skirted past the burly man and into the main dining area. As they passed by the dessert table, the tantalizing aroma of chocolate and apple pie accosted his senses, making his mouth water even more.

Cash wandered up to the table where Finn and Teague sat, finally gaining their attention.

Teague was finishing a loaded baked potato while Finn gnawed away on a rib bone.

"How's the food?" asked Cash.

Finn flashed a bar-b-q-covered thumb into the air and grinned. Sauce and tiny flecks of pork spread all over his face.

"How the hell did you two get in here?" demanded Cash.

"Yukuko," replied Teague.

"Who?"

"Someone's little Japanese grandma," answered Finn. He pushed the plates around the table in search of something. Teague handed him a napkin, and he nodded a thank you.

"It was her way of thanking us for helping her win," explained Teague.

Finn wiped his face. "She kissed him on the mouth."

"You sound a little jealous," chided Zac.

"I ain't jealous," defended Finn.

Cash chuckled. "Yeah, that sounds like jealousy to me. Wouldn't you agree, River?"

"Yep," she concurred, giggling.

Finn stood up and tossed his napkin on the table. "Not jealous," he said, then he stalked off toward the Italian food.

"With that," said Zac, "I'm getting some of that prime rib over there." He held his arm out to Beth. "Care to join me?"

She chuckled and took his arm.

"I'm gonna go try some of the Cajun," said River.

Teague wiped his face and scooted his chair back. "Hold up, I'll go with," he said, "I need to have some more jambalaya; it's pretty good. Could use some more spice, though."

Cash chuckled and followed. They might not have come out on top of this whole side quest, but he was going to make sure he'd get his money's worth out of the buffet.

Chapter 16

HEAVY SMOKE, CARRIED ON A LIGHT, WARM BREEZE, BILLOWED AROUND Daniel, burning his eyes, causing them to water. While uncomfortable, it was not nearly as bad as sitting too close to some of the drifters who made up the camp. The stench of body odor was practically enough to make him want to pack it in and go home. It was so strong it overwhelmed the smell of the burning wood. Daniel promised himself that when he finally caught up with Finn, he would make the little bastard pay for every bit of discomfort he suffered along the way.

For the past several months, Daniel studied the world of train hoppers. He lurked online in their forums and interacted with whoever would respond. This allowed him to learn most of their lingo; a required skill if he was to fit in. He didn't enjoy these in-person forays among the rabble. But if he was going to find Finn, he had to get out and learn about their world. These Nomads didn't make it easy. Some of them had attitudes that made it impossible to get close enough to learn anything. Hard edges all around, and unfriendly as hell. While others were almost too friendly, those were usually the ones who smelled the worst.

Shortly after discovering the Nomad Girl's profile online, he created a profile of his own. One that hid his identity while also making him desirable for a teenage girl to interact with. It wasn't diffi-cult at all to find a suitable, young male to steal images from. This generation was all online. They photographed and shared everything. How naïve of them.

Profile set up, Daniel immediately went about connecting and adding friends. After all, he had to appear legitimate. This was prob-ably the worst part of the whole thing. All the hours spent online chat-ting with the mindless, narcissistic fools. All he had to do to get in with them was stroke their ego. A compliment here, a friendly post there, and he was a shoo-in. It was almost too easy. These kids were desperate to be popular online.

The easiest one of all was the Nomad Girl herself; it was almost sad. He first started following her and liking her posts. Gradually, he posted comments, always flattering to her, of course. Constantly letting her know how cool she was and how much he admired her. It took him less than two weeks before she sent him a "friend" request.

Of course, he waited two hours before accepting—wouldn't want to seem too eager after all. She would comment on his posts from that point on, and in return, he would comment on hers. Her posts told him where the group was at a particular time, but he needed different infor-mation. If he was ever going to catch up with them, he needed to know where they were headed before they arrived. He needed to be one step ahead of the group. The only way to get that information, was to ask. Not wanting to be suspicious, Daniel waited for the right time to send a private message. A few more interactions, and it would be time. After all, how else was he going to find his son?

"Oh, I love this song!" shouted a young woman, on the other side of the fire. She hopped to her feet, pulling the young man whose lap she had been sitting on with her. She folded her arms around his neck, and the two slowly swayed to the music.

Daniel watched, transfixed. Young lust. He could still recall the days of unbridled desire when a young firefighter, just out of the acad-emy, met a young woman at the beach. The week they spent together, they could hardly keep their hands off of one another long enough to eat.

When his buddies suggested joining them for a week at Port Aransas, his first inclination was to decline. Daniel was never big on partying. His real ambition was to find the right girl, marry and have a family. He didn't like drugs or alcohol, and in his opinion, partying was just a waste of time.

After much prodding, his best friend, Corey, finally convinced him to go. The next thing he knew, he found himself in Corey's old dually, barreling toward the Texas coastline. Corey seemed determined to hit every bar on the island. Daniel obliged begrudgingly.

It was their fourth stop and third round of tequila shots when Daniel first spotted Tricia. Sitting alone at the bar, sipping an oversized margarita, she looked lost and out of place. There was a quiet sadness to her. A solemn look on her face as she swirled the yellow liquid in her glass. He scanned the room to discern whether she was there with a date. As far as he could tell, she was alone.

Daniel wasn't what anyone would call a ladies' man; he was shy and awkward when talking to women, especially pretty ones.

He took one more shot of tequila and his nerves were steady enough to mosey over.

"Is this seat taken?" he asked, voice quaking. His mouth was dry, his throat constricted. Music blasted over the speakers, mixed with the voices of dozens of people.

A sudden smile spread across her face. Her eyes lit up. "No, go ahead. You can sit there," she replied. A rogue lock of hair fell across her face; her first attempt to move it was a gentle puff of breath. The lock remained, so she sighed and flipped her hair over to the other side.

Nervous but optimistic, Daniel took a seat. "It's loud in here, isn't it?" he said clumsily.

She shrugged. "The noise is kinda nice. Allows me to think."

Suddenly self-conscious, heat spread up from his neck, turning his face red. "I'm sorry, I didn't mean to bug you—"

"No, no," she responded quickly. "You're not bugging me. Not at all." She placed a soft hand on his arm and smiled again. "I'm Tricia." She held out her other hand.

"Daniel."

Tricia nodded toward Corey and the others. "How come you're not hanging with your friends?"

"Between you and me?" He grinned. "They're a little too loud."

Laughter erupted across the bar as Corey chugged down a beer, prompted by all the people around him chanting, "Corey, Corey, Corey."

"I see what you mean." Chuckled Tricia. "You're welcome to stay on this side of the bar. To avoid all the noise, that is."

"Well, thank you for the generous offer. I believe I would be a fool to not take you up on it."

Time slowed, lost in deep conversation, the bar emptied around them. The only interruption was when Corey came up, drunk and nearly falling over, to tell Daniel it was time to leave. After Tricia offered to drive Daniel back to his hotel, Corey flashed a drunken wink, then disappeared through the door. Not long after, the lights came on, and the bartender suggested they take their conversation elsewhere.

They spent the night at Tricia's hotel—and every subsequent day and evening after. The days and nights blended together. Between bouts of lovemaking, napping, and endless conversation, they hardly left the room.

Daniel had fallen hard. He didn't want the week to end. Tricia lived north of Dallas; he was west of Austin. The odds of them working out a way to see each other more than every few months were slim.

As he hugged her in the parking lot, he leaned down and kissed her forehead. "Promise we'll see each other in two months."

Tricia snuggled close to his chest and breathed deeply. "Two months. Promise."

They kissed one last time, then she climbed into her car and drove away.

The entire ride home, Daniel sat quietly staring out the window, daydreaming. The scent of her perfume still clung to his clothes. He could still feel her hands on his body.

He tried to call her several times, but she never answered her phone. He left messages, but she didn't call back. Corey told him to let it go. He had a new job to focus on; responsibilities to take care of. There were plenty of other fish in the sea.

Gradually, Daniel let his dream of being with the girl at the beach slip away into oblivion. He loved his job, and eventually, he began dating Corey's sister Erin. Memories of his wild week at the beach gave way to cozy nights snuggled up on the sofa with the beautiful red-head. They talked about marriage and how many children they would have. They settled on three. On New Year's Eve, nearly eight months after his wild, summer affair with Tricia, Daniel proposed to Erin. They set a date for the following spring.

His life was perfect.

Two months later, Tricia called. Her voice quaked when she spoke; catching in her throat mid-sentence. She pleaded with him to meet her, claiming they had to talk.

A deep sense of foreboding set in—something was off. Daniel told himself he needed to go, just to make sure she was okay to drive all the way home, not because he still had feelings for her.

Sitting in his car outside the hotel, he convinced himself he was not lying to Erin. She would want him to make sure Tricia was okay. After all, it was a long drive to North Texas. Erin cared about others that way. He was doing what she would want him to do.

He paused at the door of the hotel room and breathed deep. A pang of guilt stabbed his chest.

A baby cried out. Daniel leaned close and pressed his ear against the door, pulling back when he heard the unmistakable sound of a baby wailing inside the room.

His heart raced. Maybe he had the wrong room. He pulled out the slip of paper with the address and room number—it was the right one. Inside, the baby continued to wail.

Palms sweaty, he knocked on the door.

It opened with a gush of air and a plume of cigarette smoke. Somewhere inside the room, a baby's high-pitched cries pierced the air.

Flustered, hair a mess, wearing rumpled clothes, Tricia stood before him. She blew a lock of hair away from her face, then leaped forward, wrapping her arms around his neck. "Oh god," she whispered, "I am so glad you came." She leaned forward to kiss him; he pulled back and gently unhinged her hands from his neck.

The baby wailed a bloodcurdling cry.

"What's going on?" he demanded. Nervous that he might already know the answer.

Tricia sighed. "Well, you might as well come on in and see." She gestured for him to enter.

Beneath the scent of cigarette smoke, the room reeked of old takeout and dirty diapers. The television was on, playing some daytime talk show. A tiny baby, dressed in a light-blue sleeper, lay sprawled out in the middle of the bed. Body tense, arms stretched out in a claw-like pose. Face red, it inhaled, screamed, then choked.

"Jesus Christ!" shouted Daniel, as he dashed across the room and scooped the baby in his arms. In his line of work, he handled enough newborns to know how to calm them down. He held the tiny, feverishly warm head against his throat, rocking back and forth, he whispered, "Shh, shh, little guy. It's okay."

The baby responded immediately. He calmed down and became slack in Daniel's arms. His tiny body shuddered with each intake of breath, but he no longer cried.

"What the hell is going on?" he asked Tricia. Mindful of the baby in his arms, he spoke in a subdued tone that masked his rage.

Tricia scoffed and lit another cigarette.

"Put that damn thing out!" he snarled. The baby startled, his tiny hand grasping Daniel's collar.

After taking one long drag, Tricia put out the cigarette and exhaled. The noxious cloud drifted across the room to Daniel, who batted it away to keep the baby from breathing it in.

"Don't even act like you don't know," she hissed.

Daniel knew what she was alluding to, but he needed her to say the words out loud. He needed to hear them outside of his own brain.

Tricia chuckled. "I guess I'll just say it then. Daniel." She gestured toward the baby. "Meet your son, Finn."

The words hit him like a blast of fire. His heart raced. Breathing was difficult. Was this what it was like to have a panic attack? He sat heavily on the edge of the bed; blood pounded in his brain. He took a deep breath and held the baby out in front of him.

Daniel stared down at the tiny being in his hands. The baby lay calm—relaxed, staring up at him with one blue eye and one amber brown, a shock of dark hair on the top of his head. He touched a chubby, dimpled hand. The baby wrapped his tiny fingers around Daniel's.

So small.

"How you doin' little guy?"

The baby cooed and let out a tiny yawn. He stretched and smiled the most beautiful smile Daniel had ever seen. At that moment, Daniel knew he loved this tiny, little human more than he thought possible. He would do anything for him.

"Hey, Finn." Tears welled up in Daniel's eyes.

The baby stared.

Daniel's heart melted. "You will always be safe with me."

That night, he went home and told Erin. The only honorable thing for him to do was marry the mother of his child and give them a proper home. After a big fight and many tears, he packed his bags and moved into the hotel with Tricia until they could find a home of their own.

He and Tricia married at the courthouse a week later, just the two of them and their newborn son, Finn. Corey never spoke to him again, neither did Erin.

A cold, wet nose brushed up against his hand, causing Daniel to jump. "What the—" A small, dirty, white dog sat staring up at him.

"Gypsy! Here!" barked a gruff, commanding voice.

The little dog waddled over to the muscular, blond man, standing a few feet away from Daniel.

"Sorry, man," said the dog's owner.

"No worries. No worries," replied Daniel. "Aside from being dirty, she's kinda cute."

The big man smiled. "Yeah, she is kinda dirty. Our last ride was a grimy one."

The dancing girl sauntered up. "Gunner, why don't you come join us for a drink."

"Sorry, Ella, our ride is heading out in a few minutes." He gave out a sharp whistle. "Nate. Stop fucking around. Time to go."

Ella's bottom lip jutted out in a mock pout. "Aw, too bad," she said. "Y'all meeting up with River and the others?"

At the sound of River's name, Daniel's ears perked up. He had spent enough time on Nomad Girl's account to know the names of their entire group. He studied the big man more closely. The posture, the confident swagger; Daniel had spent enough time around ex-military to know one when he saw one. A distinct bulge in the back of his jeans, just below the belt, told Daniel that Gunner was packing a handgun.

A young man, who reminded him of a lighter-haired version of Finn jogged up alongside Gunner.

"Nah," replied Gunner, "They're heading to Flagstaff. We're goin' the other way."

Flagstaff.

Daniel stared, unmoving, as Gunner and his young companion, Nate, waved their goodbyes, then disappeared into the darkness, taking the little, white dog with them.

The night wasn't a bust after all; he now had a concrete lead. Time to hit the road. Daniel wondered what the weather was like in Flagstaff this time of year.

Chapter 17

THE AMARILLO TRAIN YARD WAS A GOOD FEW MILES UP AHEAD. OVER the past few days, they had messed up so many rides that when this one came up as an option; they jumped at it. No one considered the ramifications or complications of riding a freight train straight into the heart of one of the largest train yards in the middle of the day. At least, not until the very moment they were rolling through the city in broad daylight. To their left, vehicles streamed by on the freeway—to their right, tall office buildings obscured the view of the landscape beyond.

The plan was to meet up with Bells, D.B., and Max at the Cadillac Ranch just west of the city. Since it was daylight, they didn't have the option of riding straight through the city to their destination. Instead, they would have to hop off before the train got to the yard, then make their way across the city via bus, ride, or walking.

The train slowed and blasted its whistle, signaling its arrival.

"This is it," said Finn, as he rose to his feet and readied his pack. All around him, in the boxcar, the others were busy doing the same.

Zac peered out the door. "Time to go!" He tossed his pack, then jumped.

One by one, the others leaped from the car. Finally, it was Finn's turn. He tossed his gear, then leaped into the air. A warm rush of dry, desert air, carrying the scent of oil and metal, whirled around him. He inhaled deeply; he loved that smell.

His feet hit the gravel. Acting on pure impulse, his body rolled with the landing, coming to a stop standing on his feet. He paused long enough to run his fingers through his overgrown hair, then picked up his pack and gathered with the group.

"Any word from Max and the others?" he asked Teague, who was looking at his phone.

"Ya, they're almost at the ranch. It shouldn't take us long to catch up with them."

"There a bus stop anywhere nearby?" asked Cash.

"Looks like one's about a half-mile away," replied Teague, as he pinched and pulled the map on his phone. He glanced around the area. "That way." He pointed west.

The city was alive all around them. Vehicles of all types and sizes clustered on the streets while men and women dressed in tidy, office attire bustled about, sipping from their paper coffee cups. The buses crowded with commuters made Finn feel constrained—he hated it. Two more stops, and they'd be off this damn sardine can. Staring out the window, he counted streetlights. Twenty-two, twenty-three, twenty-four —.

When the bus pulled over at their destination, he was the first to bolt for the door. Once outside, he breathed in deep, letting the fresh air calm his nerves. Finn hated being packed together with so many strangers, too many people breathing the same stale air. It made him queasy.

Their destination was a couple of miles up the road. Finn walked ahead of the others, ignoring their lighthearted banter. A light, persistent breeze blew in his face, keeping his hair from falling into his eyes. He focused on the sound of his boots striking the pavement, counting every step. Three hundred forty-five, three hundred forty-six —.

He passed the Cadillac Ranch RV Park and crossed the road. The air immediately took on a chemical odor, like spray paint. They were close. Dozens of parked vehicles lined the roadside. Graffiti appeared on the blacktop. At first, intermittent and easy to read, it gradually gave way to a rainbow of colors and words with the odd drawing mixed in. Behind him, the others took to reading aloud the messages and names.

The chemical smell was potent. Finn wrinkled his nose, holding back a sneeze.

"Hey," came a familiar, feminine voice. "Howdy, my people." Bells hopped off the fence rail she was sitting on and sauntered over to Finn. She wrapped her slender, muscled arms around his neck and pulled him in close.

Thin of frame with her shaggy, straight, blonde hair, Bells stood a few inches shorter than Finn. She stepped back and studied him; her piercing, brown eyes peered through long, spikey-cut bangs. A satisfied smile spread across her face.

"Finn, you scruffy bastard, you look great." She tussled his hair as though he were a little brother. She worked her way through all the others, one by one, each time saying something endearing and unique to each individual. "Hey Beth," she said, as she paused in front of her. "Finally! We meet in person!" She took hold of Beth's shoulders and pulled her in for a fierce hug.

"Where's Max and D.B.?" asked River.

"They're over by the cars," replied Bells. "Last I saw, D.B. was creating one of his works of art while Max was busy chatting up some Swedish tourists; gotta earn his dollar." She winked. "I couldn't take the smell of all that spray paint, so I came out here to wait for y'all." She tapped her chest. "No telling what all those chemicals will do to your lungs."

"I can't believe he's still at it," said Cash, shaking his head.

Bells smirked. "My boy is nothing if not determined."

"Still at what?" asked Beth.

"You'll see," chuckled Bells. "It's best if he explains it." She took hold of Finn's arm and led the group toward the gate.

The chemical stench of spray paint permeated the air. Finn couldn't help but wonder whether they could get a contact high outside in the open air. Up ahead, the famous row of Cadillacs stood half-buried, nose-first at an angle. Cans of used spray paint littered the ground while crowds milled around between the vehicles, reading the various tags or posing for pictures.

Four cars down, he spied D.B., crouching down close to the ground, focused on his latest creation on the underbelly of a car. Finn strolled over and peered past D.B.'s shoulder to see what he was working on. It was a blood-red Nomad compass.

"Nice," said Finn approvingly.

D.B. put on a few finishing touches, then stepped back and inspected his artwork. "I'm hopin' it'll stay solid for a while since it's so low to the ground."

A dense cloud of spray paint floated past, making Finn sneeze. "Dude, I can't believe you aren't high just bein' out here in this."

D.B. chuckled. "Who says I ain't?"

Beth wandered up, phone in hand. "Come on, stand next to the car so I can get a picture of you with your work of art."

D.B. shook his head. "Nah, I'd rather not be associated with my tags, even if it's legal to do them here." He and Finn backed away and let Beth take her picture.

Max sauntered up with a family of four in tow. "Ah, here're my friends," he exclaimed. "Finn, this is Ville," he pointed to the tall, slim blond man at his side, then gestured to a blonde woman. "This lovely lady is Kajsa." He pointed to two children, one blond boy, and a redhead girl. "The two shorter folks behind her are Viktor and Amalia."

Ville moved forward, reaching his hand out to Finn. "Nice to meet you," the man said, with a heavy Swedish accent. "Max has been telling us about his adventures."

"Don't believe everything he says," warned Finn. "He talks a lot of shit."

Ville laughed. "I'm glad we stopped here. It wasn't something we planned, but you have to ask, when will we have another chance to see such a display of American culture. Besides, where else would we have met Max?"

Kajsa leaned close and whispered something to Ville. "Oh, yes," he replied aloud. "Looks like it is time for us to leave. We have several more hours before we reach Dallas."

"It was great meeting y'all," said Max. "Before you head out, can I ask a quick favor?"

"There's no harm in asking," agreed Ville.

"Can you spare a buck?"

A look of confusion spread across Ville's face. "A buck?"

"Yeah," replied Max, "a US dollar."

Ville pulled out his wallet. "Of course." He picked out a ten-dollar bill and handed it to Max.

"Nah, Nah," protested Max, putting his hands out in front of him. "Just a buck. No more. Though, I could take a buck from Kasja too." He winked.

Kasja pulled her wallet from her bag and fished out four one-dollar bills. "Here, there is one from Ville, me and one each from Viktor and Amalia." She smiled as she passed the bills to Max.

"Thank you. I appreciate it very much," responded Max.

The couple said their goodbyes and headed back toward the parked cars along the roadside.

Max took out a fat roll of bills from his front pocket. He wrapped the new bills around the others and twisted the rubber band around, securing the stack.

"That's quite a haul you got there," said Finn.

"You should've seen the wad he put into the bank a couple of weeks ago," said D.B.

"So, what is the deal with the dollar bills?" asked Beth, as she watched Max stuff the roll into his pocket.

"Go ahead, Max," said Bells, "explain it to her."

Max grinned and cleared his throat. "Statistically speaking, the average person can meet about ten thousand people in their lifetime. I'm not average." He lit a cigarette, took a puff, and exhaled. "I imagine I meet about that many new people every year or so."

"Still not sure what that has to do with the dollar bills," said Beth.

Max took another drag. "Hold up, hold up, I'm gettin' to that." He exhaled a plume of smoke. "Now, I figure, if I could get a buck from every new person I meet, that would add up."

Beth nodded. "Go on."

"Like, say I meet ten thousand people and get a buck from each of them. That would be ten thousand tax-free dollars every year." He took another drag and snuffed out his cigarette. "Over time, I bet I could end up making a million dollars—one buck at a time." He brandished a wild grin.

"Except it's gonna take you a hundred years to do that," interjected Cash.

Max wagged his finger. "Now, now, you and I have had this conversation before. If I bump it up and go the extra mile, I could do it in less." He smirked. "Or if some folks, who still owe me a dollar, would pay up, it would be that much faster."

Cash shook his head. "I am not giving you a buck. I'm not participating in your game."

"You'll cave," retorted Max. "They all have." He smiled at Finn. "Ain't that right?"

Finn shrugged. "What can I say? You wore me down, man."

Cash shoved Finn playfully. "Sell out."

Beth giggled. "I'm in," she said, as she handed a dollar bill to Max. "Here's my contribution to your millionaire fund."

"Oh, come on, Beth, don't encourage him," warned Cash.

"Well, thank you very much, my lady," replied Max, as he added the bill to his roll.

"How do you keep from spending or losing it?" asked Beth.

Bells stepped forward. "He makes us stop by his bank so he can make a deposit whenever we pass one."

Max nodded. "This is true."

"How much do you have so far?"

He flashed a satisfied smile. "Last deposit, the account was just over twelve thousand."

"Wow!" exclaimed Beth.

"I've only been at it for a little over a year and a half."

Bells scoffed. "He came up with the theory one night when he was super high."

Everyone laughed.

"I can see that," said Beth.

"Ha, ha, ha," responded Max sarcastically. "Y'all laugh away. We'll see how you feel when I'm a millionaire."

"We'll all be dead," countered Cash, "cause it's gonna take you a hundred years!"

"Well, I, for one, am rooting for you," stated Beth.

Max wrapped his arm around her shoulder. "Beth, I'm gonna like having you around."

Chapter 18

THE MOON HUNG LOW IN THE SKY, CASTING ITS BRILLIANT LIGHT UPON the train yard. Ordinarily, Cash enjoyed catching on by moonlight; however, in this specific circumstance, it complicated things. The cool, white orb shined down without preference. The same bright light that helped Cash and his friends also aided the yard crew by making it easy to see any and all activity. This would not be an easy hop. It was bad enough with all the extra people; the illumination exacerbated things. This made him nervous.

He peered up at the sky. "Damn moon," he muttered.

"On the upside," said Max, "at least we can see exactly what we're doin'."

"Yeah, and so can everyone else," admonished Cash.

"Nah, you worry too much. We just need to keep our heads down. Piece of cake."

Cash sighed. "I seriously hope so."

The train rolled forward—he braced himself. Max was right; the moonlight was a bonus. At least he didn't have to worry about tripping over something or stumbling into any of the others.

Bells, River and Beth ran forward first, followed by Max Teague and Zac. Now it was Cash's turn. With Finn and D.B. in tow, he dashed toward the train.

Cash crept close along the side of the car to minimize casting a shadow. The train was not moving fast, which made it easy to keep pace. He took hold of the rusty metal ladder and climbed into the gondola with ease, landing softly on the grit-covered floor.

"Looks like your concern was misplaced," said D.B.

The phone in Cash's pocket buzzed with an incoming message. "Everyone's on," he said, after reading the text, "we're on our way."

The train rolled out of the yard. With each passing second, the lights of the city receded farther into the distance until, at last, the only light was that of the moon, surrounded by billions of tiny stars. Leaning back against a pile of coal, Cash took in the glittering spectacle overhead. Cool air swirled around him, carrying with it minute particles of dust and the familiar scent of metal, rock, and grease. Cash breathed in deep. Was there anything better? He smiled to himself because he knew the answer to that question—No, there wasn't. He wondered where they were. Had they crossed over into New Mexico yet? Or were they still in Texas?

A small, glowing, red object sailed over the rim of the car and landed atop the pile of coal. It bounced off the rocks, falling to the floor, where it detonated with a loud pop!

"What the hell was that?" Cash shouted, as he jumped to his feet.

"Looks like they're fucking with us," replied D.B. He picked up the small paper remains of what used to be a red and white firecracker. "We got a bunch of these earlier today at one of those roadside stands."

Cash climbed to the car's rim and found himself staring directly at Max, Teague, and Zac. All of them sporting huge grins.

"Nice," he said, "that could have hit one of us."

Max's face became serious. "Did we hit anyone?"

Finn and D.B. appeared alongside Cash.

"Nah," replied Finn, "you missed us by a mile."

D.B. held up a pack of firecrackers. He sparked a lighter and lit several fuses at one time, then tossed the fiery mass over to the other car. "Heads up!"

The metal walls of the gondola multiplied tenfold, the sound of the bursts.

Bells, River and Beth peered over the rim of the car they were riding in.

"Incoming!" shouted Bells, as she lobbed another flaming pack into the middle car.

"That all ya got?" teased Max. "You're gonna have to do a lot better than that," he declared, as he pulled a roman candle from his pack. He aimed it at the girls and ignited the fuse.

"Oh, shit!" shouted one of them, then all three ducked down out of sight.

Glowing red orbs erupted from the tube, flying overhead, exploding in a riot of bright light one after another.

"You asshole!" cursed Bells, as she leaned over the rim. "You wanna play, huh?" In her hand, she dangled a roman candle of her own.

"Shit!" yelled Max, then he turned and ran for the far end of the car, taking cover behind the pile of coal.

Grinning viscously, Bells ignited the tube. Flaming balls flew out, bouncing atop the coal. One landed on Max's backpack. Smoke billowed as the fabric caught fire.

"Holy shit!" he cursed, as he stumbled and slid over the loose rocks. He grabbed hold of his pack and batted furiously at the burning embers. "All right, that's it. This is war!" he announced.

"Yeah?" replied Bells, "That's exactly what I figured." She wiggled another roman candle between two fingers.

Max pulled another from his still smoking pack. "Gloves are off, sister," he warned. "You're goin' down!"

"Bring it!" taunted Bells.

Both of them lit their candles and aimed directly at one another. Bells' went off first, launching a fireball that struck Max in the side. He yelped and swatted it away, causing his first charge to fly astray— directly at Finn, Cash and D.B., barely missing them as they ducked just in time.

"Watch it now!" warned D.B. "Keep the fireworks over there. We're just spectators over here."

"Consider it a fully immersive experience," quipped Max.

The train jerked, then slowed as the steel wheels squealed on the tracks. The rapid shift in forward momentum almost knocked Cash off his feet. He grabbed hold of Finn for balance.

They were in the middle of nowhere. Why did the train stop so abruptly? Cash thought he knew the answer; he just didn't want to believe it.

"This ain't good," whispered Finn.

Glancing over at the other cars, everyone stared out with the same look of confusion on their faces. A blinding spotlight burst out from the front of the train. "Stay right where you are!" A voice ordered over a bullhorn.

No way was that going to happen. Like mice scurrying from a barn cat, everyone grabbed their gear and scattered in various directions.

Cash followed Finn and D.B. out of the car, running as far away from the train as possible. The moon illuminated their way, making it, so they didn't end up stumbling into a thorny desert shrub. They vaulted over a slight rise and came to a stop, peering back at the tracks. It stunned Cash at how far they had run in such a short time. Scanning the horizon, he could see no trace of the others. A narrow beam of light weaved and bobbed along the tracks. The engineers were walking the length of the train, searching for them. The light shaft turned and skimmed the darkness in their general direction. Cash, D.B., and Finn ducked down. They waited several moments before peering back again; the beam was slowly making its way back up to the front, engine car.

They watched quietly in the darkness as the train rolled forward, picked up speed, and moved away. Moments later, there was no sign the train had even been on the tracks.

The melodies of the evening desert surrounded them. Cicadas and crickets sang their choruses, echoing out across the wide-open wilderness.

Cash pulled the phone from his pocket—no connection. He nudged Finn. "Where's your phone?"

Finn shrugged. "Maybe the outside pocket." He turned his back to Cash so he could access the pockets in his pack.

After rummaging around for several minutes, Cash found the phone, only to realize it was completely dead. "Dude, do you ever charge this thing?"

Finn shrugged.

"I got mine," said D.B., "and it looks like I got a couple of bars." He texted a message to the others.

```
D.B.: Where y'all at?
Max: The desert.
D.B.: Smartass. Any notable landmarks?
Max: Rocks, shrubs, oh, and sand. Lots of sand.
Teague: I slapped him for ya.
D.B.: Thanks!
Bells: I owe ya one.
River: We all do.
D.B.: Again, are there any notable landmarks
around?
Max: I can't really see. My vision's blurry from
a head injury.
```

Cash chuckled while D.B. sighed.

```
Teague: There're some lights in the distance. It
might be a town.
Bells: We see them too.
```

Cash looked out upon the horizon. There was a faint glow in the distance. It was hard to tell if it was a glow of lights or his mind playing tricks in the night. He pointed. "That might be what they see."

"Yeah, was just thinkin' that," replied D.B. He turned back to his phone.

D.B.: I suggest we head toward that light and see
if it's a town or something.
Max: Head toward the light, Carol Anne.
Bells: Teague, please hit him again.

Silence

D.B.: So we all good? We're gonna head toward the
lights.
Bells: Sounds like a plan.
River: Got it.
Max: Which lights? The ones over the hill or the
ones behind my eyelids from the brain trauma
after being abused?
Teague: We'll see you there. I can't guarantee I
ain't gonna slap him again just so you know.

Cash, D.B., and Finn plodded their way toward the lights, hoping that at some point, a town would come into view. All around them, the dark desert teemed with life.

They came to a gravel road, the first sign of civilization—a welcome sight to see. A perfect spot for a quick break, Cash tossed his pack on the ground and sat down. Exhaustion taking hold in the wake of waning adrenaline.

"Do you hear that?" asked D.B.

"Hear wha—?" asked Finn.

D.B. put a finger to his lips. "Shh, shh."

Cash perked up his ears, trying to hear the mysterious sound. Other than the wind and various desert creatures scurrying around in the dark, he heard nothing out of place.

Head tilted at an odd angle, D.B. climbed to his feet and slowly wandered down a gravel path.

"Looks like the rest is over," Cash said to Finn. "Come on."

The gravel path turned out to be a narrow driveway that curved around a grove of trees. Beyond that sat a small, desolate farmhouse. A dilapidated barn stood halfway between them and the house. Undaunted, D.B. continued to pursue the elusive sound straight into the barn. Even though he didn't want to, Cash followed.

A small, almost impossible to hear whimper was barely audible. It wasn't a whimper though; it was more like a cry or call out—like the sound baby animals make for their momma. Following the sound, they crept around a rusty, old tractor, stopping in front of a pile of rotting wood and hay. The sound was much louder now. It was definitely a baby animal.

D.B. gently pulled away some of the hay. Sitting in the middle, they found a tiny, mottled, black and orange kitten. Scrawny and covered in mange, the kitten trembled and let out a pathetic hiss, pawing at the air.

"Hey there, little fella," whispered D.B. "You here all alone?"

He reached his hand toward the tiny thing. It tried to growl and swiped at D.B.'s hand—which was giant compared to the pathetic thing. D.B. ignored the feeble attempts and gently placed his hand on the head of the creature. The kitten responded by leaning into his hand and purring.

"That's a good boy," cooed D.B. "You want some food?" He scooped up the kitten and walked back over to his pack. The kitten sat exactly where D.B. placed him, watching patiently as D.B. dug around, finally pulling out a small packet of tuna. "How about some of this?" He wiggled the pack in the air.

The kitten meowed as if it were responding.

D.B. tore open the packet and handed a bit of tuna to the kitten. "All right, here ya go."

The kitten pounced and gobbled the chunks of tuna noisily. Meowing loudly when done, asking for more. D.B. fed the entire contents of the packet to the tiny creature, one handful at a time.

"Where do you think its momma is?" asked Cash.

D.B. glanced around the barn and shrugged. "He looks like he's had nothing to eat in days."

Cash reached out and pet the little animal. Skin and bones. D.B. was right; this little guy hadn't eaten in a while. It was a good thing they stumbled upon him. He might not have made it much longer. A flea jumped onto Cash's hand; instinctively, he jerked his hand away and shook it off.

D.B. was unfazed.

Finished cleaning itself, the baby animal stretched and curled up on D.B.'s lap, purring.

"Looks like you got yourself a permanent friend," quipped Cash. "He's kinda cute, don't ya think?" He asked over his shoulder, expecting Finn to reply. When no response came, he looked around. "Where's Finn?"

"I don't recall seeing him when we came in here."

Cash walked over to the door and peered outside toward the house. Illuminated by the moon, a shadow moved across the side toward the back.

"Shit!" said Cash, over his shoulder. "Looks like he's checking out the house. You stay here with your buddy; I'll go with Finn."

The closer Cash got to the house, the more clear it was that the building was abandoned. A strip of yellow police tape dangled off the frame of the front door. He walked around back to find the door ajar.

Leaning his head inside, he called out in a whisper, "Finn. You in here?" Why he was whispering was beyond him. The house was empty. Who was he going to disturb?

"Yeah, right here," replied Finn from the dark.

Cash pulled out his flashlight and clicked it on, only to be blinded by the explosion of light all around the room as Finn clicked on the kitchen light.

"The place is empty," said Finn.

"Figured as much," replied Cash, shielding his eyes from the bright light to give them a chance to adjust.

He examined the room. A few dishes sat on the drying rack, covered in a thin film of dust. One bowl, one mug, and a fork. Whoever lived here did so alone. Following Finn, he entered the living room. Metal crosses of various sizes and detail covered one wall. Opposite that stood an old television. It was hard to tell how old the device was, but Cash was pretty sure it was older than him.

Past the staircase, down a narrow hall, was the bathroom, followed by a small bedroom. Across the hall was a larger room. A creaky floorboard overhead told him that Finn was already upstairs. He walked back down the passageway and made his way up, coming to a stop in an open loft area.

Finn stood in the middle of the room, staring up at a giant, crimson stain covering the entire wall. A small collection of photographs littered the bloodstained floor around his feet.

Cash lifted one photo. Dried blood spatter speckled the faces of the smiling young children. Revulsion overcame him—he flicked the photograph to the floor.

"Holy shit," he said. "What the hell happened here?"

Finn ran his hand over the stain.

Don't touch that! The sight of Finn's hand on the blood made Cash's stomach turn.

"Looks like someone hit the eject button," replied Finn. He had a lighthearted tone. He poked his finger inside the bullet hole.

Cash grabbed Finn's hand and yanked it away from the wall. "Stop that," he admonished.

Finn smiled. "It's just a little blood."

"A little blood?" demanded Cash. "This what you call a little?"

"You feeling okay, Cash? You look a little gray," teased Finn. He turned back to the wall. "It ain't nothing to be freaked out about. Just someone who cashed in his chips."

Finn's tone was a little too jovial for Cash.

"Come again?" he asked, still stunned by Finn's reaction. Please don't start fondling the damn wall again.

"You know, check out for good. Took the one-way ticket," replied Finn, with a gleam in his eye. He pointed two fingers to his head and pretended to shoot himself.

"You're a strange, little man."

"Come on," said Finn, "everyone knows they have an out. If things get too much, you just hit the eject button."

"No," responded Cash. "Everyone does not."

Finn shrugged. "Of course, they do."

Cash shook his head. "No, they do not. That's not a normal thing for anyone to have. No one thinks that way."

"I'm gonna say you're wrong."

"No. No, I'm not. I know I don't think that way."

Finn bowed his head toward Cash. "All right then, I stand corrected."

They stood there in awkward silence, staring at one another. Cash struggled to find something to say, a way to change the conversation and lighten the mood.

Behind him, the stairs creaked as D.B. stepped up into the loft, the tiny kitten on his shoulder, tail wrapped around his neck.

"I think this'll be a good place for everyone to meet up," said D.B. "I'm gonna send a text and let the others know."

Chapter 19

FINN STOOD ALONE IN THE LOFT, STARING AT THE ENORMOUS bloodstain on the wall. The bullet hole was dead center of all the gore. Scattered across the floor, crimson splatter covered photographs of smiling children with birthday cakes, athletic uniforms, and school books. If they were so happy, how did this person end up like this? Of course, Finn knew the truth; it was all a lie. There was no such thing as a loving, happy family. People pretended for pictures; it was always just an act.

Downstairs, the others had arrived. Happy chatter floated through the air as they greeted one another. A moment later, Teague materialized at the top of the stairs.

He let out a slow whistle as he scrutinized the wall. "Mais la! What the hell happened here?" he murmured, as he got down on one knee and looked over the images. Darkness swept across his face as an old demon reared its ugly head.

Years ago, before meeting up with Finn, Teague had a close run-in with suicide. He never got over it—barely even spoke about it. Finn understood the need to keep private things private, so after the initial conversation where Teague told him the entire story, Finn never brought it up again. Leaving it buried deep like a thick, nasty scar permanently etched on Teague's soul.

Teague stood up and rubbed his hands on his thighs as though he were wiping away his own memories. "Let's get back to the others," he said. Without waiting for Finn, he descended the stairs.

Finn remained a minute longer, taking in the space's vibe. Death never disturbed him; it was a natural end to things. Someone calling it quits on their own terms was normal. Why the notion of controlling your own destiny was so unsettling to some was beyond him. It was just a part of life. He shrugged and followed Teague.

The others were lounging in the living room on tattered furniture that had seen better days. Finn recognized the sofa from the pictures upstairs. Old magazines lay askew all over the coffee table. A thin layer of dust covered every surface. Though he hadn't noticed it earlier, the entire house had a faint odor of age, like mothballs mixed with memories. No matter where the home, or who the former occupants, old places had the same familiar odor.

"This dude really liked his crosses," said Max. "I mean, how religious you gotta be to cover an entire wall like this?"

Max was right. Whoever the previous resident of the house was, they sure had a thing for crosses. Big ones, tiny ones, ornate and plain. There must have been fifty in total.

"He might not have been religious," replied Finn. "If he were, he probably wouldn't have offed himself upstairs. Ain't that some kind of taboo?"

Max nodded. "Maybe his wife liked them."

Finn shook his head. "No woman lived here. At least, not for a long time. Besides, none of the pictures upstairs had a woman in them." He studied the wall. "This guy lived here alone."

"It's still kinda weird," said Max. "And what's with this one?" He pointed to a plain, stainless-steel cross sitting almost dead center among all the others.

The cross was out of place. Small and simple, surrounded by all the other, more ornate crosses, this one disappeared. Something Daniel once said came to Finn's mind—something about people hiding the most essential things in plain sight.

Finn took the cross down off the wall. It was heavy, like solid steel. He rolled it around in his hand, trying to coax forward whatever memory it was that scratched at the back of his mind.

"He had a weird taste in magazines, too," said Cash, as he shuffled around the old magazines on the coffee table. He lifted one up. "Modern Survival," he read the title aloud. "Ten things you and your family can do to ensure you survive a catastrophe." Cash chuckled and tossed the magazine onto the table and picked up another. "Five tools you must have in your go bag."

The others laughed.

"Sounds like this dude was a prepper," said D.B., as he meandered into the room, munching on a handful of stale crackers. He broke off a piece and fed it to the kitten, still perched on his shoulder. "Too bad he didn't have any of those prepper meals. The cupboards are pretty bare." He fed another piece to his furry pal. "Sorry, buddy, I tried to find you some tuna or something." The kitten meowed in response, then licked its mangy paw.

Finn glanced around the room, turning the small, metal cross around in his hand. A memory was clawing its way to the surface, but it just wasn't there yet.

"Modern Homesteading," River read the title of another magazine. "I bet there's a garden somewhere outside. Sometimes they continue to grow if left alone. Might still be some veggies there."

Finn's memory ruptured to the surface. "Plain sight," he said aloud, though not really intending to.

The others ceased talking and stared.

He turned to Max. "Gimme your pocket knife."

Max nodded and fished the knife out of his pocket, setting it down in Finn's open hand.

Finn popped open the blade and held the cross over it, hovering just above the surface. The blade lifted off his palm and attached itself to the back of the cross with a metallic clink.

"Holy shit, it's a magnet!" exclaimed Max.

A satisfied grin spread across Finn's face. "Yeah, it is."

Across the room, Teague chimed in, "So why would he have a magnetic cross hanging on the wall?"

Finn wiggled the cross in the air. "Because it's a key."

Max scoffed. "Key to what?"

"Not sure," replied Finn. "That's what we're gonna find out."

He placed the cross against the window frame, gently sliding it all around. "Preppers like to hide things in plain sight. It makes it easier for them to get to it when they need it." He moved across the room to the threshold frame. "It also feeds their sense of superiority."

"Superiority?" asked Bells.

Finn nodded. "Yeah, some of them like to believe they could outsmart everyone else in an apocalypse." In his hand, he felt a tiny click as the magnetic cross hit a concealed latch. He pulled open the trim hung by a single hinge, exposing a narrow set of shelves.

An audible gasp spread throughout the room.

Several boxes of ammo rested neatly on the shelves, along with a .22 handgun. A Swiss Army Knife sat on the shelf below.

Finn tossed that over to Max. "Here, replace that crappy pocket knife of yours with a real one."

Next were the floating shelves that hung above the sofa. Finn pushed back the knick-knacks and swept the cross over the longest one first. A slight click, then a hidden drawer slid open. Inside was a sawed-off shotgun.

"Jesus," gasped Cash. "This dude must have guns hidden all over the place."

Finn slid the magnet over one of the shorter shelves. "There's probably ammo in these two. The drawer slid open, exposing three boxes of ammo. Pleased with himself, he grinned at the others.

"I'm gonna bet those stairs are hiding some cool shit," said Finn.

He swept each tread, finding nothing.

"Maybe he didn't get around to those," offered Teague.

"Nah, he did so much with the smaller spaces over there; he wouldn't leave this alone." Finn continued to slide the cross along every surface. Stairs were great places for hiding things. When he was small, Daniel had once taken him to one of his prepper buddies' homes. The man was so proud of his ingenious hiding place at the bottom of the stairs, he spent the entire visit talking about it. Finn never forgot the beaming look on the man's face—couldn't remember his name, though.

He moved to the side of the staircase. At the base of the newel post, he heard the telltale click. A narrow slit opened up between the floor and the first riser.

"What did I say?" exclaimed Finn. "This one might hold something useful."

He lifted open the false door, exposing a large, hidden compartment big enough for him to crawl into. A crossbow hung against the back wall. Three full quivers of arrows lay on the floor just below. As an extra bonus, a box of emergency ration bars sat unopened on the floor.

"Heads up," he called out, as he tossed the package to Teague.

Max examined the crossbow in astonishment. "This is so weird," he said, practically whispering. "It's ingenious. I never would have thought to look for anything like this, let alone a secret magnetic key."

Finn crawled out of the compartment and took a seat beside Teague.

"I wanna try," said Beth. "Can I have the cross?"

"Go for it," he replied. "There's probably another key hanging on the wall somewhere else. I'm gonna bet there're multiple."

Beth spun around and headed into the kitchen; D.B. followed close behind.

"Let's see if we can find some more food," said D.B. He rubbed the kitten's head. "Tuna would be nice. Right, Spyder?"

"Spyder," said Beth. "That what you calling him?"

"Seems fitting," replied D.B., "He sure climbs like one."

River, Bells, and Max took off down the hallway, searching for more magnetic keys and secret compartments.

Over by the stairs, Zac was busy looking over the crossbow. "I wanna take this out back and try it."

"Too dark," replied Teague. "But we could do it first thing in the morning, right when the sun comes up."

Zac nodded. "Sounds like a plan," he replied, as he stared down the sight.

In the kitchen, Beth squealed with glee.

"Looks like we struck the mother lode" called out D.B. He sauntered into the living room carrying several MREs. "There's a hidden door behind the pantry wall. Had a crap ton of these stashed away in the secret room." He tossed one to each of the others, then cut open his package and shuffled around until he found the pouch of tuna.

"Look, little buddy," he cooed, "got some more food for ya."

From the hallway came another exclamation of joy. Max strolled into the room, holding a roll of bills.

"Nah, we found the mother lode," he exclaimed, as he unrolled the bills and counted. "There's five hundred dollars here."

"Plus a bunch of silver and gold coins," said Bells. She dumped a load of coins onto the coffee table.

"Hoo Lawd!" exclaimed Teague. "This old man thought of everything."

"He even remembered the booze," said River, as she strolled in carrying a bottle of whiskey.

"I ain't gonna lie," said Max. "I'm actually glad we got chased off the train."

Chapter 20

"THERE'S ONE!" SAID TEAGUE, POINTING TO THE STAR-FILLED CANOPY. Laying on the ground, he and Finn gazed up at the sky, watching the meteor shower play out overhead. The desert air was crisp and calm. An earthy scent hung heavy in the air.

"How many does that make?" asked Finn.

Teague counted in his head. "Ten."

Finn grunted.

Teague chuckled. Now and again, the old man that Finn would grow into one day rose to the surface. Crotchety was the first word that came to mind. Most people wouldn't like him very much. Hell, that was kinda the case now. But Teague knew him better than that. Sure, Finn could be an absolute jackass and certainly was capable of violence from time to time, but that was only because of the way he was raised. The real Finn, the one Teague knew, loved passionately, laughed readily, and lived instinctively.

"There's another one." Finn pointed. "Just over that hill."

"I missed that one," replied Teague, "but there's another one!" He pointed. "Oh, and another!"

"There you are." Beth stood above them. "What're y'all doing?"

"We're watchin' the meteor shower," replied Teague.

"Oh, I didn't know that was happening tonight!"

"It's a birthday gift for Teague," replied Finn.

"Wow, you remembered," replied Teague, somewhat surprised.

Finn sat up and faced him. "I remember a lot of things."

"Ahem," Beth interrupted. "So, ah, can y'all come inside?"

"Nah," replied Teague, "we're good."

Finn smiled, kissed Teague on the forehead, then hopped to his feet and reached out a hand. "Come on, let's go inside. See what the others are up to."

Teague didn't want to go. He wanted to stay outside, lying in the dirt, alone with Finn. But, for whatever reason, Finn was insistent, so letting out a deep sigh, Teague took hold of Finn's hand and followed him inside.

Candlelight flickered, illuminating the kitchen with a dancing, golden glow. The delicious aroma of chocolate filled the air.

Teague breathed it in. "Somethin' smells amazing."

"I hope so," replied River. She twirled around, holding a cake with candles in front of her. A proud smile stretched across her face as she set the cake on the table in front of him. "We found all the ingredients in the cupboards. Even the candles."

The smell of warm chocolate made Teague's mouth water. Heat radiated from the myriad of mismatched candles, burning away atop the thick chocolate frosting. Tapers, votives, a couple of tea lights and even a few birthday candles littered the top of the cake.

"There're only twenty candles," said Beth. "That's all we could find. You've undoubtedly already noticed; they're a little mismatched." She smiled.

"Hold up!" exclaimed Max. "I can fix that!" He foraged around in his pack for a minute, then came back carrying a sparkler. He leaned the tip into one candle and let it catch. A rainbow of colors exploded, sending tiny sparks into the air. "There!" He stuck the sparkler in the center of the cake. "Twenty-one. Now it's perfect."

"I can't believe y'all did this," said Teague, forcing back tears of bliss.

"To be honest, we almost didn't," replied River. "We didn't know how we were gonna celebrate. This house was a precipitous find." She rested back on her heels. "When I saw the cupboards full of all the ingredients, I got the idea. When Beth found the candles, well—," She smiled. "It was a done deal." She leaned close and kissed him on the cheek. "Happy Birthday, baby."

"Go on," interjected Finn, "blow out the candles."

"We have to sing happy birthday first," insisted Beth.

"Okay," said Max. "Somebody kick it off. I'm fixin' to die if I don't get me some cake in the next minute."

The start was slow, but soon the entire group was belting out the happy birthday song. Teague was glad the candlelight wasn't too bright; otherwise, the others could see how red his face had become— how choked up with emotion he was. As soon as the song ended, he leaned forward and blew out the candles. In the center, the sparkler burned momentarily, then sputtered out.

Applause and whistles.

River picked up the cake. "Okay, presents first."

"Wait, I thought it was cake time," grumbled Max.

River slapped him on the arm. "In a minute. I wanna do gifts first."

Max whimpered and let his head drop heavily onto the table in mock dismay.

River disappeared into the living room, returning with a gift wrapped in newspaper.

"Happy Birthday," she beamed, as she handed the package over to Teague. She wrapped her arm around his shoulder. "Go on, open it."

Teague untied the bow and pulled away the paper, exposing a black knit beanie. The wool was luxuriously soft. He placed it on his head. "Thank you," he said, to River, who smiled back at him.

"My turn now," said Zac, as he thrust a gift wrapped in a blue bandanna in front of Teague.

Cash cleared his throat. "Our turn, this one's from both of us."

Zac nodded and stood back proudly.

Teague pulled apart the twine that held the fabric together. Based on the weight and the size of the item, he had a pretty good hunch about what it was but pretended to have no clue, anyway. Dragging it out as long as possible, he peeled back the fabric, exposing a beautiful Bowie Knife. The sheath was dark, brown leather with a fleur-de-lis burned into the center.

Teague smiled.

"We figured it was time to replace the one you lost a while back," said Zac.

"At least now you can stop using that tiny pocket knife all the time," said Cash.

"This is great," replied Teague. He pulled the knife out and moved it around in his hand. The blade was sharp and clean, the knife was solid.

He looked around at all the smiling faces. "Thank you, all of you. I would've never imagined something like this."

"Hold on," interrupted River, "It ain't done yet." She shifted her attention to Finn, nudging him. "Go on, get it."

Finn smiled and disappeared into the living room, returning a moment later, carrying a crumpled, brown, paper bag. He placed it lightly on the table.

Teague stared at the wad of paper, confused.

"Interesting choice in wrapping paper," teased Max.

Finn shrugged. "It ain't the wrapping; it's what's inside that counts." He prodded Teague. "Go on, open it."

Teague didn't know where to begin. The bag was more of a tube with both the ends twisted like a giant popper. He wasn't sure which one to open.

"Just tear it," said River, unable to contain her excitement.

Clearly, she and Beth knew exactly what the package contained.

Teague did as she suggested and tore open the center. Inside was a coiled length of leather cording, only it wasn't cording; it was more like a long, skinny strip of leather. One side soft as suede, the other smooth as leather. It was a wrap-around bracelet with a knot and loop closure. Anchored along the length of the strip were three objects. The first was a small, red-orange piece of crystal wrapped in copper wire.

"Wulfenite," said Finn, "I picked it up the last time we were out in Yuma. That's the best one I could find."

Teague remembered Yuma. That was over a year ago. *How long have you been planning this?*

"I helped him secure it to the leather," declared Beth proudly.

"There's more," said River. "Check out the other things."

Teague moved his attention to a thin strip of metal, smooth on one side, numbers etched on the other. He read aloud, "Lat: 30.265063, Long: -97.75688." He glanced up at Finn, who was gnawing on his nails.

Finn paused and nodded toward the bracelet. "That's the coordinates of where we met," he said excitedly.

Staring at the tiny engraved piece of metal, Teague ran his finger across the surface. His throat tightened. He could think of no words to say.

"One more," prodded Finn.

Teague inhaled deeply and moved his focus to the other strip of metal. "1115 Palmetto St., San Antonio, TX."

"Where's that?" asked Max.

Tears welled up in Teague's eyes. "Blue house," he choked.

The small ramshackle house on the corner lot of a cozy neighborhood flashed in his mind. He could feel the cold air streaming through holes in the walls and hear the creaky floorboards on the front porch. He could practically smell the heavy perfume of jasmine, carried on the warm, summer breeze from the jungle of shrubs outside.

Finn nodded. "It wasn't really blue, we just imagined it should be, so that's what we called it," he explained to everyone. "We had to share it with a pack of feral cats. They were there first." He grinned. "It was home." He leaned close to Teague. "Well, Did I surprise y—"

Teague interrupted him with a kiss.

Wiping away tears, Teague glanced around the room. Not a dry eye in sight. Even Max stood red-faced and speechless, and that was no small feat.

"Dude," sighed Bells. She sniffled and wiped her face with the back of her sleeve. "That is the gayest thing I have ever seen you do."

She clapped a hand on Finn's shoulder. "It's also the sweetest thing I've ever witnessed anyone do in my life. And I'm here for it."

A round of laughter gave Teague a chance to collect himself. He wrapped the bracelet around his wrist and tied it into place. He would never take it off.

Chapter 21

Ten more followers! That was on top of the other twenty Beth gained over the past twenty-four hours. The content she posted over the last few days was some of her best. Her followers loved it. They told her so all the time. Had she known that running away and hopping trains would make her so popular, she would have done it a long time ago.

Sitting on the back porch, a plume of weed smoke billowed around her, held in place by the low ceiling. Max and Cash were having an intense conversation about how long it would take Max to meet one million people, while Bells and D.B shared a joint. Spyder chased a large moth, pouncing and clawing at the air; he was not the best hunter. A few yards away, River and Zac lay sprawled out on the ground, gazing up at the meteors. Beth tried to hang with them, but it was just too boring for her. Since heading out, she had done plenty of sky watching. Sure, it was cool at first, but after a while, she realized the sky was the same wherever they went. Who cared if there were meteors or not? It just wasn't that impressive anymore. You could go online and see videos of it anytime. No need to lie in the dirt. She made her final edit to her latest video and hit post. They're going to love this one.

"What's so fascinating?" asked Max.

Beth looked up to find both Cash and Max staring at her. She shrugged. "Nothin' really."

"Beth likes her phone peeps," said Cash. "Apparently, online is way more interesting than just about anything else."

It bothered her when they picked on her like that. It made her want to hide every time she pulled out her phone. That only made her angrier. If she wanted guilt or judgment every time she went online, she would have stayed home with her parents.

Max and Cash showed no signs of going away or leaving her alone, so she put her phone away.

"So Max," she said, "tell me about yourself."

He grinned. "What do you wanna know?"

"Where'd you grow up?"

"Texas."

Just off the porch, Zac whistled. "Yeah, boy! Texas!" he cheered.

Max whistled and cheered in agreement with Zac. "Outside of Fort Worth."

"Oh, cool!" replied Beth. "I have a cousin that lives near Fort Worth. What school did you go to? You might know her."

Max shook his head. "Didn't go to school. I was homeschooled—well, technically unschooled."

"That's why he's so weird," chided Cash.

Beth had only ever known one homeschooler before. It was a kid who lived down the street from her when she was around ten years old. She recalled wondering what he did all day. When she left for school in the morning, he would be outside. When she came home, he would still be outside. A few times, she came home to find him leaning under the hood of her dad's truck asking questions—lots of questions. Her dad didn't even seem to mind. Not long after that, his family moved away. Her dad said something about Seattle.

"What was that like?" she asked Max.

He shrugged in response. "Not much different from now, I suppose. The scenery was stagnant but pretty much similar."

"Did you ever miss not going to school?"

"Never."

"Seriously?" said Beth. "I couldn't imagine not being around my friends all day. I think it would be boring."

He grinned and leaned back against the rail. "And I couldn't imagine being in the same building day after day doing mundane, superficial tasks over and over again."

"Yeah, school work is stupid," admitted Beth, "but at least you get to be with your friends."

"What about freedom to do whatever you want with your day?" asked Max.

"We weren't trapped," replied Beth. "It's not like we had no freedom."

"Did you have to ask permission to go to the bathroom? Could you eat whenever you were hungry? How about going outside; could you walk outside whenever you felt like it?"

Beth rolled her eyes. "Well, of course, you couldn't do all that whenever you wanted. It'd be disruptive."

"Can you do all of that now?"

"Well, yeah," replied Beth, not sure if she liked the way this conversation was going. "It's different."

"What's different?"

She shifted in her seat. "I don't know. For one, I'm an adult now."

Cash chuckled.

Max grinned. "So, we agree, as an adult, you don't ask for permission to do anything."

Beth responded with an uncertain nod.

"Why not?"

"Why not, what?" asked Beth.

"Why don't you ask for permission to go to the bathroom or to move about and do whatever you want?"

Beth scoffed. "Because that's stupid and degrading."

Max's eyes were on fire. He was relishing this. "So, if it'd be degrading and stupid to ask for permission to do the most basic of human things, why did you have to be trained to accept that when you were a kid?"

She didn't have an answer for that. Truthfully, she had never thought about it before. She didn't want to think about it now. It made her head hurt. "I don't know," she whined. "Because it's what you do when you're a kid."

"I didn't. Neither did any of my friends who were homeschooled."

"Sure," responded Beth, "but most people need structure. Kids need to learn how to function in society."

"Asking permission to pee is a societal norm?"

"Well, no. I didn't say that. You're awfully hung up on the need to pee."

Cash snickered.

"It's a basic, bodily function," replied Max. "I'm merely using it as an example of one of the more extreme tactics of control that is deployed in a school setting."

"They have to do that," argued Beth. "How else would they be able to teach an entire class of kids?"

Max leaned closer. "Now you're getting to my point. What exactly are they teaching by forcing kids to ask permission to do the most basic of bodily functions?"

"To read, to do math," answered Beth.

"Funny," said Max, "My moms taught me how to read and do math, but I never had to ask them permission to pee."

Beth was finished playing this game. She didn't like the turn it took, and she didn't like the questions it was bringing into her mind. She didn't want to think about this anymore. Homeschoolers really are weird. She needed to change the subject.

"Was your mom a stay-at-home mom? she asked.

"One was," replied Max, "the other one worked for the city. She's an engineer."

"So, like, which one is your stepmom?"

"Neither. They're both my moms."

"Oh," said Beth, "like, together?"

Max pulled a photo from his wallet and handed it to Beth. Five smiling faces beamed up at her. A younger Max stood dead center with another boy, maybe older, to his left. On his right stood a girl; she looked younger. Behind them were two women. One thin and tall with short hair, wearing an elegant, floral dress. She had the same sparkle in her eyes and friendly smile as Max. Next to her stood another tall woman. Wearing jeans and a button-down shirt, she had a muscular physique, like someone who spends a lot of time at the gym. Her hair was long and up in a ponytail. She, too, had an easy smile, though not at all like Max. Come to think of it, as Beth looked closely at the people in the image, she realized that the older brother resembled the athletic mom—same eyes, hair, and build. Whereas Max and the sister both looked like the other mom.

"So, tell me who everyone is," she said.

"That's my brother, Alex." He pointed to the girl. "That's Becca." He pointed to the woman in the pretty floral dress. "This is my mom, Michelle, and this is my mom, Stephanie." He grinned. "That's me in the middle."

Beth smiled. "I figured that one out already." She handed the photo back to him. "Tell me about them? How did they meet?"

Max stuffed the photo in his wallet. "They met in college. Got married in a private garden on campus and have been together ever since."

"Wasn't that illegal back then?"

Max flashed a proud smile. "They had a friend who got her license to perform ceremonies, just so she could do theirs. Yeah, legally, according to the government, they weren't married, but in their eyes, it was totally legit and forever."

"When the government finally pulled its head out of its own ass, we had a big celebration with all our friends and family."

"Sounds wonderful," said Beth. "So, what are they all up to now?"

"Becca is in college. She's studying to be a veterinarian. Alex went to college, then took a break. So far, he hasn't gone back. He works for a construction company, operating big machinery."

"What about your moms?"

A gloomy cloud settled on Max's face. The shift in his mood was drastic compared to his usual light-heartedness.

"My mom, Michelle, was diagnosed with dementia a couple of years ago."

Beth's heart sank. "I'm so sorry."

"It is what it is," he replied. "The only thing we could do was learn to live with it. She was afraid of losing her memory, so we came up with a solution. We painted a huge family timeline all around our house. A mural highlighting all the noteworthy events, starting where they met at college and going all the way through the years. We hung framed pictures in different spots."

"That sounds lovely."

Max nodded. "Whenever something new happens, we add it."

"Your mom must love that."

A melancholy smile passed over his face. "We sent her away for a weekend with my aunt and grandma when we did it. We wanted it to be a surprise. When she got home, she cried so hard I wondered if it was a good idea." He sighed, lost in the memory. "She walked the rooms following the line, stopping at each picture. She loved it—still does."

"Your moms sound amazing," said Beth.

"They are."

"What do they think about what you're doing?"

"Michelle has this whole romantic idea about it all. Early on, Stephanie let me know she was disappointed. She wanted more for us; expected more from me. But she also understands that we all have to travel our own road. Both of them love it when we go home for a visit."

"So, you think when you're done, you'll go back home to stay?"

Max shrugged. "It's as good as anyplace else, I suppose. We'll have to see when that time comes. I ain't there yet." He smiled. "I think I need some more cake." Glancing around at the others, he asked, "Anyone else care to join me?"

Max and Cash took off inside, leaving Beth alone with D.B., Bells, and Spyder.

"So, what's your story?" she asked Bells.

Bells shook her head. "Don't have one."

"Come on," prodded Beth, "what made you strike out on your own?"

"It just came up as an option, I suppose."

"Okay," said Beth, "Why the name Bells?"

"My last name is Belleveau, Bells just stuck."

"What about your family?"

"Ah, my family," replied Bells. "My older sister blew all of that up years ago. She fell in with a group of miserable assholes and got a bunch of bullshit crap in her head. She then blew everything up, like tossing a hand grenade in the middle of our living room." Bells sighed and watched Spyder. "Unable to take the heartache of having her life torn apart before her eyes, my mom gave up. She packed a bag, and left. Never said goodbye, or anything."

An audible gasp escaped from Beth's lips. Instantly regretting it, she clasped a hand over her mouth.

Bells continued, "My dad fell into alcohol and drugs, then found Jesus and got clean. He's remarried now, living in Ocala." She peered up at Beth. "I don't know where my sister is. As far as I'm concerned, she's dead. I'll never forgive her for the damage she did to my family with her bullshit."

Spyder leaped into the air. Claws outstretched, he snatched the moth, pulling it down to the floor, where he promptly ate it.

"I'm sorry to hear about your mom," said Beth, unable to come up with anything else to say.

Bells scoffed. "It's all water under the bridge. The past is the past, ya know?"

Beth nodded in agreement.

"D.B.," said Bells, "tell Beth a little about yourself." She smiled and struck his arm.

Spyder finished cleaning himself. The little kitten stretched and curled up on D.B.'s lap, purring.

D.B. shrugged. "What do you want to know?"

"Well, for starters," replied Beth. "What does D.B. stand for?"

"Dirt Bag," he replied with a smirk.

"Dumb Bastard," interjected Bells, snickering.

"Seriously though," said D.B. "There's not much to tell. I grew up in Oklahoma. My dad died in a car accident when I was five. I grew up with my mom and grandparents from then on. I had a good life. My grandpa taught me all I know. My family's pretty cool."

"They are," agreed Bells.

"Does your grandpa approve of what you're doing?" asked Beth.

D.B. smiled. "He did it when he was young, so did his dad before him. I guess you could say it's a family tradition, going back to A-No.1."

"So, cool," said Beth, "I bet your grandpa has lots of amazing stories."

"He does. It was his stories that made me want to try it."

The door flung open, carrying plates of cake, Cash, and Max erupted onto the porch.

"Is there any left?" asked Beth.

Max nodded with a mouthful of cake. "There's just enough for y'all if you get it now."

With that, Beth didn't need another invite. She and Bells raced inside.

Chapter 22

Daniel rolled into Flagstaff, uncertain of what to do next. Should he get a hotel or should he park the Jeep and go wander among the train hoppers? Speaking of train hoppers, where the hell was he supposed to find them? Surely they didn't gather around the station in the center of town; there had to be another area, somewhere near the train yard where they could hide out and camp while waiting for their next ride. Where the hell would that be? His familiarity with the city was limited; He had only ever visited Flagstaff once.

It was mid-summer. Craving adventure and a change of scenery, Daniel convinced Tricia that a road trip would be fun. She balked at the idea at first, insisting instead that a vacation at the beach would be more enjoyable. In the end, they agreed on a compromise; a beach vacation during winter and a mountain vacation in the summer.

Tricia didn't like long drives. She said they were dull and uncomfortable. Daniel couldn't wrap his brain around that sort of thinking. He loved road trips. The seemingly endless open road, the mesmerizing effect of watching the landscape roll by, changing ever so slightly with each passing mile.

Finn seemed to revel in the adventure. The little guy spent most of the trip staring out the window, a distant look in his eyes, calmly sucking on his two fingers, holding his bear. Every so often, he would glance up at Daniel through the rearview mirror and smile.

God, how he loved that little guy. In his wildest dreams, Daniel never imagined that he could love another person as much as he adored his son.

Mostly, the trip was everything Daniel had hoped it would be. Of course, there were a few minor blow-ups; that was to be expected. After all, Tricia was not a road-trip-kind of person. If he kept the driving down to only six hours a day, she did well. It was the long days that got her riled up and irritable.

He glanced over at her, asleep in the passenger seat, head leaning against the glass, sunglasses slightly askew on the bridge of her nose; snoring—ever so slightly. The waning sunlight cast a celestial glow across her face, highlighting the inch-long scratch across her cheek that Finn had given her earlier that day. Daniel wasn't sure what had happened. Tricia, as usual, was ambiguous on details, and Finn, well, at eight months old, he could hardly tell his side. All Daniel knew was that he went outside to load up and bring the car around. When he left, Finn was playing happily with his favorite teddy bear in the fold-out crib, and Tricia was in the shower, humming along to one of her favorite songs.

When he came back—not more than a few minutes later, Tricia was irate and yelling while standing in front of the mirror, cleaning the wound. Finn was on the floor beside the desk, wailing, fists clenched, face red, tears streaming down his cheeks, mixing with the snot from his nose. His porta-crib lay on its side; his teddy bear was across the room.

This was how it was for Tricia and Finn—one issue after another between the two. Daniel couldn't fully understand why they never seemed to get along. He thought mother and child shared a unique bond; these two had no bond at all. Tricia swore Finn was doing things that forced her to act out on him. She was insistent the baby had it out for her. That he hated her. But Finn was just a baby; babies don't have spiteful thoughts; they only have needs. Immediate needs.

Daniel scooped up the howling infant and cradled him against his chest. Swaying back and forth, he cooed, "It's okay little guy, I'm here." The wailing ceased. Finn shoved his two fingers into his mouth and relaxed against Daniel's chest, each breath catching on intake, forcing his tiny body to spasm.

"You see what that little shit did to me?" demanded Tricia, as she flew menacingly across the room.

"He's a baby," replied Daniel. "He didn't do anything on purpose."

Tricia scoffed. "That's what you think. He's a little, scheming shit. Aren't you?"

She reached out a hand to touch the baby's thigh, but Daniel shifted his body, effectively putting Finn out of her reach. When these altercations took place, it was always best to keep the two apart. He often wondered how bad things got at home when he was away for his twenty-four-hour shifts. More than once, Daniel came home to find Finn bruised or injured. Tricia always had some incoherent story about how it happened. Somehow, it was always Finn's fault.

After the dust settled and both were calm, they left the hotel. Much to Daniel's surprise, the rest of the drive that day was peaceful. Tricia played with the radio, trying to find songs she liked. Finn, harnessed in his car seat, stared out the window, watching the world scroll by. That innocent face melted Daniel's heart. He couldn't imagine how anybody could harm such a sweet, helpless thing. Of course, he had seen it every day at work, but, looking at his son—he just couldn't fathom what could happen to some people that would send them down the path where they felt it was okay to hurt their children.

Daniel parked the Jeep outside the old train station and glanced around. There had to be a rail yard nearby. He pulled out his phone and opened the map. The yard was a couple of miles east. It would be a simple task to get there quickly.

His stomach growled, reminding him he hadn't eaten in nearly twelve hours. Food was a priority, but first, he needed to check and see if there were any updates as to the whereabouts of Finn and his friends.

He opened the app and quickly navigated to the Nomad Girl's page. Sure enough, she had just uploaded a new video. Daniel grinned. Beth was indeed the most valuable asset on his journey. Without her, he wouldn't have had a clue where to search. He would have to thank her when he caught up with them.

The title of the new video was "Happy Birthday!"

Let's see what they're up to today. He hit the play button.

The camera focused on a trio Daniel had never seen before. Then it panned out, showing the familiar faces of Finn and the others. Everyone was smiling. Daniel's gut burned with hatred. The camera zoomed in on the birthday boy; the blond one named Teague, then scanned around the room, focusing on the others. Finn stood close alongside Teague. There was something about their body language that struck Daniel as odd, yet familiar. He couldn't quite place it.

He watched as each gift was opened. The sweetness of it all made him nauseous. Finn disappeared from the screen, returning a moment later with a crumpled, brown paper bag. That had to be the worst excuse for wrapping Daniel had ever seen. Teague tore right into it. *What else was he going to do? Admire the wrinkled paper bag?*

The video went silent. There was no movement on the screen. For a moment, Daniel thought it froze. He watched as Finn described the little details of his gift. Something gnawed at Daniel's brain. He wasn't sure what it was, but he knew he was witnessing something important.

Then Teague kissed Finn.

A vicious grin stretched across Daniel's face. *Well, well, well, ain't that something!* He had no idea. An interesting turn of events as well as extremely valuable information.

He laughed aloud. Once again, the Nomad Girl had come through with key details. Thanks to her, Daniel now knew exactly how to inflict the most pain on Finn; he could already hear the bastard pleading for mercy.

Hunger pangs poked at his insides. He needed to find some food. Thanks to the video, he knew that Finn and crew had not yet arrived in Flagstaff. Daniel had plenty of time to eat and find the hobo camp.

He climbed out of the Jeep and stretched his back. His legs tingled. It had been several hours since he last stopped for gas. No wonder his body felt cramped.

It was late afternoon, and daylight was waning.

Daniel inhaled. He was so close, he could almost smell it. The scent of pine needles mingled with car exhaust on the cool, late-afternoon breeze. His stomach grumbled; a little reminder that other tasks needed tending to. Might as well grab a bite while scoping out the town. Maybe he'd get lucky and run right into the scrawny, little shit.

Flagstaff wasn't so bad as far as cities go. Nestled among pine trees and mountain views, it was downright pretty. One bonus he noticed right away, there were plenty of riders all over the place. This town was a veritable hub—almost like a Grand Central Station for Hobos. With all their tattoos, piercings and laid-back bohemian style, they were hard to miss.

Across the street, a group of four drifters clustered on a metal bench. Daniel examined their faces, hoping that at least one of them would be from the videos. He was both relieved and pissed when he realized none of them were.

Intent on talking to them, he wasn't looking where he was going and nearly ran into another young drifter. Lanky but fit, the young man had greasy, blond hair, deeply tanned skin, and several visible tattoos crawling up his neck and along his jawline. Giant ear stretchers dangled from both sides of his head. Guitar around his shoulder, case open on the ground at his feet, he smiled at Daniel and held out a bag of popcorn. "You want a piece of popcorn?" he asked, jiggling the bag.

Daniel didn't respond.

The young man wiggled the bag again. "You sure? It's delicious." He smirked. "Might even be some of the best popcorn I've ever had." He shoved a handful into his mouth.

How high are you?

Daniel smiled. "You know, I think I will try some."

The young man happily handed over the bag, then held out his hand. "My name's Colt."

Daniel took his hand. "Dane."

"Nice to meet you, Dane."

His vivid, blue eyes sparkled with an inner glow of contentment that filled Daniel with rage. How dare anyone be so happy with their life! Especially someone who had nothing. Someone who probably hadn't seen the inside of a shower for at least a week.

Unfazed, Colt continued, "You passing through?"

Daniel nodded. "How about you?"

Colt strummed his guitar. "Me and a couple of buddies are heading out tonight." He nodded across the street at the group collected on the bench. "I figured I'd take advantage of the downtime and earn some money."

"Where y'all catchin' on?" asked Daniel, doing his best impersonation of a seasoned Rider.

"There's a jungle just on the edge of town." He pointed west. "Trains have to go slow through there because it's a residential area. It's a perfect spot."

A whistle erupted from across the street. "Yo Colt!"

"Well, looks like I gotta bail," said the young man, as he quickly packed up his guitar.

"Maybe I'll see ya there tonight," said Daniel.

"Right on," replied Colt, nodding in approval. He slung his guitar over his shoulder and sprinted across the street.

Daniel watched as Colt and his buddies sauntered away. It didn't take him nearly as long as he imagined to find out where he needed to go. Smiling and whistling happily, he wandered down the street in search of a place to eat.

Chapter 23

THEY LANDED IN FLAGSTAFF JUST AS THE SUN PEEPED OVER THE horizon, casting its golden, morning glow in every direction. After spending the night at the suicide house, it took them all day to figure out a way to get back on a train. It was nearly midnight when they finally caught a ride. Unfortunately, the only train available was hauling a load of truck trailers. With no other options, they split up into groups of two, climbing beneath the belly of the trailers. They rode the entire way, clinging to the metal frame, gravel, and tracks speeding by less than two feet from their bodies.

Finn took a deep breath and stretched the tightened muscles in his back and legs, while the others did the same all around him. They wouldn't be catching on until well into the evening, which meant they had the entire day to mess around. He was looking forward to that; Flagstaff was on a short list of cities he truly enjoyed visiting. Maybe it was the mountainscape or the compact nature of the old downtown area; perhaps it was the food. Thinking of food, their first order of business was to find something to eat. At least, that was his; he didn't know what the others wanted to do. He was starving. A huge breakfast of eggs, bacon, and pancakes was precisely what he intended to track down.

They stashed their gear and strolled through the quiet, morning streets, heading for a diner they frequented whenever passing through town. Finn was in the lead while the others trailed behind, embroiled in another animated conversation, of which, Max was the brunt of all the teasing.

So much chatter. It grated on Finn's nerves. Walking several yards ahead, he picked up his pace in order to put more space between himself and the others. He was hungry, and tired of traveling with a large, noisy group. He struggled with the urge to break into a jog and put more distance between them.

Raucous laughter erupted behind him, followed by a sheepish denial by Max.

Shut-up! Finn focused on the shop windows, counting the flyers as they passed by. *Twenty-five, twenty-six, twenty-seven.* The diner was in sight. Finally! Something he could look forward to.

It was late evening when they showed up at the camp. The moon hung low above the treetops, casting shadows that flitted about on the group of riders who congregated around the bonfire. Finn counted roughly ten people. Not being one for jumping right in when it came to gatherings, he hung back and watched.

From what he could see, they were just another group of riders, nothing unique. However, one man caught his eye. Something about the stranger made him uneasy. His clothes were too clean, his hair too well-groomed. Even his boots were almost pristine. Keeping close to the shadows, Finn moved along the periphery of the fire to get a better look at the man's face.

The stranger was much older than most riders—older than Spinner. He had gray hair around his temples, and his neatly sculpted beard was half white, half dark brown. The man was conversing with a young woman; well, he pretended to be at least. His eyes told a different story as they tracked River and Beth. When he noticed Cash, the odd stranger stopped pretending to pay attention to the conversation and searched the crowd of people.

Who are you looking for?

Finn watched as the man studied the faces of everyone around him, then he searched the tree line. He was searching for someone. Finn stepped back into the trees as the man's eyes crossed over the area where he stood.

The soft sound of pine needles rustling under footsteps disrupted Finn's concentration, then Teague's arm wrapped around his shoulder. Finn leaned back against him, feeling the rhythm of Teague's heartbeat.

"We gonna stand in the shadows all night?" asked Teague. "Not that I'm fussin' about it; I like the company."

"Did you get a good look at the old guy?" asked Finn.

Teague nodded. "He's out of place."

"That's an understatement."

"Cop?" asked Teague.

"Definitely," replied Finn. "Who else would wear shoes like that?"

Teague chuckled. "No pack either, as far as I can see."

Over by the fire, a woman twirled a flaming stick, attracting the attention of everyone—everyone, except the stranger. He continued to study the trees, coming to focus directly on where Finn and Teague stood. Unnerving as it was, Finn knew the most the odd man could make out was their silhouettes.

"Local or Bull?" asked Teague.

"Hard to tell," replied Finn. "Railroad would know better than to show up lookin' like that. A cop wouldn't."

"He's right." Zac materialized from behind.

"So what d'you imagine he's here for?" asked Teague.

Finn shrugged. "Railroad makes sense. Cop, not so much. Surely there are better ways to do a drug bust."

Cash sidled up alongside the trio. "Checking out the old guy?"

"You got closest to him," said Finn. "Anything you wanna share?"

"Other than he's law enforcement, I got nothing."

"That's what we were thinkin'," said Teague. "I'm gonna get close and check him out."

"Hold up, I'll come along," said Cash.

Finn watched warily as Teague and Cash wandered close to the group around the fire. They shared various greetings with the other riders, then split up. Cash on one side of the unusual stranger, Teague on the other, both keeping a safe distance, yet close enough to get a good look.

Something in the woods caught Teague's attention, causing him to spin around abruptly and stare into the trees. His body tense, he seemed to have forgotten all about the man.

Finn's nerves were on end. He strained his eyes, staring into the woods to see whatever had Teague so intrigued.

What is he staring at?

A moment later, Teague turned away and strolled back along the perimeter, carefully making his way back to Finn and Zac.

"What was goin' on in the trees?"

"Don't know," replied Teague. "I thought I heard a twig snap like someone was lurking out there. Gave me the frissons."

"See anyone?"

Teague shook his head. "Couldn't see anything. It was too dark."

"Maybe it was just an animal then," said Finn.

"Nah," replied Teague. "Someone's out there. I could feel it. Whoever they are, they ain't showin' themselves." He looked back at the group around the fire. "Maybe it's the person the cop is lookin' for."

They watched as River strolled away from the bonfire, disappearing into the tree line. A moment later, the cop rose abruptly to his feet and followed.

"That doesn't look good," said Teague, tracking the stranger's progress.

Finn and Zac were already several steps ahead.

Splinters of moonbeams illuminated the forest floor as they followed the sound of footsteps up ahead. They came to a stop along the edge of a small clearing. Hidden among the trees, the cop hovered, his eyes fastened to a specific spot several yards away. Behind a tree, a telltale, blonde dread peeked out.

The sick bastard gets off on watching girls pee.

Finn gestured with his hands for the others to create a circle around the creep. Once the perimeter was set, they closed in, encircling the cop, who was too busy watching River to notice Finn and the others. Startled, the man jumped back, looking nervously at the group. His eyes locked on Teague, then he quickly glanced over, eyes wide, at Finn.

The stranger forced a nervous smile. Palms up, still facing Finn, he sputtered, "H-hey guys." He glanced around at the others, then back at Finn. "This isn't what it looks li—"

Zac's fist connecting with the man's face cut his words short. Too busy staring at Finn, the dumb bastard never even saw it coming. He collapsed in a silent heap at their feet.

"What the hell is goin' on?" demanded River, as she stomped up, buttoning her pants.

"This creep was watchin' you pee," replied Teague.

"Ew," exclaimed River. She kicked the unconscious body. "Creep."

Finn was already digging through the man's pockets. He pulled out the wallet. No badge, no cop ID, not even a concealed carry permit. He didn't even have very much money on hand—just a twenty-dollar bill, which Finn handed to Teague.

"Looks like Derrick here is an idiot, or he went to great lengths to make sure no one could figure out why he was here," said Finn.

"So, what are we gonna do with him?" asked River.

Finn smiled. "I got an idea."

"Hurry, it's gonna leave soon," urged Finn.

"I'm workin' on it," replied Teague, as he zip-tied the still uncon-scious cop's hands to the frame of a grain car.

"I can't believe we're doing this," whined Beth.

"He deserves it," said River.

"Sure does," interjected Max. "What a creep."

"He's lucky this is the only thing that's happening to him," said D.B.

Beth shifted on her feet. "What happens if he can't get loose?"

"Railroad security will spot him as soon as they pull into the next yard," replied Zac. "They'll cut him loose, and then he can explain himself to them. He's just goin' for a ride. Don't worry about it."

"All set," announced Teague. He hopped off the car, landing beside Finn just as the train jerked and pulled forward.

Two tracks over, another train pulled forward, heading in the opposite direction; right on time, this was their ride. Without another word, they hopped on, leaving Flagstaff behind.

Chapter 24

When Daniel came upon the encampment, the sun had just dipped behind the mountain. The camp was busier than he imagined; these riders didn't even try to hide their presence. He glanced around at all the youthful faces; except for Colt, he recognized not a single one. No sign of the Nomad Girl, nor any of the people she was traveling with, and no Finn.

Daniel sauntered around the bonfire, looking over all the revelers. He said hello to Colt, who was just as happy to see him as he was on the street corner. Since embarking on this journey, Daniel met many train hoppers. It never ceased to amaze him how open and friendly some of these kids were. Fearless and happy, they were high on life. Daniel found this both intriguing and enraging.

Colt made it a point to introduce Daniel to whoever would listen, each time presenting Daniel like a kindergartener showing off his new, best friend. God, the kid, annoyed him. When a girl wandered up and asked Colt to dance with her, Daniel seized the opportunity, encouraging the younger man to go, then quickly backed away.

For the most part, the usual types had gathered around the fire, including a man with a guitar. There was always someone with a guitar, mindlessly strumming away in between bits of conversation.

The smell of whiskey and weed drifted through the air, mingling with the scent of burning wood. Daniel always loved the smell of a wood fire. He breathed in deeply and scanned the faces of everyone around the camp, noting one in particular that stood out.

Older than the others, this man was visibly out of place. For one, he was too well-groomed. His hair neatly combed, his beard trimmed and clean; Daniel could practically smell the man's aftershave. There was no sign of dirt or wear to his clothes. His jeans and shirt were almost brand new, as though he bought them specifically for this trip.

A cop.

Daniel sidled up for a closer look, keeping a safe distance, of course. This man reeked of law enforcement. It seeped from every pore; every gesture screamed it.

Seeming to sense Daniel's presence, the man gazed up at him. The two locked eyes and shared a moment of acknowledgment. Neither belonged there, and they both knew it. The man stared at Daniel with a sense of familiarity that made him uneasy.

Daniel searched his memories for any recollection of this person—nothing. He was positive he didn't know him, nor did they ever cross paths before. At least, if they did, Daniel had no memory of it. For a tense moment, he wondered whether the man was an undercover cop searching for him. He shook that thought away; there was no reason anyone in law enforcement would look for him. Even if they found what remained of Tricia's body in Florida, it would take months to connect any of it to him. And even then, it would be a real stretch. Daniel made damn sure he covered his tracks. There was no connection to be made.

Whatever this man was doing here, it had nothing to do with Daniel. It was far more likely the odd familiarity was nothing more than an age thing. At any rate, not wanting to get any closer to the man, Daniel pulled back into the trees, hiding among the shadows, where he could watch and wait patiently, out of the way from prying eyes.

Laughter erupted as three people came into the light of the fire. Daniel recognized them right away; The Nomad Girl herself and the blonde with all the dreads—River. Behind them, a tall man with dark hair appeared. Daniel didn't know his name, but he recognized him from the videos; then came Teague.

Daniel's heart raced. Finn was nearby; he could sense it. The hair on the back of his neck tingled. Teague worked his way through the crowd around the campfire, greeting each one, coming to a stop a couple of yards from the treeline.

Blood pounded in Daniel's skull. He fought back the urge to reach out and grab hold of Teague. The kid was fit, and they were about the same height; he looked like he could put up a good fight. Daniel made a mental note of that.

If Teague was here, Finn was not far. Elation buzzed throughout Daniel's body. This was the closest he had come to the bastard in years; he needed to lay eyes on him in person. He moved sideways to look beyond Teague. Inadvertently stepping on a twig, a loud snap erupted at his feet.

Teague spun around and stared directly at Daniel. At least, that's what it felt like. The kid stood stark still and peered into the trees. Time suspended. Icy panic welled up inside Daniel, extinguishing his excitement. He was not ready to be seen. If this kid saw him, his plan would be toast. He stared back, holding his breath, watching as the kid studied the darkness.

He can't see me.

Daniel slowly realized the density of the surrounding forest obscured his presence. Try as he might, Teague could not see him; he undoubtedly perceived a presence, but he saw nothing. After several tense minutes, the kid backed away.

Daniel gave a sigh of relief. That was close. He watched Teague as he skirted the perimeter of the camp, stopping alongside two shadows standing back among the trees.

There you are!

Daniel could tell Finn's posture anywhere. He grinned, his pulse quickened. Rage roiled inside his belly like hot, molten lava radiating throughout his entire body.

Some sort of ruckus erupted by the fire, causing Daniel to look away from the silhouettes. A young man breathed fire into the air; a woman ignited a branch at both ends and twirled it around like a baton. Music blared, the youngsters cheered, and there, still seated in the middle, trying desperately to fit in, sat the cop. Awkward and out of place, the old man did his best to engage the youngsters in conversation. It was almost sad.

When Daniel looked back for Finn, he was gone; Teague also was nowhere in sight. Searching the darkness, he found no sign of either. He studied the revelers around the bonfire; the dark-haired man had disappeared as well. The only people left who were a part of Finn's group were River and Beth. He kept his eyes on them, afraid if he looked away, they too would disappear.

A few moments later, River trudged off into the woods.

Determined to not lose sight of her, Daniel followed, being sure to keep a healthy distance. He wondered whether it would be better for him to just grab her first. She wasn't Teague, but she certainly was close enough to Finn to warrant his compliance with Daniel's demands.

River wandered farther away from the light of the fire.

Daniel was just about ready to make his move when a branch cracked. He spun around and stood several yards from the cop. They locked eyes.

What the hell?

Pine needles and dead leaves rustled on the ground while tree limbs shook and shivered; the forest seemed to come to life. Shadows moved swiftly.

Daniel stepped back behind a large pine tree. Peering out, he watched as Finn and his group emerged in a circle around the cop. With one mighty blow, the big, red-haired one knocked the cop unconscious.

Safely hidden among the shadows, Daniel watched as they dragged the body away toward the train yard. Maintaining a safe distance, he lagged, following as close as possible. By the time he reached the train yard, they had already tied the cop to the rear end of a grain car. Hiding behind an idle engine, Daniel watched as the unconscious man rode away to points unknown. A moment later, Finn and the others hopped on their ride heading south.

Daniel's mind told him to sprint, he struggled with the decision to jump on or not. Were it not that his gear was in the Jeep, he would have run out and caught that train.

The whistle blew, the engines picked up speed, leaving the yard behind.

Dammit!

Cursing under his breath, Daniel trudged back to his vehicle in the dark. There would be another chance. Next time, he'll be better prepared. His phone chimed with a notification. He opened the app to an image of Beth making a silly face. The words "Tempe, here we come!" were typed in the description.

Daniel chuckled. See ya real soon, kid.

Chapter 25

THE BOXCAR PROVIDED AMPLE ROOM TO STRETCH OUT OR MOVE around; it was a welcome departure from the gritty gondolas of the past few days. River sat by the open door with Cash, watching the desert scroll by.

"It's pretty, isn't it?" she said.

He nodded and sighed. "Mesmerizing. Sitting here makes it easy to forget everything, to leave problems and hang-ups behind. It's like meditating—but with better scenery." He took a drag from his cigarette.

She leaned her head against his shoulder, and the two rode in silence. Overhead, billions of stars twinkled in the black sky. Pine trees disappeared, giving way to shrubs that ultimately gave way to the giant saguaro. They were close. The lights from the city lit up the sky, blocking out most of the stars. The scent of petrichor hung heavy in the air; she breathed it in.

"I love the smell of the desert after it rains," she said.

"Yeah," agreed Cash, "it's up there as one of my favorites too."

"What're some others?"

He smiled. "Well, let's see. Pine forest in the early morning."

"Early morning? Why so specific?"

"Because that's when all the dew is still on everything."

River chuckled.

"Seriously," he continued, "the dew makes the pine scent more potent."

"All right, I'll give you that one. What else?"

"Decaying leaves on the forest floor."

"Oh, I love that too!" she agreed. "It's sweet and floral, almost like flowers."

"Fresh laundry," said Cash. "You know, like when it's hung outside in the summer sun."

"These are all interesting scents, Cash," teased River, "I had no idea you were such a romantic."

"You telling me a man can't get a little romantic every now and again?"

"I'm just surprised at you."

"Okay, smartass," said Cash. "What are some of yours?"

"Honeysuckle." River closed her eyes and breathed deep. "It reminds me of summer when I was a little kid, back in Memphis. Dawn and I would go to this park about a half-mile from our house. To get there, we had to cut through a grove filled with old-growth trees and such." She opened her eyes and smiled. "There was a wall of honeysuckle that lined the perimeter. The scent was intoxicating. It was like walking through a fragrant cloud." She looked out at the horizon. "We used to pluck the little flowers, roll them between our fingers and rub them on our wrists. I'd spend the whole day sniffing my wrists."

Cash sat silent, listening to every word. A sublime smile on his face.

"What's that look all about? Asked River.

"I just had a vision of a freckled, messy-haired, little River; dirty-faced, scabby-kneed and all, sniffing her wrists."

River shoved him. "Don't laugh. I was a cute kid."

Cash nodded. "I don't doubt that."

"I see you as the type of kid who was always dirty," said Bells, as she took a seat by the door.

River smiled. "What about you?"

"I was a perfect train wreck," replied Bells. She lit a cigarette.

"I get a distinct, scraped-knee, tree-climbing vibe from you," teased Cash.

Beth sidled up and thudded heavily on the floor. Phone in hand, she sighed as she stared at the screen.

"No service?" asked River, with a grin.

Beth shook her head and stuffed the device in her pocket.

"Uh, oh," quipped River, "Looks like you're gonna have to hang out with us, old school."

"So, what are y'all talking about?" sighed Beth.

"Just chattin' about our childhood," replied Bells.

"Sounds interesting," said Beth. She turned her focus to Bells. "How did you start hopping?"

"I started dating this girl who did it off and on," replied Bells, "she convinced me to try it, and well, here I am."

"Where is she now?"

Bells shrugged. "That relationship didn't last more than a few months. She was way too controlling. I honestly don't know where she might be right now." She pointed across the car to Max. "I met him outside of Chicago. Had to save his ass from getting beat."

"Hey now," protested Max, "I had it under control. I was just about to talk my way out of it when she came along."

"Pssh," scoffed Bells, "If that's what you wanna call it, who am I to argue?" She turned back to Beth. "We kept running into D.B. in different places." She shrugged. "One day, he decided to come along with us."

The train jerked, causing River to tumble into Cash. They were entering the city. Staying out of sight, they rode the train into Tempe, hopping off near the bridge. The city was alive all around them. Bright lights blocked the evening sky. Partiers wandered from bar to bar while music poured out into the streets. The tantalizing aroma of pizza, burgers, Thai and Mexican food wafted through the air, making River's mouth water. She made a mental list of the places she wanted to visit, but first, they needed to secure a couple of rooms at a nearby motel for the night.

Once settled, they hit the town, and she was ready for it.

The main drag was a hive of activity. Lights flashed, beats pumped, and people milled around everywhere. The live music was exhilarating, the food intoxicating. River convinced Cash to hit the dance floor with her more than once. She was having so much fun. When Bells approached to tell them the others wanted to leave for some party, she tried to convince Cash to stay on the dance floor. He insisted on at least hearing what they had in mind.

Back at their table, River found a stranger standing next to Max. She was a pretty girl, about college age, with red hair and perfect, white teeth. So perfect; River found them distracting.

"Just in time," said Max.

"In time for what?" asked River.

The girl's name was Alex, and she seemed friendly enough. Still, River didn't want to leave, so Alex better have something great to offer.

Max grinned. "There's a party going on at a dorm nearby."

"And?" asked Cash.

"She's inviting us to go."

"Everyone's really friendly," interjected Alex. She smiled nervously.

"I'm in," said Cash, a little too hastily.

"You're in?" asked River, not even trying to mask her irritation. "Do you even know what you're in for?"

Cash shrugged. "It's a party. There're college-age females and booze, maybe even weed." He smirked. "What more do I need to know?"

River shook her head and scoffed. Glancing around at the others, she could see that Beth was totally on board, as well as Bells and D.B. When she locked eyes with Zac, he nodded, signaling he was up for it.

"What do you two think?" she asked Finn and Teague, hoping that Finn would not want to go.

"Is there food?" asked Finn.

Dammit.

Alex piped up. "Yes! Are you hungry?"

"Always," he replied.

"Well, there're lots of snacks. We set up several tables earlier today,"

"Looks like we're in," said Teague, on behalf of himself and Finn.

That settled it; River had no other choice but to resign herself to the dorm party. As they left the bar, she pulled Cash aside. "This better be worth it. Nothing weird better happen. I was having fun."

"It's a bunch of college kids," he quipped. "What could go wrong?"

Chapter 26

Concrete triangles crisscrossed over windows, like a man-made exoskeleton. Not a fan of modern architecture, Teague found the sterility and lack of fine details off-putting; it was almost prisonlike. Entering through the large glass doors, he secretly hoped that his unease was more attributed to the institutional feel of the building rather than a harbinger of things to come.

Inside, a spacious room opened before them with a cold, linoleum, tile floor and scant few windows. The entire space had a bland, corporate feel to it. Overhead, string lights dangled from small hooks fixed to the ceiling; a rainbow of color twinkled in time with the music that thudded in the background. Across the room, a small group clustered around a pool table. Cash, Max, and D.B. walked over to it right away while River, Beth, and Bells followed Alex over to the sofas.

Not up for socializing, Teague remained with Zac and Finn, keeping to the room's perimeter. Food being their sole reason for coming along, they headed straight for the tables.

A menagerie of food sat atop a colorful tablecloth. Savory aromas mixed with sweets and chocolates. Teague could hardly wait to dig in.

The first table had bowls of chips with various dips alongside trays of cookies and brownies; bottled water and soda covered the second.

Passing the fruit and veggie table, Teague grabbed a couple of small carrots and popped them into his mouth.

Finn hovered over a plate laden with what appeared to be buffalo chicken nuggets while Zac was set to destroy a plate full of miniature corn dogs. As for Teague, a pile of pepperoni caught his eye.

"Ugh!" shouted Finn, his mouth still full of chicken. Refusing to chew or swallow, he snatched a napkin and cleared the offending food from his mouth.

After witnessing Finn's antics, Zac warily eyed the mini corn dogs on his plate. Reluctantly, he took a nibble out of one and promptly spit it out.

"That is vile," said Finn. "Something's wrong with that chicken."

Zac grabbed a bottle of water and chugged.

Teague glanced down at the contents of the table again. "What's wrong with it?"

"It tastes like ass," replied Finn.

Crushing the now-empty plastic bottle, Zac chimed in, "Can confirm. It tastes like ass."

"Think it's bad?" asked Teague.

"It's not bad, and nothing's wrong with it," came an arrogant voice, "It's vegan."

Teague turned his attention to the skinny, short man who was standing beside him. Easily a foot shorter than he, Teague had to bend down to look the man in the eye. A name tag on his chest read Jae.

"Why?" asked Finn.

"Because real meat's disgusting," scoffed Jae. He rolled his eyes.

"Nah." Finn shook his head. "This stuff's disgusting. Real meat is great."

"This is true," agreed Zac.

Jae was clearly offended. "Eating meat is unhealthy and cruel. It's also bad for the environment."

"Then why make food look like meat?" demanded Finn. "Why not just eat your plants and paste?"

"Because it's all about the presentation," replied Jae, now visibly irritated. "I don't even know why I'm trying to answer your questions. Only assholes eat meat." He shot a snarky glance at Zac and smirked.

"Hear that?" said Finn, his tone dripping with derision. "Apparently, we're assholes."

Jae didn't seem to be aware of the thin ice he was skating on. Looking at Zac, he touched the side of his face and said, "Nice tattoo." He rolled his eyes again, making sure that Zac and the others understood he was not giving a compliment. "Is that the Texas star?" He didn't wait for an answer, which was good because one was not forthcoming.

Jae shook his head and sighed. "Of course, someone from Texas would be clueless. I wouldn't expect anything different."

"You're kind of a prick," stated Finn, venom dripping from each word. He stepped forward, towering over the short man.

Jae turned and glared up at Finn, oblivious to the danger that hovered close.

"What's wrong with Texas?" asked Zac.

Undaunted and clearly unable to read the room, Jae continued, "Nothing, if you like racist, homophobic, losers."

Finn's nostrils flared, his jaw clenched. He was about to close the remaining gap between himself and Jae when Teague stepped in the middle.

"Look," said Jae, more to Teague than the others, "It's clear you don't belong here. Maybe you and your friends should just leave." He stepped backward and pointed toward the exit door.

Teague had to agree, it was time to leave. He didn't care much for Jae or the food.

"Come on," he said. "Let's go outside." To his relief, Finn didn't argue.

They stepped out into a small patio. Moonlight glinted off of a small pond. As the heavy door closed behind them, the music faded, giving way to the evening melody of crickets and cicadas.

"Shitty food, shitty people, and shitty music," said Finn. "A trifecta."

"Well, if you weren't such a homophobe," said Zac, "we'd be

inside right now enjoying all the fake meat we could eat." He snickered.

"Goddamn Texans," replied Finn, shaking his head.

Laughter.

"Where do people come up with such stupid shit?" asked Zac. "I used to think people in college were so smart." He shook his head.

Teague couldn't recall the last time he had spent any real time around college kids; he wondered if that was how they all were.

They took a seat on a metal bench.

"So, what do y'all want to do now?" asked Teague.

The door to the building swung wide, club music poured out, disturbing the quiet night with its heavy beat—then once again, silence. Cash, Max, and D.B. stepped onto the patio; they strode over upon seeing Teague and the others.

"Man, what happened to the college crowd?" asked Max. "These people have no sense of humor." He glanced over to D.B. "I don't remember them being like this. Do you?"

D.B. shook his head. "But then again, I never spent much time around them." He sank to the ground.

"Man, these people are some of the most uptight people I've ever met," stated Cash. He sat down on a large stone and pulled out a joint.

"What happened?" asked Zac.

Cash scoffed. "We were playing pool." He took a hit then exhaled and passed it on to Max. "These kids suck at pool, by the way."

Max took a hit and handed it off to Zac. "I made a joke about muh balls and they got all weird." He flashed an impish grin. "Suffice to say, every joke from that point on dropped like a lead balloon. I don't even know which one offended them or why."

"Why are you out here?" asked Cash.

Zac exhaled. "Apparently, we're homophobes," he replied, indicating himself and Finn.

A smile stretched across Cash's face. "Come again?"

Zac nodded at Finn. "Apparently, all Texans are racist, homophobic, losers." He mimicked a deep southern drawl, "I heard it from a college kid so it must be true."

Laughter broke out in their little circle.

The door to the building swung open again, this time spewing Bells and River into the cool night.

"Max," said River as she approached. "This party sucks. Your college kids are no fun." She halted in front of Cash, who passed her the joint. "I vote we go back to the bar we were at before all of this."

"I second," said Cash.

River glanced around at the group. "Why are y'all out here?"

"We're homophobes," replied Finn proudly.

"Racist losers too," interjected Teague. "Don't forget those. Apparently, it's a Texas thing." He looked up at River and laughed.

"Do I wanna know?" She exhaled and handed the joint over to Bells. "Never mind." She shook her head. "I think I already do."

"Who's up for heading back to the main drag?" asked Cash.

Teague was more than ready to go. "Looks like the only one we're missin' is Beth," he said. "Who wants to go in and find her so we can get out of here?"

Zac exhaled a cloud of smoke. "I'll go." He sauntered over to the door. "Wish me luck, I'm goin' back in."

Chapter 27

BETH HAD ALWAYS WONDERED WHAT IT WOULD BE LIKE TO LIVE IN A dorm. She couldn't help but wonder what life would have been like had she stayed home and not left with the Nomads. Not that she regretted her choice, she just wondered about it from time to time.

The building loomed large before her, a vast, modern creation covered by a concrete facade in the shape of triangles; she wondered whether one could climb out of a window and sit out there. She imagined what it would be like to live in the building. What it would be like to have a roommate—to go to all the parties on campus.

Beth's belly quivered as though millions of tiny butterflies fluttered around inside. She fretted about saying the wrong thing or worse, coming across as stupid.

As her anxiety took over, she realized she hadn't felt that way for a long time. Such a contrast. Mulling it over in her mind, Beth realized the stress and the need to fit in were two of the reasons she left. Joining the Nomads was the right choice. She would take dirt, cold, smelly hotel rooms and bears any day above, stressing over acceptance or walking on eggshells to avoid offending someone.

The heavy beat of dance music vibrated through her body as they entered the building. Everywhere she looked, people lounged about on chairs and sofas, all seemingly deep in conversation. Thump, thump, thump, the beat pounded in her head.

Beth thought she recognized the band; at least they sounded familiar, but she didn't recognize the song. She used to be up on all the latest info about her favorite bands. For reasons she could no longer recall, it used to be important to her. Funny how things that once seemed so vital slipped away overnight. She made her way across the room toward the makeshift sound table, which was just a table with a few people huddled around, staring down at their phones.

Palms sweaty, heart racing, she stepped up alongside a young man. Dark, brown hair pulled into a tight bun atop his head; he had the patchy beginnings of a beard growing along his jaw. As soon as he noticed her, he flashed a big smile with perfect white teeth.

"Hello," he said.

Beth's mouth went dry. She swallowed, suddenly overcome with the fear she might say something stupid. *Why are you so nervous?* She knew why. She had a lifetime of feeling this way.

"H-hi," she choked out. *Oh god! Did my voice just squeak? Maybe she could slink away into the crowd and get away.*

"You're new here, aren't you?" asked the young man.

"That obvious?"

He chuckled. "A little." He turned to face her directly, showing his name badge. Pointing at the piece of paper, he said, "I'm Ryne."

"I'm Beth."

"Nice to meet you, Beth." He looked around the room. "You live in this dorm, or are you here for the party?"

"The party," she replied.

"Do you know anyone here?"

Laughter erupted over at the pool table. Beth glanced over and saw that whatever was going on, Cash and Max were at the center. They laughed loudly, bantering back and forth while nearly all the other people around the table stared with stony faces.

Across the room, River and Bells were chatting with a group of men and women. From what she could tell, it appeared as though things were going well over there. Her eyes passed over the food tables, where she glimpsed Finn spitting food into a napkin. Beside him, Zac did the same.

Beth shook her head. "Nope, I don't know anyone here."

Ryne flashed a gorgeous smile and placed his arm around her shoulder. "Well then, Beth, let's introduce you around."

Suddenly, Beth found herself trying to keep up with a whole list of unfamiliar names. It reminded her of a day not long ago at a secluded hot spring along the Rio Grande. This time was very different, however. The faces weren't nearly as friendly, and there was no sense of ease among the guests. It was as though everyone was hiding behind walls. Afraid of saying something that would make her sound stupid, she chose her words carefully. Smiling politely and trying desperately to avoid embarrassment, she feigned interest in their conversations. A few times, she would understand what they were talking about while others, well, she just couldn't keep up. Someone placed a red cup in her hand. She took a sip, cold beer washed down her throat. Hoping it would help her lighten up, she took a large swallow.

Ryne brought her over to another group and made the introductions. While the previous groups left a lot to be desired, this new group was terrible. One girl went out of her way to make Beth feel like an outsider. It brought back feelings she would prefer to be buried in the past. Whenever Beth would say anything, the girl rolled her eyes, sometimes leaning over to whisper in her friend's ear.

Laughter and chatter revolved all around the room. Dorm life sure seemed as though it was everything she imagined it to be. She wondered if she would have fit in. Would she even want to?

"So." Ryne leaned close. "What do you think of the place now?"

"It's nice," responded Beth. "I've never been in a dorm before, so I don't have much to compare it to."

"Seriously? You've never been in a dorm before?"

Beth shook her head. "I used to wonder what it would be like to live in one."

"Want to come up and see my room?" asked Ryne, flashing the sweetest smile.

Beth agreed eagerly. The only time she had ever seen the inside of a dorm room was on television.

Ryne took her hand in his. It was soft and warm; she wasn't entirely sure she liked it. He guided her toward the stairs.

"The elevator's out, so we have to use the stairs," he explained apologetically. "I hope that's okay."

The stairs were concrete, indistinguishable from every high school she had been in. The music faded into the background, but the beat still pounded through the walls and under their feet.

Beth lost track of how many stairs they climbed; it sure felt like a lot. The shuffling sound of her footsteps echoed off of the bland concrete walls. Just when she thought they were going to climb to the top floor, Ryne pushed open a metal door, exposing a long, narrow corridor.

An endless line of wood doors, all decorated with notes, posters and various other items, stretched out before her. She stepped across the threshold and onto the carpeted floor, letting the heavy door whoosh closed behind her. Silence. The music from downstairs was gone; she could no longer feel the beat thumping.

"Wow," she said aloud, "It's so quiet."

"It's one of my favorite things about this building," replied Ryne. "The elevator situation sucks, but it's nice and quiet when you get up here."

They stopped in front of a door. A riot of rainbow-colored post-it notes surrounded a whiteboard. Beth took the marker and scrawled a message, "Beth was here," followed by a smiley face.

The room was clean. No pile of dirty laundry on the floor, no empty pizza boxes or food-crusted dishes. Even the bed was made.

Beth sauntered across the threshold, checking out the posters on the walls and the pictures atop the bookshelves. She ran her hand over the spines of the books; people she had never heard of before wrote most of them. Over at the desk, a corkboard hung on the wall. Beth studied the items on display; a couple of ticket stubs and photographs of smiling people. A slight smile spread across her face, recalling a time when she had one similar.

Ryne wrapped his arm around her waist and pulled her close.

She leaned against him, breathing in the scent of his aftershave mixed with his laundry detergent. Their lips touched.

Beth was expecting fireworks or warmth that spread throughout her body. At least, that was how kisses were always described in books. Whatever she was supposed to feel, she felt nothing.

Ryne's hand slid across her body, reaching for places she didn't want him to touch. She pulled back, trying to put some space between them, but Ryne held tight, not letting her go.

Panic welled up inside. Her fight or flight instinct kicked into overdrive. Beth pushed harder, hoping he would get the hint.

He did not.

Angry and scared, Beth shouted, "Stop it!" She reared back and shoved him away with all her strength. He stumbled backward onto the desk.

Gone was the pleasant smile. An angry sneer flashed across Ryne's face for a moment, then it disappeared, hidden behind a mask of perfect, white teeth and a smile that never made it to his eyes.

"Come on, Beth," he cooed and moved closer. "Don't be like that."

Once again, his arms snaked around her waist. He pulled her close and kissed her neck, then bit her earlobe.

The pain was immediate. Beth cried out and struggled against his grip, but this time, he held on tighter. Try as she might, she couldn't get free. He continued to kiss her neck as his hands pried and prodded for a way under her shirt.

"Get off!" she shouted. "I don't want this!" The terrified sound of her own voice was foreign to her own ears.

River's voice crept into her mind. "Sometimes, you just gotta use what's available." Beth relaxed her body and pulled her head back. Ryne stopped and gazed at her face with a warm smile. His grip loosened, allowing her arms to swing freely. Beth smiled sweetly, then punched him in the nose.

"Stupid bitch!" exclaimed Ryne, cupping his face.

Beth spun around and ran for the door. She only got a few feet away when he grabbed hold of her long hair and flung her across the room, slamming her head against the bookshelf. She hollered out in pain.

The room spun out around her. Her face, just below her eye, throbbed.

Then the door to the room crashed open, throwing splinters into the air. Zac stormed past Beth, heading straight for Ryne like a heat-seeking missile.

A flurry of punches slammed one after another right into Ryne's face. Beth imagined those perfect white teeth would need some repair. Her desire to see him in pain surprised her. She had wished no one harm before. She brushed away her conscience, realizing this was probably not the first time Ryne had pulled something like this.

Glass exploded scattering across the floor. Outside, Beth thought she heard Cash shout, "Holy shit!"

She ran over to the window as Zac pulled Ryne back inside and dumped his limp body on the floor like a wet pile of laundry. She peered out the window; all the others were staring up at them in shock.

This was going to be a story to tell.

Zac gently touched her chin and lifted her face up into the light. After wiping the tears from her face, he ran his thumb over the welt under her eye. She had no idea his touch could be so soft.

She wrapped her arms around him, buried her face in his chest and sobbed.

Chapter 28

ZAC WASN'T SURE WHAT HE EXPECTED TO FIND WHEN THEY WENT TO the party at the dorm, but he never could have imagined it would be as bad as it was. Over the years, he had a few run-ins with spoiled kids his age. He fought with more than a few of them when he was in high school. Zac knew the type, and he didn't care for them.

When he was younger, he used to think it was their intellect that set them apart. He read and studied and tried to make conversation—still nothing. Ultimately, he realized it wasn't intelligence that set them apart; it was their arrogance. He was taught to treat everyone as equals; they were taught to treat most people like underlings.

After the encounter at the food table, Zac was ready to head out. He knew if they hung around much longer, someone was going to end up in a fight, and odds were that someone would be him. He didn't hesitate when the others agreed to leave.

Now, to find Beth.

He went back inside the building and strolled around the different groups, hoping it would be easy and she would just be sitting somewhere chatting away. No such luck. She was nowhere to be found.

The first group of people he tried to ask were less than friendly. When he tried to engage, two of the girls rolled their eyes at him. The next group was better, though not helpful at all. It seemed none of these people put any effort into anything that wasn't right in front of them.

He stepped back and surveyed the room.

"Are you looking for one of your friends?" Came a voice beside him.

Zac turned around, finding himself peering down at a petite, round-faced girl with short, pale blue hair.

She smiled at him.

"I noticed your group when you came in with Alex," she blurted. "You guys kinda stick out."

"We do, huh?" He glanced around the room. "I suppose you're right; we do stick out around here."

"I'm Skylar." She thrust out her hand.

"Nice to meet you, Skylar. I'm Zac."

"I couldn't help but notice that you and your friends didn't get along well with everyone."

Zac scoffed. "That's an understatement."

She chuckled. "I saw you talking to Jae earlier." She shook her head slowly. "I'll agree, some of these folks are hard to be around; Jae, in particular, is a real challenge. Please don't judge us all based on him." She smirked. "After all, everyone can't be as awesome as I am."

"That's some serious self-esteem right there," teased Zac.

"Well, I mean, come on." She gestured with her hands. "Look at me. Who could not like this."

Zac couldn't help but smile. "Skylar, you're startin' to grow on me."

"Well, slow your wagon, cowboy." She winked. "You're not exactly my type. But we can still be friends."

Zac let loose a hearty laugh. "All right, I'll bite. What exactly is your type?"

Skylar ran her fingers through her hair. "Where's your blonde friend?"

"You're gonna have to be a little more descriptive than that." He smirked. "You talkin' male or female? Short or long hair?"

Skylar laughed. "The hot female with short hair and attitude."

"Bells," replied Zac, "You, have excellent taste."

"Would you seriously say anything different if I were talking about the other two blondes?"

Zac grinned. "Absolutely not."

"A man who's loyal to his friends," she laughed. "I wouldn't have expected anything different, Zac." She pulled a folded piece of paper from her pocket. "Do me a favor, would ya?" She handed him the paper. "Could you give this to Bells?"

"I can," replied Zac, as he stuffed the paper in his pocket. "Well, Skylar, it's been great meeting you, but I've got to get on with what I came here to do."

"That's right." She snapped her fingers. "Which friend is it you're looking for?"

"She's about this tall." He held up his hand about chest high. "Long, brown hair and young lookin'. Might've even been starin' at her phone for a while."

"I remember her," replied Skylar. "But she wasn't staring at her phone; she was too busy staring at Ryne."

"Who?"

"Ryne," replied Skylar. "His room is upstairs." She pointed to the staircase. "Second floor, fourth door on the right."

Without another word, Zac headed that way.

"Be sure to knock before you enter," called out Skylar. "Ryne's got a reputation."

Zac wasn't sure what Skylar meant by that comment, but it made him uneasy. Deep in thought, he climbed the stairs. *Beth, what are you doin'?* He shook his head and wondered whether he even wanted to go any farther.

He paused before the door. Post-it notes with hearts and smiley faces were stuck all around. In the center of it all, a whiteboard boasted multiple messages intended for Ryne, including one from Beth.

Well, this is the right room.

A loud bang came from the other side of the door, followed by muffled voices, one of which was a high-pitched, female voice. Another bang, this one followed by a squeal.

That was it. Zac was going in.

The door was locked. Zac stepped back, reared up, and kicked the door. It flew open with the splintering sound of cheap wood slamming against the wall. The whiteboard crashed to the floor, followed by a flurry of post-it notes wafting to the floor like snowflakes.

Beth was on her knees, holding her head while Ryne hovered above, ready to grab hold of her again.

Fury exploded in his chest. The world turned crimson. Zac stormed across the room, fists ready. He landed the first blow to Ryne's face, feeling the snap of cartilage through his clenched fist. Blood ruptured from the young man's face.

He stumbled back.

Zac followed, punching again and again. One more blow, and Ryne stumbled backward into the large window. Glass shattered, and the young man fell back through the jagged opening. The only thing preventing him from falling to the ground was the concrete facade.

"Holy shit!" came a voice from below.

Zac pulled Ryne into the room and dropped him on the floor. He peered out the window. Broken glass glittered on the grass. Standing a few yards away from all the debris, the others peered up at him, their faces a mixed array of confusion, shock, and humor.

"Be right down," said Zac nonchalantly.

"A'ight," came a reply from Finn.

Zac pulled his head back into the room and inspected Beth. Her face was red and blotchy, her cheeks covered in tears. He wiped them away and inspected the purple welt below her eye. It was one hell of a bruise, but it didn't appear to be broken.

Beth wrapped her arms around him and sobbed.

He stood there, holding her for what seemed a long time, with no intention of letting go of her until she was ready. He could only imagine how scared she must have been.

Beth pulled away, sniffled, and wiped her face with both of her hands. She adjusted her clothes and tucked her hair behind her ears. "Thank you," she whispered.

Zac smiled. "You ever need someone to throw a loser through a window for ya, I'm your man."

Beth giggled. The redness in her face subsided a little.

It was good to see her smile, even if it was pathetic. "You ready to head out of here? You're gonna need some ice on that." He tilted his head toward the window. "And I think those sirens we're hearing are headin' our way."

Beth nodded. "It's probably a good idea if we're not here when they arrive."

As they left the room, Zac paused and surveyed the damaged door frame. Cheap wood. He turned to Beth, "I'd offer to hold the door open for you, but, uh, there isn't much left."

Beth laughed; this time, it was far less pathetic. It was good to see her bouncing back so quickly.

Chapter 29

THE ENTIRE WALK BACK TO THE HOTEL, BETH PLAYED THE ORDEAL over and over in her head. Shame, regret, and anger roiled inside. She couldn't believe she was so stupid. What would she have done if Zac hadn't come in when he did?

When she and Zac emerged from the building, the expressions on everyone's faces made her want to run and hide. She would never be able to forget their faces. She would never overcome the embarrassment of it all.

After a brief round of questioning, silence settled in. Everyone focused on getting as far away from the campus as possible.

The entire walk back to the hotel, Zac kept pace with Beth. He wasn't right next to her, but close enough for her to sense his presence and see him in the corner of her eye. Knowing he was there made her feel safe. For that, she was thankful.

As soon as she got to the room, she went straight into the bathroom, where she splashed cold water on her face and sobbed softly, away from the others. A gentle tap on the door interrupted her self-loathing. It was River, holding a small bag filled with ice. Beth let her in, then broke down, weeping, while River stroked her hair.

"I keep playing it over in my head," said Beth. "I can't understand why he would do that."

River sighed and swept a lock of hair out of Beth's eyes. "Some people don't need a reason. They're just assholes."

"But, he didn't look like that type of person."

"They hardly ever do, sweetie," replied River. "It's always the ones you don't suspect who turn out to be the real creeps. The real monsters in life have the best manners."

"I didn't even see it coming," said Beth. "How could I be so stupid?"

River wet a face cloth and wiped away the black mascara that streamed down Beth's cheeks. "You weren't stupid. You just put your trust in the wrong person." She rubbed a spot on Beth's cheek. "Girl, this mascara you're wearin' was not meant to come off."

Beth chuckled softly.

"There, I think I got it all," said River, as she moved Beth's head from side to side, making sure she was clean. She gently touched the bruise under Beth's eye. "How bad does it hurt?"

"Not too much," replied Beth.

River placed the ice on the bruise. "Keep this on. It'll help with some of the swelling."

She stared Beth in the eyes. "Look, Beth, don't beat yourself up about this. Learn from it. That's about all you can do."

Beth nodded.

"Sometimes, the people with the finest clothes and best manners carry the most evil in their hearts," said River. "Never let your guard down around people you don't know."

"Thank you," said Beth.

"For what?"

"For being you. For making me feel better." Beth smiled. "And for getting all the mascara off my face."

River laughed softly. "That was no small feat. That stuff was on there like you drew it on with a Sharpie."

Beth hugged River tight.

"But seriously, girl," said River. "I heard you got a good hit in."

"You sound like Zac," replied Beth.

They chuckled together for a few more minutes, then joined the others.

All the chatter stopped when Beth entered the room. Suddenly self-conscious, she wanted to turn around and lock herself in the bathroom again. The tantalizing aroma of fresh, hot pizza wafted through the air. Her mouth watered and her stomach grumbled. Her hunger won; she decided it was best to get over the awkwardness as early as possible. She snatched a big slice, then plunked herself down in the nearest chair.

An uneasy silence hung heavy in the room. Spyder jumped off D.B.'s lap, where he was nibbling a piece of pepperoni, and stalked across the floor. He hopped up on Beth's lap, where he leaned back and purred.

"Looks like you have a buddy," said D.B.

Beth smiled and scratched the little kitten under his chin. "I'm sorry I ruined everyone's night."

"You didn't ruin anything," replied Bells.

"Yeah," replied Teague, "you can't ruin what already sucked."

"Was it just me," asked Max, "or was that the worst college party ever?"

"It was awful," agreed D.B. "A bunch of people walking around on eggshells. I can't think of a more miserable way to be."

Max shook his head. "I just don't understand the kids these days."

Laughter.

"They seemed normal, at first," said Beth. "A few of them had seen my posts online."

"Your what?" asked Max.

"I post pictures and videos online," replied Beth.

Max pulled out his phone. "What's your profile?"

"Nomad Girl."

"Look, Beth," said Bells. "Don't beat yourself up about what happened. That could've happened to any of us."

"She's right," said Finn. "You ain't the first person to put your trust in the wrong person."

The look on his face was pure compassion. He was sincere. It dawned on Beth that he was probably the one person in the entire room who knew exactly how she felt inside.

"Damn Beth," said Max, staring down at his phone. "seventy-four thousand followers!" He glanced up. "Our girl here is popular." He scrolled through her posts.

Bells peered over his shoulder. "That's a good shot," she said.

"Y'all do some dumb shit," quipped Max. He held his phone up, the screen facing out so the others could see the video playing. "Seriously, rustlin' cows?"

Beth glanced over at the others; their faces were solemn—unreadable. Everyone except Finn, that is. Gone was the soft, kind expression. In its place was a dark scowl. An icy chill ran up her spine.

"Nice video of Teague's birthday," said Max. "You got my good side in this one."

Bells scoffed and shoved his head playfully. "You don't have a good side."

River and Cash walked over to get a better look.

"Look at that follower count," said Max, "I am seriously impressed." He held out his phone again, so the others could see a picture of Finn. "Very photogenic."

"You need to take down my pictures," ordered Finn, his words dripping with suppressed rage. "And all the videos too."

"It's too late for that, buddy," said Max. "The internet is forever. Like it or not, you've gone viral." Max looked up at Finn. "You're internet famous."

Finn sprung to his feet, hovering above Beth menacingly. Teague stepped in front of him, creating a barrier with his body. Undaunted, Finn pushed back. Glaring at one another, they stood in deadlocked silence.

Oblivious to the growing tension in the room, Max continued, "Dude, you've got this whole fan club."

Finn seethed. He pushed harder against Teague, who had to push back, using the full weight of his body. Finn's eyes could melt iron.

"There're even people from Europe who follow!"

"Stop talking!" shouted Bells.

A cloud of angry silence covered the entire room. The mood was dark and foreboding.

"Beth, what were you thinking?" asked River. Her tone was one of deep disappointment. "I warned you about this."

Finn stepped back from Teague and rounded on River. "You knew?"

River nodded slowly. "I didn't think it was a big deal."

"No big deal?!" bellowed Finn. "She's plastered our goddamn faces all over the internet!"

"It's all positive," defended Beth. "Everyone loves what I post."

Red-faced with rage, Finn flew toward Beth. She jumped to her feet, knocking Spyder off her lap, and backed up against the wall.

The terrified kitten scurried over to D.B. and climbed up his leg.

Once again, Teague stepped in front of Finn, using his body to stop his forward momentum. Finn pushed back, but Teague held his ground. Neither said a word.

Finn sneered, then shoved Teague backward, nearly knocking him off his feet. "Get the fuck away from me!" He headed straight for Beth.

Having seen enough, Zac stepped in and grabbed Finn from behind, pinning his arms behind his back.

Finn struggled, but could not free himself. "Let go!" he demanded.

"I ain't letting go until you calm the fuck down," hissed Zac, through clenched teeth.

After several tense minutes, Finn finally gave in. Zac shoved him into a chair by the door and stood close, just in case.

Teague spun around, his face red with fury. "What the fuck were you thinking?"

It occurred to Beth that she had never seen him angry like that. Unlike Finn, his rage was calm, more calculating. For the first time, she saw the darker side of Teague, and she found it terrifying.

Cash and River were busy scrolling through Beth's feed. When they finished, they gave the phone back to Max.

Silence. The only sound was the hum of the air conditioning unit under the window.

"Come on, Beth," said Bells, "Why don't you come with us to our room so everyone can calm down."

Beth skirted past Teague, who made no effort to move aside. His eyes were cold, his body standing firm as she squeezed between him and the television cabinet. Walking by the others, River didn't even make eye contact while Cash stared blankly. As she skirted past Finn, Zac placed a firm hand against his chest, holding him in place in the seat.

When the door closed behind her, Beth wondered if this was the end of their little group. Once again, tears spilled down her face.

Chapter 30

TEAGUE SAT AT THE TABLE, STARING DOWN AT THE FLOOR, HIS MIND A whirlwind of thought, while Finn gnawed his nails and paced around the room like an irate, caged bear.

Like a computer glitch, the moment Finn shouted and shoved him backward played over and over in Teague's mind. He fidgeted with the leather bracelet around his wrist.

Until that night, Teague had never been at the receiving end of that cold, hateful glare. In all the years together, through all the fights they had; Finn had never stared him down that way. Teague didn't like it at all; those eyes were dark, cruel, and alarming.

"Are we gonna sit in here and stew in our own thoughts?" asked River, her tone nervous. "Or are we gonna talk about this?"

There was a long pause before Cash chimed in, "I agree with River. We should at least talk about this."

"Fuck that!" cried Finn, never making eye contact, still pacing back and forth. He stopped in front of Cash, his body twitching with pent-up energy. "She has to go."

"Where?" demanded River. "Where exactly is she supposed to go?"

"Back home," replied Finn. "Where she should have stayed."

"I'm not gonna say what she did was no big deal," said River. "But sending her packing without a chance to redeem herself is extreme."

"How are you not even bothered by this?" demanded Finn. "She plastered our faces all over the damn internet!"

Finn's rage was boiling out of control. Teague wondered whether he should try to intervene. He thought about what transpired a few moments ago and realized that trying to calm Finn down when he was in such a rage, was like handling a red-hot coal with your bare hands. If, by some rare chance, you could cool it off, you'd be scarred forever. He could still feel the glare of those hateful eyes, or was it just his emotions getting the better of him? Get over it.

Over by the door, Zac stood sentinel; arms crossed, face solemn, he tracked Finn's movements with a wary eye.

Meanwhile, River continued her attempt to work out a solution.

"Maybe we can tell her if she wants to stay, she has to delete her profile," offered River. "Erase it all, and no more uploads."

"And what? Just forget what she's done?" seethed Finn.

Until that moment, Cash observed, deep in reflection, tugging at the facial hair around his chin. "I think River has a good point."

"Fuck you!" boomed Finn.

Cash stepped forward. "Do not get up in my face," he hissed. "I'm not Teague. I'm not gonna take it."

Those words stung Teague like a slap to the face. He stared down at his hands, his mind blank. This was spiraling out of control, and for the first time, he wasn't sure there was anything he could do to stop it.

"I think everyone needs to calm down," said Zac, still standing cross-armed at the door.

The stare down between Finn and Cash ended with them both stepping back from one another.

River glanced over at Teague with the look of someone wondering why he hadn't stepped in yet. Teague quickly turned away. He was too deep in his own head to be of any help to anyone.

Cash stepped toward Finn, palms out in front of him. "I realize you're pissed," he said. "And rightly so. It was an awful thing to do."

Finn grunted and crossed his arms.

"But hear me out," said Cash, "we've all fucked up." He pointed to Finn. "That includes you. No one kicked you out. In fact, none of us were ever threatened with being ostracized for fucking up."

"He's right," agreed River.

Cash continued, "What have we always done when one of us does something that pisses off the rest of us?" He paused.

Tension hung over the room as they waited for Finn's response.

With no answer forthcoming, Cash continued, "We've always given one another a chance to correct the problem or at least make up for it."

Finn shook his head in disgust and went back to pacing and gnawing at his fingernails.

"I'm not saying we brush it aside and forget all about it," said Cash. "All I'm saying—all River is saying, is we should give Beth a chance to redeem herself."

"I agree," stated Zac.

Finn stopped in front of Teague and scowled, nostrils flaring, jaw flexing. "Well?" he sneered.

Teague wasn't sure what the proper response should be. The only thing he knew was that he was done being threatened. He was finished cowering as though he had done something wrong. Teague stood up, back straight, chest out, and stared directly into Finn's eyes. He took a step forward. If they were going to fight, then so be it.

Finn stepped back, blinked, and redirected his eyes toward the floor. His shoulders sagged.

"I agree," said Teague, never breaking his gaze.

Finn stepped away and plopped down onto the edge of the bed, where he stared at nothing while biting his nails.

"All right then," said Cash. "I think setting the condition that if she's gonna stay, she will need to delete her account and stop with the online posting is a good start."

"Aside from erasing her online stuff, what else would we want her to do?" asked River.

Teague shrugged. "Don't know," he replied. "But I know she has to earn our trust again." He looked down at Finn. "I'm fine with giving her a chance to do that. How about you?"

Finn did not look up, nor did he reply.

"All right," said Cash. "So, we're all agreed, we're gonna give her a chance to stay with us."

Everyone except Finn, agreed.

"On the condition that she delete all of her online posts," said River. "And not post anymore."

Teague, Zac, and River agreed.

Finn sat silently, staring at Teague.

Something about the look in Finn's eyes made Teague uneasy. No longer angry or contemptuous, it was calm and almost resolute. Teague had the unmistakable notion that a deep crevasse had opened between them.

Finn got to his feet and walked toward the door, pausing in front of Zac without saying a word. After a silent exchange between the two, Zac stepped aside, allowing Finn to pull open the door and storm outside.

"I'll go with him," said Zac, then he too left, leaving the door open.

Silence descended on the three remaining friends.

Thoughts churned in Teague's head. A sense of dread gripped his gut. He pulled his phone from his pocket and texted Gunner.

Teague: You there?

After a hot minute, the screen lit up.

Gunner: Always. What's up?

Teague stared at the screen, struggling to put words to his confusion. Should he tell Gunner he had a strange feeling? About what? What the hell could Gunner do about that? Why the hell did he even text him?

Teague: Nothing. You just popped into my head, so
I figured I'd check in.
Gunner: Everything okay there?
Teague: Yes. Just wanted to check on you.

Another hot minute. This pause seemed to take an eternity, leaving Teague to wallow in his own regret for acting like a fool and bothering Gunner. Finally, his phone lit up.

Gunner: How's Finn?

I don't know. Teague shook his head. He raked his hand down his face. What the hell did that even mean? They had a fight. It wasn't even a fight at all; Teague could recall several instances in the past where they actually broke out into punches. None of that took place this time. How stupid could he be? Why is he making such a big deal over this, let alone go whining to Gunner?

Teague: He's fine. Just went out for a walk
around town with Zac.

Once again, a long pause. Is it me, or are these pauses getting longer? Teague was now worried that he panicked for no reason and got Gunner involved over nothing at all. The longer his screen remained dark, the more his discomfort grew. Unable to take it any longer, he wrote another text.

Teague: I'm fine, he's fine, everyone's okay
here. I just wanted to check on you.

Mais la! Now he's gonna know something's up.

Gunner: I'm fine. And for the record, I'm always
here. I'll leave my phone on, so feel free to
text or call if you want to talk.

Teague swallowed against the lump that had somehow materialized in his throat.

```
Teague: Thanks, I'll remember that. Gotta go.
Gunner: Goodnight.
```

U

Chapter 31

BETH WIPED HER FACE WITH HER SHIRTSLEEVE. THE PAST SEVERAL hours had been a nightmare of emotions. When River came to get her, she didn't know what to expect. In her opinion, they had blown the whole thing out of proportion. She still didn't quite understand what the big deal was. Who wouldn't want to be famous? It's not like people hate them; it was very much the opposite—people loved them. And they loved her for sharing their adventures. Why do the things they do, if they won't post about it? What was the point?

As she crossed the threshold into the room, the mood was somber. The tension was so thick; it was a wonder anyone could breathe. Finn was not there, neither was Zac. She wondered where they had gone off to.

More than a little nervous, Beth took a seat on the edge of a bed and braced herself for the "talking to" she was about to get.

Their demand was simple. She was to delete her account and never post about any of them again. Beth thought they were joking at first, she quickly realized they were dead serious.

In the end, she agreed to shut down her social media account; she had an alt account, anyway. Beth would have liked to keep the primary account, but she had no other choice than to comply with their demands. Bells, Max and D.B. hadn't suggested she come along with them, so it was either shut down her profile or be left alone in Tempe. "I'll do it right now," she said. She pulled her phone from her pocket and opened the app. After a few swipes and taps, she had deactivated her account. She held out the device so the others could see. "There, done!"

After both River and Cash confirmed it was done, River smiled and gave Beth a hug, thanking her for doing the right thing—though Beth didn't see it that way at all.

Across the room, deep in his own thoughts, Teague didn't stir. He showed no sign of being interested in what was taking place. He simply stared down at his phone. His face was a mask of dismay.

Whatever his issue was, it had nothing to do with Beth. She forgot all about him and spent the remaining hours of the night with River and Cash, happy to put the last few hours behind her.

She awoke in the morning to the dim glow of sunlight peeping through the nicotine-stained curtains. Beside her, River snored quietly.

Rubbing the sleep from her eyes, Beth sat up and glanced around the room. On the small sofa lay Cash, curled up under a light blanket. On the other bed, Teague slept, his arm draped across his face. Beside him lay Zac, sprawled out, sleeping soundly. Beth didn't even hear him come in last night. It had to have been very late.

In the corner, partially hidden by the chest of drawers, Finn sat wedged between the wall and the large piece of furniture. Knees up, his head resting atop his arms that were wrapped around his knees. Beth wasn't sure if he was sleeping or not. She couldn't imagine someone being comfortable in that position.

She slid off the bed and quietly padded across the floor toward the door. She glanced around the room, making sure she didn't wake anyone, then went outside and sat on the curb, taking in the sunrise.

Three doors down, an older couple loaded their bags into their sedan. Across the parking lot, a lone man leaned against the corner of the building, smoking a cigarette. Something about him was familiar, but she couldn't quite put her finger on it. He was fit with a dark suntan. His salt-and-pepper hair was messy, but not overgrown. He clearly hadn't shaved in a few days, and his clothes were slightly disheveled. Maybe he's a Nomad like us. He could certainly pass for one. She waved at the stranger, and he nodded in response.

The door to the room creaked open and River stepped out. She yawned and stretched, then took a seat alongside Beth. "Good morning," she said. "What ya doin' out here?"

Beth smiled. "Just taking in the sunrise and people watching." The older couple had finished loading their car and drove away. The smoking man was gone. He must have gone back into his room.

"Well, as soon as the others are awake," said River, "we're heading to the river."

"You sound very excited."

River smiled. "It's pretty. The water is nice, the area is quiet, and there are wild horses. Just wait. You're gonna love it."

The door to the next room opened, and Max wandered out. Yawning and rubbing his head, he sat down on the curb. "What're y'all up to?"

"Just talking about today's plans," replied River. "Are you coming with us?"

Max shook his head. "I think we're gonna stick around here for another couple of days. At least that was what we talked about doing last night." He studied Beth, then River. "Besides, it appears y'all have some reconnecting to do. Probably best if we gave y'all space to do that."

"Sounds like a good idea," agreed River.

Beth had hoped that last night was behind them. Max didn't seem to think it was; this made her worry. How much more guilt was she going to take before everyone let it go? Wasn't giving up most of her online following enough? She decided she would give it till the end of the river trip, and if things weren't better after that, she would ask to tag along with Max, D.B., and Bells.

It was almost noon when they left the motel and caught a ride out to the national forest. The city fell away, opening up to rolling hills filled with saguaro, catclaw, cholla, and prickly pear. The desert was such a fascinating place, full of cruel beauty.

For the most part, the others were in good spirits. No one brought up the internet or anything about the night prior, which was okay with her. She had no desire to keep bringing that up. Even Finn was in a decent mood, or at least, he seemed to be. He hadn't said over two words to her since he woke up. Come to think of it, he spent more time with Zac than any of the others, including Teague.

Whatever. It wasn't her problem.

All in all, it was going to be a good day. She looked forward to sitting by the campfire when the sun went down. She loved the sound of the desert at night.

Their ride dropped them off at the entrance to a recreation area. After backtracking across the bridge, the group hiked along the river's edge for a couple of miles, choosing a secluded spot along the edge of the water.

Beth placed her pack on the ground and took in the gorgeous scenery.

"I told you it was amazing," said River.

"Wait till you see it at night," said Zac, as he strolled past her carrying a load of firewood.

Cash pulled a bottle of whiskey from his pack. "I've been holding on to this, just for tonight." He placed it down beside the newly built fire pit.

"Woo!" shouted Teague, as he stood knee-deep in the water. "That is cold, cold."

Finn plunged into the river, creating a giant splash of water that soaked Teague. He laughed and dove in.

"Come on," said River, grabbing hold of Beth's arm. "Let's go for a swim."

Beth peeled off her shorts and T-shirt, exposing her swimsuit beneath. She took a step into the water, feeling a shiver run through her whole body. It was cold.

"Teague, you're right," she said, "this is cold, cold."

"It's okay," he called back. "You get used to it. Just jump on in."

River stood on the beach. "How cold is it?"

"You're about to find out," replied Cash. He scooped her up in his arms and ran into the water.

River let out a scream as she crashed down into the water. She resurfaced and splashed water at Cash. "Come on, Beth, just jump in," she prodded.

Beth took a tentative step forward; the cold water was now up to her knees. She shivered.

Zac waded up alongside her. "Come on, let's do this together."

Beth nodded, her teeth chattering from the cold.

"Okay, on the count of three," he said.

Counting together, "One, two—"

Before she could say three, he had grabbed hold of her arm and tugged her into the water with him. She hollered right before going under. The cool water enveloped her body, surrounding her head. Her long hair billowed with the soft weightlessness of the current. The cold dissipated, leaving in its wake a sense of cool weightlessness. She breached the surface and floated, staring up at the sky, reveling in the sensation of the warm sun against her face and the cold water around her body.

Back at the campsite, sitting on the beach, Beth wiggled her toes in the soft, warm sand. The sun was setting on the horizon. Behind her, Cash and Zac prepared dinner.

"I'm glad you're still with us," sighed River.

"I am, too." Though she would have liked to keep her account.

A sharp whistle echoed across the tiny valley. Beth looked up to see Teague standing atop the hillside. Waving his arms overhead, he pointed behind him. "Horses," he shouted.

Beth jumped to her feet. "Did he say horses?"

"He sure did," replied River.

They took off toward the hill, meeting up with Teague.

"Keep the ruckus down," he warned. "There's a mama and her foal just around those rocks, drinking."

Beth did her best to keep up, but the rocks made it difficult. Up ahead, Teague moved along like a mountain goat. She picked her way carefully, doing her best to avoid slipping.

Teague stopped and pointed down to a quiet lagoon.

A loud sigh escaped Beth's lips. Below, standing in the calm water, heads down, a brown and white mare and her sweet, little foal were drinking. A cluster of horses, black, dark brown, and more paints like the mama and foal, nibbled at the nearby plants on the shore. Finn was busy stroking the nose of a handsome, dark, brown horse with a shiny, black mane.

"They're gorgeous," whispered Beth.

"Wanna pet 'em?" asked Teague.

"Yes!"

"Come on then," he said.

More crawling along sharp and jagged rocks. This time, Beth could keep her mind off the pain by focusing on the horses. She was sure by the time they got to the bottom, the horses would bolt.

But that wasn't what happened.

The small herd milled about as though the humans weren't even there. Beth wanted to run right up and wrap her arms around all of them, but she knew better. Walking carefully and with purpose, she crept up alongside Cash and touched the brown horse.

A large, paint pony approached Beth. She rubbed his nose. Behind her, she heard footsteps in the water. A soft nose gave her a firm nudge. She spun around to find the mama mare standing there, regarding her with dark, brown eyes. Her little foal stood close, partially hidden by the mama's body.

"Give her some of this," said Zac, as he handed her a bunch of grass. "They like it."

Beth held the clump of grass out, and the mare nibbled away. Something cold and wet brushed up against her thigh; she looked down to see the foal peering up at her with big, brown eyes. It took every ounce of restraint she could muster to avoid squealing with delight.

Standing there in the waning light of dusk, surrounded by wild horses, was the most magical moment of Beth's life. She never wanted it to end. She wished she had her phone to record it.

Somewhere deep in the hills, a coyote called out, startling the horses. The dark, brown horse gave out a nervous whinny, then the herd disappeared into the thick desert shrubs, leaving Beth and the others standing on the shore in silence. After several minutes, they picked their way back along the path to their campsite.

The warmth of the fire was a delight against Beth's skin. Overhead, a blanket of stars glittered against the black sky. The fire crackled and popped as red and orange flames licked away at dry logs. The bottle of whiskey made its way to her. She took a full swig, reveling in the warm sensation that spread throughout her body. By no means a connoisseur; there was a different flavor to this whiskey. She took a second sip, then turned the bottle in her hand to read the label; her vision blurred. *Something's wrong.* The world swirled and spun out in a kaleidoscope of red, black, and white. She closed her heavy eyelids and fell into a deep sleep.

Chapter 32

It took Daniel a lot longer than expected to find a country veterinarian whose office was fully stocked with ketamine. He had to break into two different facilities between Flagstaff and Phoenix before he found one with everything he needed.

Thanks to Beth's posts, he knew the kids were going out for a night on the town in Tempe.

When he arrived in the city, the streets were teeming with revelers moving from one bar to another. Having no idea where to look, he pulled out his phone to see if Beth had posted anything new. Nothing.

Not only was there no new post, but her profile was nowhere to be found. Positive it was a glitch, Daniel closed the app and relaunched it. He searched for her user name—it was gone.

Shit! Did she close her account? Dammit! Now, how was he supposed to find them? Anger and confusion churned in his guts. He couldn't possibly have come this far—gotten this close, and have it all slip through his fingers because some teenage girl closed her social media account. Goddammit!

Daniel stood on the corner observing the people pass by, his anger increasing by the second. No, no, no-no. He did not get this far, only to have it snatched right out from under him like this. Without Beth's social media, Finn was a ghost. A specter in the world without a trace. Daniel had no other way to track him. If he went back to creeping around hobo camps, he could be out there for years and never even get a nibble.

He spied a small dive bar tucked away between two more prominent, trendy bars. A perfect place for him to have a few drinks and sort his thoughts. He needed to cool off; anger leads to rash decisions. A rash decision, more often than not, was the wrong decision.

After ordering two double whiskeys on the rocks, Daniel took up a seat in front of a set of open garage doors. Sipping his whiskey, he studied the seemingly endless parade of twenty-somethings.

The street was teeming with drunk, horny, young people. A trio of friends strolled by, one of their members clearly drunk, staggering between his two buddies. He could remember a time, long before everything went to shit when he was just like them. Young, healthy, and full of promise for the future.

A throng of young women clustered on the sidewalk, blocking Daniel's view. There was a time when he would have enjoyed the scenery. But those times were long past. The scent of their perfume made him nauseous. Their inane chatter and constant giggling irritated the hell out of him. He fought the urge to yell at them and tell them to shut the hell up.

The women were obnoxious. Their gaggle of chaos made it impossible for anyone to get past without first stopping and then weaving their way through the bottleneck they created. Judging by the facial expressions of all the other people who had to weave their way through the mess, they were every bit as annoyed as Daniel.

One of the women stumbled and landed against her friend, causing her to bump into a passerby. This brought the whole clusterfuck to a near-dead stop.

Daniel was just about to pick up what remained of his second drink and move to a different seat when he glimpsed a familiar face.

The young man stood less than ten feet away. Dark hair, wearing sunglasses. A sneer of irritation set across his face. The same bottleneck that prevented Finn from moving forward created a perfect camouflage for Daniel, who was so close he could almost smell Finn.

Daniel's pulse quickened. Here he thought his luck had run out, that he had hit the end of the road. Fate had delivered his prey directly to him. Daniel could hardly believe his luck. He looked around for the boyfriend; he was nowhere to be found. The only other friend around was the red-headed linebacker.

Up close, the kid's size was impressive, much larger than Daniel— for that matter, much bigger than many full-grown men. Indeed, the redhead was going to be a tough one to handle. Luckily, Daniel came prepared.

Daniel moved his focus back to Finn. Oblivious and looking quite annoyed, the kid was too busy in his own head to realize he was standing within touching distance of his worst nightmare.

The bottleneck loosened, and the foot traffic could move forward once again. Finn and the redhead weaved their way through the mess, breaking free on the other side.

Determined not to lose sight of his quarry this time, Daniel followed close on their heels. How neither of them noticed was a mystery. Very lazy to let your guard down like that.

This went on for hours until the revelers dissipated and the bars closed. That was when things got tricky. More than once, Daniel was forced to duck into an entry or slither around a corner. Still, Finn and his friend never saw him; they never even showed any sign of being aware they had a tail.

Their wandering ended at a cheap, seedy motel. Just looking at the exterior made Daniel's skin itch. He watched as they disappeared into a room.

This time, Daniel would not take any chances. He would be damned if he left, and Finn slipped away again. Not this time. There was the issue of transportation that needed resolving. He didn't know how the kids would travel when they left the motel, but he wanted to be prepared to follow. The best solution was to get a room, park nearby and wait till sunrise. He paid the clerk to monitor the room, then left to retrieve his Jeep.

Less than an hour later, he was settled in his own room, just a few doors down from where Finn and his friends slept. It reeked of stale cigarettes. His body alive with anticipation, Daniel spent the next several hours moving inside and out, keeping a watchful eye on the other room.

The evening sky gave way to the icy blue of dawn. The door to the room opened, and Beth wandered out. She sat heavily on the curb and looked out above the building, tilting her chin up to the sky. She was so young. Naïve would be another good word to describe her. It never occurred to her that some people in the world would do her great harm —people like Daniel. He almost felt bad for the girl. She noticed him leaning against the building and waved. He nodded back. As soon as she looked away, he slithered into his room, peeping out through yellow curtains.

A couple of hours passed, then a big, black SUV pulled up, the logo of one of those rideshare companies visible in the window. Finn and his friends loaded up and drove away—with Daniel not far behind.

More than once, Daniel wondered where the hell they were going as he followed the vehicle through the city streets and onto the freeway. It all made sense when they crossed into the national forest. He couldn't ask for a better location to carry out his plans.

After being dropped off, Daniel hung back, watching as the group of young travelers crossed over the bridge and trekked their way down into the valley, following the river. He parked his Jeep, gathered his backpack with supplies, and headed down the same path.

His mind was filled with fantasies of what he would do with his life after finally being rid of Finn. Maybe he would travel—he did enjoy the past several months on the road. The accommodations would have to be much better, though. Or perhaps he would just find a piece of property in the middle of nowhere and live off the grid for the rest of his life.

Hidden among the brush, he watched as they horsed around in the water. The sound of their laughter grated on his nerves like nails on a chalkboard. Their happiness infuriated him. When they took off over the hills, he crept into their campsite.

Daniel had a clear plan. All he had to do was find the right way to administer the ketamine. As luck would have it, a bottle of whiskey rested alongside the fire pit. A vicious sneer crept across his face. He unscrewed the cap, took a swig, then poured the ketamine inside. He swirled the bottle in his hand, a satisfied grin settled on his face as he studied the caramel-colored liquid.

He placed the bottle back where he found it and crept back into the brush.

Now all he had to do was wait.

Chapter 33

Wake up!

Disembodied voices echoed in the blackness.

Something's wrong!

A woman's voice.

River?

Teague couldn't make out what she was saying; the only thing he could make out was her tone. She was upset.

Wake up!

Why couldn't he open his eyes? Teague's head lay heavy on the dirt, gritty pebbles dug into his cheek. His mouth was dry, his head throbbed, while the rest of his body was numb. He struggled to open his eyes, but each time he opened them, they would roll back into his skull before focusing. His arms were bound behind his back; he could not move them.

Two male voices were in a heated exchange.

Cash? Who the hell is the other voice?

The shouting intensified then—Bang!

A gunshot rang out.

Cash howled in pain.

River screamed.

Teague's eyes shot open; this time, he could focus. Several feet in front of him lay Zac, unconscious and hogtied.

Teague craned his neck toward River's voice. She was on her knees, hands behind her back. In front of her lay Cash, a pool of crimson blood puddled on the ground beneath him. A third person, a man, paced just out of Teague's view.

"Better put some pressure on that if you don't want him to bleed out right away," suggested the man.

Teague tried to get a better glimpse at the stranger, but his restraints were too tight. He could hardly move.

"Fuck you!" shouted River. She wriggled her body in such a way, so she could set her hands on Cash's thigh. Blood, like thick, red ink, oozed through her fingers.

"Thanks for the offer, Darlin', but I'm gonna have to pass," countered the man. "Now, fifteen or twenty years ago, would have been a different story—"

Cash did not move. His face pale with an angry red welt around his right eye, clothes disheveled, hands and legs not restrained.

The man moved into Teague's view, an ominous shadow hovering over Cash, followed by the sound of a zip tie.

"Wouldn't want our boy here to get any ideas about being a hero again," said the man. "Though, between you and me, I don't think he's gonna be a problem for anybody anymore." He paused. "At least not for much longer."

River sobbed, no defiant cursing or yelling; she held her tied hands against Cash's leg.

Where's Finn? Teague wriggled around to see the rest of the encampment. In front of him, Zac stirred, just waking. A few feet away from Zac lay Beth. Her eyes were wide with fear, face covered in muddy tears.

"Well, hello sleeping beauty," said the stranger in a throaty, cruel voice. He grabbed Teague by the hair and hauled him to his knees.

The stranger bent down on one knee in front of him, allowing Teague to get a good look at him.

Deep-set wrinkles surrounded the stranger's dark, cold eyes. A thick, salt-and-pepper beard covered the lower half of his face. His shark-like smile was as soulless as his eyes.

Teague did not recognize him.

"I was wondering whether you'd sleep through everything," said the man malevolence dripping from each word. "We can't have that, can we?" He swayed his head. "No, we need you wide awake, crying and begging for your life." He held a bottle of water out. "You've gotta be thirsty. That ketamine has quite the kick. Water will help with the headache."

The stranger pressed the bottle up against Teague's lips; he yanked his head away. There was no way in hell he was going to take anything from this bastard.

The man snickered. "Feisty. Well, I thought y'all would be. That's why I got the drugs. There was no way in hell I was gonna go up against that big, red-haired beast." He pointed a thumb at Zac. "I have to say, I didn't think that one would fight back," he said, pointing his chin toward Cash. "Too bad for him."

The man paused and stared at Teague, his face a mask of sociopathic calm.

An icy chill ran down Teague's spine.

"I see you're still trying to figure out what's going on." The man flashed a wicked, toothy smile. "I'm Daniel. You might have heard about me."

Teague's stomach sank—the world zoomed in and out of focus. He was staring face to face with a monster. His heart raced in his chest, threatening to beat itself free of his rib cage.

Daniel chuckled. "Judging by your expression," he said, "I see you have." He leered at Teague. "So, you know exactly what I'll do if you even try to do something stupid." His face went serious. "Let's be honest, I'm gonna do it, anyway."

Teague's mind spiraled. Finn! He searched the area, hoping to see him tied up somewhere near.

Daniel got to his feet. "Oh, I know what you're looking for." He lumbered over to a dark lifeless shape lying in a heap in the dirt and grabbed a fist full of dark hair. He dragged Finn across the ground, dropping him several feet from Teague.

Panic surged throughout Teague's body. He wanted to scream, but there was no way he would give Daniel the satisfaction of seeing him terrified.

A nasty red gash on the side of Finn's head oozed a crimson rivulet across his face. Hands and legs untied—there was no need. The seizures would keep Finn under control.

"Don't worry," said Daniel. "He ain't dead. Yet. I have to admit, the temptation was enormous." Daniel shook his head. "He put up one hell of a fight while y'all were out." Daniel dabbed a small gash in the corner of his mouth. "Evidently, ketamine reacts differently in some people. I'll have to make a note of that." He kicked Finn in the gut, causing him to convulse in the fetal position. "See?" said Daniel, "He's still alive. Not really with it, but still alive. If it's any consolation, he'll be the last one to go. I want him to see every one of his friends suffer and die first. After that, I'll put the little mutt out of his misery."

A fiery, red tempest of hate churned inside Teague. Behind his back, he tugged at his restraints, trying to free his hands.

Finn tried to push up on his hands and knees, only to have Daniel place one of his large, black boots in the center of his back, forcing him down. As soon as Finn collapsed, Daniel kicked him again. Holding a handful of Finn's hair, he landed a punch on the side of his head.

"Stop it!" shouted Teague.

Finn fell into a seizure.

Daniel nudged Finn's rigid body with his boot. "That's like the fourth one so far." He clucked his tongue. "That can't be good for the brain."

"You're a sick fuck!" shouted Teague.

"Now, now, you're gonna hurt my feelings."

"Fuck your feelings!"

Daniel snickered. "You are a feisty one. I like you." He shook his head. "I gotta say, I did not see you two comin'. I did not know the kid swung that way. Had I known, I might've been a little easier on him."

He halted in contemplation, then kicked Finn again. "Who am I kiddin'? I'm for equality all the way baby, it wouldn't have changed a damn thing."

He laughed the most demonic laugh Teague had ever heard.

Daniel shook his head. "It still is quite a surprise. I always heard things like the parent knows." He glanced over at Finn. "Maybe the bond has to be genetic. I mean, there ain't a single drop of my DNA in him."

Teague stared, stunned.

Daniel knelt down to face Teague directly. "I can tell by the look on your face that you're a little confused. Allow me to put it into simpler terms for you."

He leaned so close, Teague could smell his foul breath. "I may have raised that sorry sack of flesh, but I didn't make him. That clear enough for you?" Daniel glared at Finn. "Turns out, the eyes are genetic." He tapped the side of his head. "Yeah. Passed down through the gene pool. A gift from his bio dad. Some sorry sack of shit from a Podunk town in North Texas." He stood up. "The blonde witch ain't even his mother," he added as an afterthought.

Daniel held his arms out at his sides. "Oh, it's a whole fucking mess of lies and bullshit!" he shouted. "It'd take weeks to parse it all out for you." He sneered. "But sadly, we don't have enough time for that. Because this mess is ending tonight, and I am so ready for it." Daniel stalked away.

He's not Finn's father; she wasn't his mother. Teague struggled against his restraints.

Daniel returned and splashed a jug of water on Finn, startling him into consciousness. "Wake up, princess, time for the fun to start."

Finn coughed and wheezed as he shook his head to wake up.

"This is taking too long," said Daniel. He took hold of Finn and tipped his head up. "Wake up!" he shouted.

Finn's eyes flitted open, consciousness settled in, his jaw flexed, then he lunged forward, seized hold of Daniel's legs around the knees and yanked him down to the ground. As soon as Daniel went down, Finn landed a sharp blow to his face.

Daniel howled, then caught hold of Finn and punched him in the face several times in rapid-fire. He clambered to his feet, wiped away the blood from the side of his mouth, and spat at Finn. "Obnoxious piece of shit," he cursed, as he landed a kick to Finn's chest.

Behind his back, Teague could feel some slack in his restraints. He tugged and pulled harder.

Daniel spun around on Teague, brandishing a handgun. "Don't you dare get any ideas!"

Teague needed to buy himself some time. He scowled at Daniel. "You're a big man when people are tied up."

"Fuck you," growled Daniel.

Daniel's confidence was shaken when Finn fought back. Taking advantage of the meager opening, Teague was determined to use it to his advantage. "You're a loser. Same as always."

Daniel howled and struck Teague across his face with the gun's handgrip.

Teague toppled over sideways. His face hurt, but he would not let the bastard have any satisfaction. He gave out a quiet chuckle. "You hit like a girl."

Once again, Daniel dragged Teague to his knees by his hair. He winced in pain; every strand of hair on his head screamed in protest. Daniel loomed over him. As soon as he was close enough, Teague lurched forward and slammed his forehead into Daniel's nose. Blood burst from the old man's nose, coloring his salt and pepper beard dark red.

"Son of a—" cursed Daniel.

The pain in Teague's head was nothing short of spectacular, but it was worth it. There was no way he was going to let this asshole get the upper hand.

Daniel pressed the gun barrel to Teague's forehead.

"No!" cried Finn his voice filled with panic and fear.

The old man glanced over his shoulder at Finn and smirked; he turned back to Teague. "Your boyfriend knows I'll do it."

Finn mumbled incoherently as he struggled to raise himself off the ground. "Please," he begged, his voice breaking. "Kill me instead. Just kill me." He reached out for Daniel's leg, but the bastard easily kicked his hand away.

The terror in Finn's voice, the way it cracked and broke up, reminded Teague of a time long ago when the two young runaways first came together. He recalled the countless nights being awakened by the bloodcurdling screams of a young kid who had suffered far too much in his brief life.

Teague glared at Daniel. He wasn't so frightening. In fact, Daniel was just like every blustery asshole Teague had ever come in contact with. A loser looking to compensate for his low self-esteem by terrorizing people he thinks he can control. Teague would not give the bastard the satisfaction of seeing him beg for his life. If he was going to go out this way, he was going to do it on his own terms. He leaned forward, pressed his forehead against the barrel, and stared directly into the devil's eyes.

A sinister grin spread across Daniel's face as he cocked the hammer.

A ragged howl erupted behind Daniel. Suddenly, Finn tackled the older man to the ground, landing at the edge of the fire. Straddling the old man, Finn landed blow after blow, a primal scream emanated from somewhere deep down inside. Daniel fought back, landing his own blows. As the two clashed and battled through the fire, tiny embers flew into the air like little will-o'-the-wisps dancing about in the chaos.

Somehow, Cash materialized, hobbling his way to his pack. He pulled out a pocket knife and cut River free, then collapsed against a tree.

Over by the fire, Daniel got the upper hand. He punched and punched until Finn was no longer attempting to fight back. He stood up, panting, then he dragged Finn's semi-conscious body to the water and plunged his head under.

"River, hurry it up!" screamed Teague.

She ran to Zac and cut him free.

He burst forth with all the power of a ballistic missile, tackling Daniel in the water.

Finn's body floated face down—not moving.

"Hurry!" Teague shouted at River. His panic grew as he stared at Finn's lifeless body.

Arms and legs finally free, Teague ran to the water and dragged Finn onto the shore. He wasn't breathing. Teague checked for a pulse —it was weak. He rolled Finn over onto his side, watching as water trickled from his blue lips. "Come on, come on," said Teague.

Finn coughed and gagged, water spewing from his mouth. His body shuddered as he struggled to inhale fresh air, only to erupt in a fit of coughing. His eyelids fluttered open. He flashed a weak, pathetic smile at Teague, then his eyes rolled up, and his body stiffened as he descended into another seizure.

Chapter 34

Finn opened his eyes and sank into a seizure. Knowing there was nothing she could do for him, River turned her attention to Cash.

His face was ashen, his breathing shallow; she had never seen him like this before. Holding back tears, she took his icy hand in hers.

"How's Finn?" he asked.

"He'll be okay. Teague's got him," she replied. "How are you feeling?"

The corners of his mouth turned up into a pitiful smile. "Nothing wrong with me that a good steak won't fix."

"Is that so?" She cocked an eyebrow.

Cash chuckled. "You know me, I'm as healthy as an ox."

Zac was still in the water, pounding away at Daniel, though, in the dark, from River's vantage point, it looked as though a giant was pummeling a rag doll.

Teague called River over, and the two of them carried Finn closer to the fire. As soon as he was settled, they did the same for Cash.

"I'm gonna have to cut your jeans to get a good look at your leg," said Teague.

"Aw man," whined Cash, "these are my favorite jeans." He grinned. "They make my ass look great."

River laughed, then she instantly wanted to cry.

Teague moved the fabric out of the way, no longer gushing; the wound still seeped an alarming amount of blood.

"Did it hit an artery?" asked River, attempting to mask her concern. "I don't know," replied Teague. "I can't see shit out here." He pointed to his pack. "Get my flashlight."

She ran over and rummaged through Teague's pack.

A pathetic whimper came from the shadows. "River, untie me. Please."

It was Beth. In all the chaos, River had completely forgotten about her. Anger boiled up inside her. All of this was Beth's fault. A significant part of River wanted to leave Beth tied up, let her stew in the mess she made. She brushed that urge aside. Now was not the time for petty grievances. Cash was seriously injured, and they needed all the help they could get. She cut Beth free, then returned to Teague with the flashlight.

The wound looked worse in the cold beam of light.

"The good news is the bullet went straight through," said Teague.

"Well, at least there's good news," quipped Cash. "Unfortunately, my pants are done for."

Both River and Teague smiled. Even in his current state, Cash was making jokes.

"The bad news is," continued Teague, "I don't know how bad it is in there. It looks like the blood is slowin', so odds are, the bullet didn't hit the artery." He picked up the bottle of whiskey. A little over a quarter of the liquid remained. "Daniel said he put ketamine in this bottle. Here." He passed it to Cash. "Sip this. It should help with the pain."

Cash stared at Teague. "So, we're really gonna trust the psycho who just tried to kill us?"

"He had no reason to lie when he told me."

"That does not instill confidence," replied Cash. He held the bottle up. "For the record, if I die after drinking this, I'm coming back to haunt your ass."

Teague nodded and smiled. "Just take a little sip. We don't want you unconscious."

"Hey, I'm the one who's shot. I get to choose whether I wanna be unconscious," quipped Cash.

River chuckled.

"Just hold off on being comatose until we get out of here," said River.

"You have a point," agreed Cash. He raised the bottle to his lips. "Well, here goes the tiniest of sips."

River turned to Teague. "What are we gonna do now?"

"We need to get the hell out of here," he replied. "We need to get him some real medical help." He gave out a sharp whistle, then called out, "Zac!"

Zac stopped and waded out of the water, releasing what remained of Daniel, leaving the body to float face down in the river.

"How's he doin'?" asked Zac.

"We need to get out of here," replied River.

Zac nodded. "I'll go see about a ride." Soaking wet, he plodded off into the darkness toward the rest area.

All they could do now was wait, and that was killing River. She hated feeling helpless—hated seeing someone she loved in pain.

Someone she loved.

In need of a distraction, she busied herself by gathering all their gear. Even Beth, to her credit, helped out, though River did her best to avoid talking to her.

Sorting through her thoughts and emotions, River replayed the events of the past hour.

When she first awoke, her eyelids felt like lead blankets covering her eyes, making it impossible to keep them open for more than a few seconds at a time. She caught a glimpse of the fire as a large shadow flew past. Sparks erupted into the air, followed by grunts. Something was scuffling in the dirt. River's mind was foggy, her vision blurry. She could not make out who was moving around, but she thought she heard Finn.

She moved to touch her head, but her hands were pinned behind her back. Panic took hold. She jerked her arms, feeling the restraints tight around her wrists. Adrenaline surged throughout her body, giving her the energy boost she needed to break through her mental haze.

Eyes wide, she searched the campsite. Cash lay beside her, unconscious, with his arms behind his back. Across the camp was Zac; he too appeared to be out cold and tied up. Teague lay close to the fire, his back to River. She could not tell if he was awake or not.

She set her focus on the ruckus a few yards away; a muscular man sat atop Finn, punching him. From her perspective, she could see that Finn was doing his best to fight back, but when the man banged his head against the rocky ground, it was all over.

The stranger got to his feet, brushed himself off, and stormed over to River. She scurried back, kicking her legs.

"Where do you think you're going?" said the man.

As soon as he came into range, River kicked out with all her strength. The man staggered back, nearly falling on his bottom. She smiled triumphantly. Whatever he was planning on doing, she would be damned if she made it easy.

He regained his composure and approached, this time keeping a healthy distance. "I knew you were a real spitfire. I could see it in all of Beth's videos." He stared at her for a long, uncomfortable time. "Yeah, you ain't like a lot of other women today. You're not some simpering girl-child yammering on about girl power while standing on the shoulders of men." He paused. "No, you're what those other women wish they could be."

River sat in silence, unblinking and listening, ready to kick out again if he tried to move an inch closer. Her mind kept pulling her back to something the man said, "Beth's videos." He was at the campsite, doing whatever he was doing to them because of Beth's videos.

"Yeah," continued the man, "You're a unique woman, River." He glanced over at Beth's body, tied up beside a tree. "You know she looks up to you." He turned back to River. "Don't be too hard on her; that internet's a hell of a drug." His jaw clenched. "Social media especially. All those people putting their lives on display, screaming, look at me. All for the dopamine." He shook his head in disgust.

"Luckily for me," he continued, "Beth is hooked. Had she not posted all those videos, this little father-son reunion would not have been possible."

Father? A cold realization settled in River's soul. He's Finn's father! *This is bad; this is really bad.*

Across the fire, Finn stirred, pulling himself up on his hands and knees, shaking his head.

"Be right back," said Daniel. He stomped over and leveled a kick to the ribs so hard, Finn flew back, landing in the dirt with a soft "oof."

A quiet moan made River glance to her side. Cash was stirring. His eyes opened and blinked, then settled on her. She tilted her head sharply in the direction where Daniel hovered over Finn.

Keeping a wary eye on Daniel, Cash worked to untie himself. Much to River's astonishment, it took him no time to get his hands free. She wasn't sure how he did it; her ties were almost too tight. The more she struggled against them, the more they dug into her wrists.

Daniel leveled a powerful stomp on Finn's head for good measure. Then he stormed back over to River.

Cash lay still, pretending to be out, waiting for the right moment.

"All right, I'm done fucking around," declared Daniel, "Time to finish getting you all tied up."

River kicked.

"Don't make this harder than it has to be," said Daniel, as he batted her feet out of his way.

She landed a blow to his mid-section. He stumbled back, then grabbed her legs and jerked her forward, scraping her back across the dirt.

Cash leaped to his feet and grabbed Daniel from behind.

The older man gave out a low chuckle, then bucked backward, slamming them both to the ground, knocking the wind out of Cash. When the dust settled, Daniel had the upper hand. He got to his feet and pulled a handgun from the back of his pants.

"That is it," he seethed, "I'm done fucking around with you two." He fired one shot into Cash's thigh.

Cash hollered out in pain.

River screamed and moved closer to Cash. Warm blood seeped through his jeans.

"Better put some pressure on that if you don't want him to bleed out right away," said Daniel.

"Fuck you!" shouted River. She wriggled her body in such a way, so she could put her hands on Cash's thigh. Blood, like thick, red ink, oozed through her fingers.

"Thanks for the offer, Darlin', but, I'm gonna have to pass," replied Daniel. "Now, fifteen or twenty years ago, would have been a different story—" He stalked off toward Teague.

River frantically tried to apply pressure. She didn't know how severe the wound was. Did he hit an artery? "Please, Cash, you stay with me," she whispered.

His hand gently stroked her back. "I'm not going anywhere," he said. But his tone didn't sound so sure.

Daniel was busy over by the fire with Teague, because of the angle, River couldn't see what was going on.

"We can't just sit here," whispered Cash.

River nodded.

"Next chance we get," he said, "I'll get the knife from my pack and cut you loose."

Sticky wetness cooled against her skin; she realized she was sitting in a pool of his blood. River didn't want Cash to worry, so she struggled to hold her tears in. The thought that she might lose him forever weighed heavily on her heart.

A primal scream echoed through the valley. Shouting and chaos ensued. Once again, Daniel and Finn were fighting.

How does he keep getting up?

The two men rolled into the fire, causing tiny embers to fly into the evening sky. Cash took off, then returned, breathing heavy, his face pale. The act of moving so quickly had taken a toll on him.

He cut her ties, then handed her the knife. "Run and untie Zac.

He'll take care of Daniel." He gave her a light shove, then collapsed against a tree. "Go now!"

River took off across the campsite, skidding to a stop behind Zac, and quickly went to work on his restraints. His body was as tense as a tightly wound coil, ready to explode. She could feel the pent-up energy vibrating around him.

With a final snap, the ties were off, and Zac bolted toward the water. Before River could even get to Teague, he was already on Daniel.

She cut Teague free, and the two of them ran over and dragged Finn from the water. He lay lifeless on the sandy shore.

When Zac returned, Finn was sitting up, drinking water, and the entire camp was packed and ready to go.

"I found an old Jeep in the parking lot," said Zac, as he approached.

"Were you able to get in?" asked Teague.

Zac nodded. "It's Daniel's. I found the keys behind the sun visor. We got a half tank of gas; I figure that'll be enough to get us out of here."

At the mention of Daniel's name, Finn startled and leaped to his feet. "Where is he?"

"Where's who?" asked Zac.

"Where's Daniel?" demanded Finn, panic in his voice.

Zac pointed to the water. "He's not a problem anymore. He's dead over there."

Finn spun around. "He's gone!"

"What the hell do you mean, he's gone?" demanded Zac. He walked past everyone toward the water's edge. Finn right alongside him.

Daniel was nowhere to be seen. River and Teague climbed to their feet and scanned the area. There was no sign of him anywhere.

"The current must've taken him away," said River.

"The fucking current?!" shouted Finn. "He's still out here."

Teague stepped up and placed a hand on Finn's shoulder. "He's a corpse floating down the river. All the more reason to get out of here now."

Finn shoved Teague's hand away. "I'm not leaving until I know he's dead."

"I ain't wasting precious time searching around in the dark for a dead asshole," replied Teague, his tone final.

"Teague's right. We don't have time to search for a body," said River. "We need to get Cash out of here and get him some help."

"I sent a message to the group," said Teague. "Stoney's meetin' us in Las Cruces. He has a friend who's a doctor."

"Las Cruces!" blurted Beth. "That's five hours from here! Why not take him to the hospital?"

"Because," explained Teague, his patience wearing thin. "It's a gunshot wound. Cops will be brought in. We just murdered a man. They're gonna want to know all about it and it could end up with one or more of us being arrested."

"We're going to Las Cruces. That's where we'll get the help Cash needs." He spun Finn around. "Now, come on, we need your help."

Still furious, Finn begrudgingly followed Teague's orders.

When they arrived at the roadside, the Jeep sat idle, exactly where Zac had left it. The inside was old and cramped, and it smelled of moldy laundry. It was a tight fit; poor Cash didn't complain when they stuffed him inside. As they drove down the road, every bump and every pothole was magnified tenfold. River couldn't recall a more uncomfortable ride.

There was no way they would make it to Las Cruces in the Jeep, so they decided to hold up in a dry building while Zac went out and found a better vehicle.

They rolled up on an abandoned mobile home set deep into the hillside, far from view of the road. It wasn't ideal, but it would do for the short time they needed.

River helped get Cash situated in the living room of the dilapidated trailer, clearing away as much of the debris as possible. Luckily, the bleeding had stopped, so at least there was no longer any danger of bleeding out.

Zac changed out of his soaking, wet clothes and, with the help of Teague, cleaned the cuts on his knuckles. "All right," he said, "I'm gonna head out and find another vehicle."

"I wanna go with you," blurted Beth.

It struck River that those were the first words she heard from Beth since the campsite.

"No," replied Zac. "You stay here. I don't have time to hold anyone's hand. I'll work better on my own."

Beth opened her mouth to protest, but then quickly slammed it shut. She turned on her heels and stomped away to a corner in the kitchen.

Without another word, Zac left on his task while River and Teague focused on Cash.

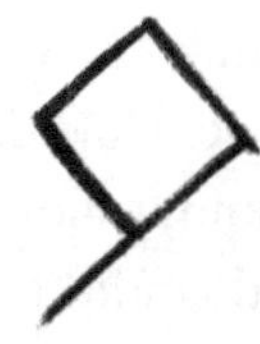

Chapter 35

THEY LEFT ME THERE! EVERYONE FORGOT ALL ABOUT ME, AND LEFT ME there!

Beth rocked back and forth, hugging her legs against her chest. In her mind, the entire nightmare played repeatedly like a cheap horror movie.

That awful man, Daniel.

Beth recalled waking up with his hands on her. She didn't struggle; she didn't fight back at all. Instead, she merely let him tie her hands and feet. Then, when he lay her softly on the ground, she simply lay there—silent. She watched in terror as his showdown with River and Cash evolved. How he beat Finn into a seizure, then turned around and shot Cash.

The way Finn screamed when Daniel pointed the gun at Teague's head. She had never heard such a sound. She never wanted to hear one like it again.

The part she detested most of all was when everyone left her tied up in the corner. Scared, uncomfortable, and alone. They left her there. No one even glanced her way. They all clearly thought of one another, but they didn't think of her. She could have been dead; they wouldn't even know. They wouldn't even care!

Relief washed over her when River cut her loose. Finally, someone remembered her. But after that, River said nothing to her. She didn't even ask her if she was all right. She didn't try to make Beth feel like it would all be okay. No more big sister act. River simply cut her loose then walked away, leaving Beth alone again.

A cockroach scuttled across the torn linoleum floor, disappearing inside the cabinet under the sink. *This place is disgusting.* She would have much rather gone with Zac. He didn't have to sit in a grungy, run-down trailer waiting for god knows how long until someone turned up with a new vehicle. How hard could it be to steal a car, anyway? The way he told her she couldn't come along made her feel small, stupid, and useless.

"I don't have time to hold anyone's hand." Fuck him! Beth didn't need anyone to hold her hand. As it was, she was the only one who knew enough not to fight back; she was the smart one who did what Daniel said. She wasn't the one who got her friend shot or got beaten within an inch of their life. No, she knew all they had to do was cooperate, and Daniel would have let them go free. He only wanted Finn. He wasn't after any of the others; they were just in the way. If they had only let him have Finn, they wouldn't be where they were right now, in a shabby, disgusting mobile home, waiting for Zac to come back with another stolen car.

Teague walked over to the kitchen sink and turned on the faucet. The pipes moaned and rattled, then vomited out a torrent of rusty, rancid-smelling water. He jumped back to avoid getting splashed, then reached out and quickly turned off the water. "That was vile," he exclaimed. "I was hoping it would work." He leaned toward Beth. "Apparently, I was wrong."

Beth stared.

"How are you holdin' up?" he asked, a look of concern on his face.

Obviously fake.

"I'm fine," replied Beth, with a wave of her hand. At least someone was pretending to notice her.

He stepped closer. "Zac'll be back soon, then we'll get out of here. It's gonna be okay."

"No, it won't," snapped Beth.

Teague's face looked as though she had slapped him.

Good. A little reality hurt no one.

"It will not be okay," said Beth. "Nothing is ever gonna be okay again."

She climbed to her feet and stared directly into Teague's stunned eyes. His surprise only emboldened her rage. That's right, asshole, Beth has something to say to y'all, and you're going to listen.

"In case you missed it," she continued, "we all just about died. Cash is over there bleeding out, and we can't even bring him to the hospital because Zac murdered Daniel."

"That's enough, Beth!" roared River from across the room. "We don't need this right now, and honestly, you've done enough already." She waved her hand dismissively. "Go sit down and shut up!"

Beth stomped across the floor, coming to a halt in front of River. "Sit down and shut up?" she shrieked. "I'm not doing a damn thing you tell me. You're the one who thought it was a good idea to fight back against a madman. Because of that decision, Cash is gonna die!" She placed her hands on her hips. "Was it worth it, River?"

River bolted to her feet and shoved Beth so hard she stumbled back into the wall.

"We wouldn't even be in this situation if it hadn't been for you," hissed River.

"Me?" Beth placed a hand against her own chest. "I didn't even know Daniel, never even saw him until tonight."

River shook her head. "If you hadn't been so desperate to be one of the cool kids online, you wouldn't have posted all those videos." She stepped closer. "Daniel wouldn't have been able to track us."

Beth blinked. Is she trying to put the blame for all of this on me? There was no way in hell she was going to take responsibility for anything that happened. None of this was her fault.

"Fuck you, River!" shouted Beth. "You don't know how he found us."

"That's where you're wrong," seethed River, venom dripping from each word. "He knew things about us, about all of us. He practically described your videos." She leered at Beth. "Also, he told me that was how he tracked us. He even thanked you for all your help."

"Wait," said Finn. "Is that true?"

River nodded.

Finn moved straight for Beth, but Teague stepped between the two, holding him back with one hand. Finn growled and slapped Teague's hand away.

Beth looked around the room. They were all staring at her as though she were the one who was at fault. None of this was her fault. "So, we're supposed to believe you, River?" she demanded.

"It's true," said Cash, his voice unsteady. He leaned up on one elbow, his body trembling from the exertion. "I heard him say it."

"What did I tell you about those videos?" shouted Finn. He paced across the room. He pointed at Teague. "I told you. Y'all thought I was overreacting."

"I don't recall anyone saying you were overreacting," said Teague.

"Shut the fuck up!" Finn roared at Teague. He stomped toward Beth. "You did this. If we had never brought your dumb ass along, we wouldn't be here right now."

Beth's anger exploded. Her fault? So now they were going to put the blame on her instead of on themselves, which was where it belonged. No! There was no way she was going to take the blame. None of this was her fault. She was the innocent victim in all of this.

"My fault?" she shrieked. "Are you serious? Am I the one with the insane father?" She stepped closer to Finn, closing the gap between them to a mere two feet. "No, asshole, this is all your fault." She pointed a finger at him. "That was your father who was trying to kill you. Yours—not mine. If you hadn't been around, none of us would be dealing with this right now. This is all because of your insane, fucked up family. Like father; like so—"

Beth's words were cut short when his hand clamped around her throat. Holding tight, he slammed her against the wall so hard, her head broke the cheap drywall. His eyes were hard, black spheres of hate, his lips turned up in a vicious snarl as he pressed his hand harder against her throat, lifting her off her feet.

Beth's legs kicked, trying to find something to stand on, but the floor was beyond her reach.

His vice-like grip closed tighter, choking off what little air could pass through to her desperate lungs.

She clawed at his hand, gasping. He was going to kill her, and no one was doing anything to stop him.

Teague materialized in her periphery beside Finn. The pounding of her heartbeat drowned out the words he said. Finn's icy hands tightened.

River showed up on the other side; she, too, said something that Beth couldn't hear.

All she could do was listen to the pounding of her own heartbeat and stare back into the wicked eyes of death as blackness closed in on the world around her.

Suddenly, the hand ripped away from her throat. She collapsed to the floor. Coughing and gasping, she rubbed her neck. A few feet away, Teague had hold of Finn from behind, pulling him backward.

River crouched down beside Beth, trying to help her to her feet. Beth shoved her away.

"I don't need your help," she coughed. Beth leaned against the wall until she could breathe again without coughing or gagging; then, she wiped the tears from her face and plodded back to her filthy corner in the kitchen.

Chapter 36

River watched anxiously as Teague released his grip on Finn. There was no telling what would happen next. To her astonishment, Finn didn't go after Beth again; instead, somehow, Teague talked him into stepping outside for a breather. She sighed in relief as she observed the two of them walk through the sliding glass door. A little space from everyone was a good thing. River hoped that Teague could get Finn to cool down. His being riled up like that was not good for anyone.

She squatted down beside Beth, seeking to help her, but Beth swatted her aside. Oh well, Beth was a big girl. She could take care of herself. River shrugged it off and set her focus on the one person in all of this who needed her attention the most, Cash.

Ashen skin, sunken eyes, Cash's entire body trembled with the exertion of holding himself up on his elbows.

She gave him the bottle. "Take a sip," she ordered.

He flashed a cocky smile. "Are you trying to get me drunk?"

"Would it make you stay put?" she asked, as she inspected the makeshift bandages on his leg.

"I can't guarantee anything," he replied, "But on the surface, it sounds like it would." His face became serious as he stared at the glass sliding door. "That is if Finn can keep his anger in check."

River tucked a towel under his leg. "We just need to get on the road. We'll get you to a doctor and him away from this place, then everything will be fine."

He took a sip of whiskey. "This stuff really helps with the pain. I can barely feel my leg." He poked his thigh. "I mean, you could stab me in the leg right now, and I'd probably not feel it."

She took his hand in hers. "I'm glad you're not feeling pain, but let's not get you all bruised up trying to prove you don't feel anything." She watched as he took another sip of the whiskey. His eyelids grew heavy.

River examined his hand in hers; even in his weakened state, there was strength in them; a warmth. She liked the feel of their hands together.

"Look, River, I don't know how this is all gonna play out," he said.

"Shh," she responded.

"No, listen," he interrupted. "Listen to me. I don't know how this is all gonna go, and neither do you. I need to tell you some things while I still can."

River nodded solemnly. She didn't want to entertain the prospect of things going horribly wrong. Hearing him talk like it was a possibility broke her heart.

"New Hampshire," he blurted.

"The state?" she asked, "What about it?"

"That's the first place I ever saw you." He smiled.

"Um, we were up there a couple of years ago," she replied, "But we were all there together." She was confused. Maybe he was hallucinating.

He shook his head. "No, no, this was a couple of years before that. Before we became a group."

River searched her memory. "Oh wow, I had forgotten about that. I went up there for a festival." She nodded her head.

He grinned. "That was the first time I ever saw you."

"That was a long time ago. Are you sure?"

"I am." He tapped the side of his head. "Because I will always remember the first time I saw you." He continued, "I was traveling with Cyrus and Craig, and we were at a camp on the north end of town, just outside the train yard."

River listened keenly.

"There must have been a dozen other riders gathered there that night. Some girl was teaching you how to spin fire."

His hand gripped hers, generating a ripple of electricity that shot through her body.

"You were so beautiful. I couldn't stop staring."

"Why didn't you come up and talk to me?"

"Because I was scared shitless," he chuckled.

"Bullshit, I've seen you pick up women before; fear and shyness are not things that apply to you."

"Maybe not to other women," he agreed, "But you, you were different. Something was totally different about you. You were so beautiful. The way the light from the fire lit up your face and your body. When you smiled." He sighed. "I can still see it today, and it still gives me chills." He paused. "I said that last part out loud, didn't I?"

River nodded.

He cleared his throat. "Craig and Cyrus tried to get me to go up and talk to you, but I was too scared. Just thinking about walking up to you gave me the cold sweats."

"You should have come up."

He nodded. "I should have. Lord knows I wanted to. I watched you try to spin those branches for an hour." He chuckled. "You kept burning yourself."

"It was a lot harder than it looked," defended River.

"You totally sucked at it," he laughed. "You set one of your dreads on fire."

River scoffed.

"I remember watching you leave." A wry smile stretched across his face. "You were traveling alone, of course."

"Of course."

"After that night, I couldn't get you out of my head. Every time we ended up around other riders, I would search around, hoping you were there." He looked up at the ceiling. "My God, the teasing I suffered." He sighed. "Relentless."

Cash looked her in the eyes. "I saw you three more times after that. Northern California, Montana, and Florida."

A warm sensation washed from her head to her toes. River was sure she was blushing. "All those instances, and you never came up to me."

He shook his head. "When I first met Finn and Teague, I told them all about this beautiful, blonde goddess who came and went like a spirit."

Heat radiated throughout River's body. *I must be so red right now.*

Cash continued, "They were with me when I saw you in Montana. Of course, I was still too scared to approach you. Which led to more teasing."

"In Florida, Teague spotted you first. He insisted we go up and talk to you," he shook his head. "I absolutely could not do that."

"Seriously, you should have come up to me. I don't bite."

"Oh, but yes, you do," he quipped and tenderly squeezed her hand. "You already know that the night we met, Finn, Teague, Zac, and I landed in Roswell by accident."

"Uh, huh."

"Does anyone go to Roswell intentionally?" he asked.

"Probably not," laughed River. Her hands were sweaty. She wondered if he could feel it. "I think it worked out for all of us."

"This is true," he agreed.

"Do you know where I first spotted you that night?"

"On the corner, when I ran into you."

He shook his head. "Nah, I saw you at a dive bar. I was playing pool with these locals when you showed up out of nowhere." He smiled. "I watched you swipe a dude's wallet. When he turned around, you gave him this huge gorgeous smile. He forgot all about why he spun around."

"Gotta use the tools you have available," she quipped.

"You most certainly do," agreed Cash. "I was so distracted by you,

I totally missed my shot and lost all the money we had left. And of course, once again, you were nowhere in sight."

She smiled.

"Do I even need to tell you how much shit the others gave me over that?"

River chuckled. She remembered the teasing. How the others continually rubbed it in that he lost all their money. She never imagined it had anything to do with her.

Cash breathed deeply. "Thanks to me, we were broke, so we had to resort to the hunter, gatherer way of getting money." He smirked. "We spent the entire night scrounging. There wasn't a lot to be found, so finally, we had given up and sat on a curb before deciding what to do next." He shook his head. "The whole time, Finn and Teague picked and picked away at me. They were relentless."

"Poor thing," River cooed.

"Tell me about it." He rolled his eyes. "I finally lost it. I spun around and told them that if we found you, I would grab hold of you and kiss you."

River blushed.

Cash chuckled. "Next thing you know, you literally slammed into me."

River recalled that night. She remembered the men following her; she had no recollection of being aware that anyone else was. Wow! I was oblivious.

"I don't remember any kiss," she teased, with a smile.

"That's because as soon as I was close enough to smell you, I lost all courage."

"Johnathan Cash Wright, are you sayin' I smelled bad?"

Cash shook his head. "No, no you smelled like River. I can't explain it; it's a scent only you have. Kind of a mix of lavender and pine needles, mixed with soil."

River stared at him. She knew he had his moments of deep thought, but she never knew he was capable of such romanticism. She looked down at their entwined hands; electric shocks pulsated throughout her body. "Sounds like you owe me somethin'," she said.

"What would that be?"

She leaned forward, their lips barely touching, and whispered, "A kiss."

The moment their lips touched, the world dropped away around River. Heart racing in her chest, the feeling of his hands slipping around the side of her neck, pulling her close, made her swoon. She didn't want to stop, but she needed to catch her breath.

As she pulled back, Cash chuckled.

"What's so funny?" she asked.

"If I knew all I had to do to get you to kiss me was get shot, I'd have gotten shot a long time ago." He twitched his eyebrows.

"Don't be such a smartass." She slapped him.

"Ouch, ouch," he protested. "Okay, that hurt."

"Oh god! I'm so sorry," apologized River. She checked his wound. It was okay. "You should rest now."

"Only if you promise to lie here with me," he replied. "You owe me now—cause you hit me."

River didn't need coaxing. It didn't take long for the drugs in the whiskey to do their thing; shortly after she snuggled against him, Cash was fast asleep. She lay beside him, her head resting against his chest, listening to his heartbeat. She breathed in deep, fully understanding his point about scent, deciding she liked the way he smelled, too.

Chapter 37

TEAGUE BARELY PROCESSED WHAT RIVER SAID ABOUT DANIEL BEFORE Finn snapped. He was genuinely worried that Finn would break Beth's neck with the amount of pressure he had been applying. Teague's first inclination was to reason with him, but Finn could hear nothing, focusing solely on the amount of pressure he applied to Beth's throat. Even River tried. It was all no use; Finn was not letting go.

In the end, Teague had to get physical.

This only enraged Finn even further.

The way he glared at Teague made his skin crawl.

"Come on," said Teague, "Let's go outside and cool off." He moved to guide Finn toward the door.

"Get your fucking hands off me!" boomed Finn, shoving Teague away.

Teague stumbled backward. The words stung like a slap across his face. He stepped aside, shoving his hands inside his pockets. His fingers brushed against the phone. Gunner flashed into his mind. In front of him, Finn paced around the room while gnawing away at his nails.

"Let's go outside and get some fresh air," said Teague. He slid open the glass door. Relief washed over him when Finn stalked through the door onto the rickety, old deck outside.

Boards protested under his feet. With every step, Teague wondered whether that would be the one where he smashes through the rotted wood to the ground below.

A few feet away, Finn paced, unfazed.

Teague tilted his head up toward the sky, taking in the sight of billions of sparkling dots in the black sky, and for the moment, he felt calm. A welcome respite from the past several hours. He breathed in the cool night air.

"Why are you choosing her over me?"

Like a knife plunged deep inside his belly, Finn's words, compounded by an icy tone, cut through the calm of the moment.

"Choosing who?"

"Beth." Finn paced frantically all around the deck. He threw his hands in the air. "All of them."

"I'm not choosing anyone."

"That's the problem."

"You're talking in circles. I don't understand what you're gettin' at."

"Me!" blurted Finn. "You're supposed to choose me!"

"Over who? Over the others? Is that what you're on about?"

Finn paused, jaw flexing, eyebrow cocked. He glared at Teague. "Every time there's an issue, you side with them."

"There is no us versus them," scoffed Teague. "It's all of us."

Finn twitched his nose and scowled. "You're right, there is no us." A wicked sneer spread across his face. "Versus them."

Teague's patience was wearing thin. This was a stupid conversation, and he would not play along. "C'est Fou," he said, tapping his head for emphasis. "Quit being stupid."

"I'm not fucking crazy!" seethed Finn. "And I'm not stupid."

Teague sighed. "You know, I'm done with this conversation. Your head's so far up your own ass, you can't even see how you're pushin' everyone away."

Finn took a step closer. "Maybe that's what I want. Maybe my life would be a lot better without haulin' this traveling circus around."

"That's not what you want, and you know it," protested Teague.

"The fuck do you know about what I want?" demanded Finn. "If you did, you'd know this ain't it."

Teague shook his head. "I'm not having this conversation with you. Not here and not right now."

"Of course, you're not," jeered Finn. "It's a nice thing you got goin' here." He stepped closer, now standing a mere foot away from Teague. "Good old Teague, honest, caring, truthful." He flashed a malevolent grin and leaned in, his face inches from Teague's. "You sure got everybody fooled."

Finn spun around unexpectedly and stepped back, startling Teague.

"Everybody thinks you're so mature," seethed Finn. "You're the big brother they always wanted." He crept close again. "Bonus, that you keep your pet dog on a short leash."

"Mais la!" shouted Teague, startled by the force behind his own voice. "Do you even listen to yourself?" He shook his head. "You know, sometimes I wonder if you've lost your damn mind. Sometimes you can be so fucking stupid."

"There you are," said Finn, "true colors comin' through now."

Frustration, exhaustion, bubbled to the surface. Teague had already gone through every emotion a man could go through in the past twenty-four hours. He didn't need this nonsense. He didn't have it in him to babysit Finn or even care about whatever problem he was having now. Teague turned to walk away.

"Do you ever wonder what it would be like if the others knew about some of the shit you've done?" asked Finn. "Maybe I should clue 'em in." He sneered and stepped close. "Maybe I should tell 'em all about Houston. Let 'em all know who their precious older brother really is. How do you think that would fly, T?"

"Fuck you!" shouted Teague. Before he even considered the ramifications, he balled up his fist and punched Finn in the face.

The force of the blow was so strong, Finn nearly lost his footing.

He wiped the blood away from his nose. The corner of his mouth twitched, then he charged into Teague. They crashed through the glass door, landing on the floor of the trailer.

Glass littered the carpet, embedding tiny shards into their clothes and hair as Teague and Finn rolled back and forth over the glittery particles.

Somewhere off to the side, Beth screamed.

River shouted. She was close—too close.

Teague wanted to warn her to stay away, let them be, and allow them to sort this out on their own, but the words never came out of his mouth. Finn sat atop him, pinning him down, so Teague bucked and knocked him off, buying the precious time and momentum he needed to wriggle out from underneath Finn. His victory came to a hasty end shortly after, when Finn, too, was on his feet. He leveled two, rapid-fire punches to Teague's face, causing him to stumble back. Finn gave no reprieve; he caught hold of Teague by the hair and slammed his head into the door frame.

The world blurred. Then suddenly Finn ripped away, his attention diverted momentarily.

Teague leaned against the wall, trying to catch his breath. Dizziness and nausea swept over him in waves. He shook his head to regain equilibrium. Blood oozed down the side of his face.

Across the room, Finn stalked toward River. In her hands, she held a two by four, using it to keep Finn at bay. She swung, and he caught hold of it, wrenching the board from her hands and tossing it to the floor. He knocked her to the floor, barreling after her.

Teague needed to stop Finn; that was all he could concentrate on. As the room swirled, he staggered up behind Finn and took hold of his arms, pinning them behind his back.

"Finn stop! Please," he begged.

But Finn didn't hear him. Showing no sign of relenting, Finn was unable or unwilling to control his rage. He reared back, hurling both himself and Teague backward, crashing down onto the floor.

On impact, Teague hit his head, shooting a spike of pain through his skull. The blow knocked the wind out of him. He lay there, gasping, trying to maintain consciousness.

"Please stop!" begged Teague, just before Finn's fist smashed down onto his face again and again.

Chapter 38

Driving away from the ramshackle mobile home, an uneasy feeling settled over Zac. The past few hours had been a nightmare. His right hand hurt, notably at the knuckles. Looking at them in the dim dashboard light, he could see a network of cracks and tears covered in dry, crusted blood. How much of it was his and how much was Daniel's remained a mystery.

Daniel's dead. Zac had no remorse for the man; instead, what he felt was relief. He hoped that somehow the end of Daniel would do something for Finn. Give him some closure or something.

Streetlights loomed up ahead; he was coming into civilization.

He drove through the small downtown, careful to drive the speed limit and mind the stops. The last thing he needed was to get pulled over. The street was clean and void of traffic. Quaint shops lined the road, all locked up for the evening.

I just have to get a replacement car, then we can get Cash help, and everything will be okay. The words played over and over in his head, like a mantra; if said enough, it would come true.

Up ahead, the bright lights of a small subdivision lit up the night like a beacon. He turned off the main road and into the neighborhood. Rolling slowly past home after home, he realized how similar each one was to the other. This neighborhood reminded him of the one that Cole lived in. He wondered how the kid was doing? Did he ever think of Zac anymore? Stop it. He shook his head. No time for that.

Zac rolled up on a house with a red minivan sitting in the driveway; it was precisely what he was looking for. A yellow sign with "Baby on Board" hung by a clear, rubber suction cup on the dark-tinted back window. Below that, a group of decals depicting a family with a mom, dad, three children of various sizes, and a dog. He would have to be silent so as not to alert the dog. He didn't want it to bark and wake everyone in the house.

He parked the Jeep around the corner and stepped out onto the sidewalk, stretching his arms and legs. His muscles were tight. The stretch felt good, but it only reminded him how exhausted he was. He leaned against the grill of the Jeep and lit a cigarette. As he exhaled a cloud of smoke, he scanned the area.

The desert night air was cool against his skin; the aromatic scent of sage floated through the air. Zac was thankful for the temporary reprieve.

All around him, A/C units hummed while the streetlights buzzed. A cacophony of crickets chirped while in the hills, a group of coyotes called out to one another.

He finished his smoke, then crept toward the driveway with the minivan. The house remained dark. Thankfully, there were no motion-sensitive lights out front. He gently touched the driver's side door, testing to see if there was an alarm. Nothing—at least so far. Now to see if the door was locked, he tugged the handle. Of course, it was, but he had to try.

Odds were, the van being a family vehicle, the owner might hide a spare set of keys somewhere on the van, inside a magnetic holder. He ran his hand under the driver-side wheel well, then to the rear tire, where his hand hit the small rectangular box. Whispering a small thank you to whatever gods were out there making things go smoothly, Zac pulled the little box free. He slid open the compartment and picked up the key. Yes! He kissed the shiny, metal object, then unlocked the door and slipped into the driver's seat.

Knees touching the steering column, head nearly brushing against the roof, Zac felt like a gargoyle. He adjusted the seat to sit like a human being, then crossed his fingers in the silent hope that the sound of the van starting would not alert the family dog. He slid the key into the ignition and turned it on. No barking. So far, so good. He pulled out of the driveway and drove down the street.

Once again, taking care to maintain the speed limit, he rolled through town, keeping a watchful eye out for any sign of police.

Up ahead, the only traffic light flashed red. He stopped and watched as a red minivan, the same make and model as the one he was driving, turned right onto the street in front of him. It occurred to Zac that he might be able to use that minivan to his advantage. He followed the vehicle for three blocks, all the way into the parking lot of a gas station. Zac waited as the driver climbed out of his car and went inside the store.

A quick glance around assured him that no prying eyes would see what he was about to do. He hopped out of the driver's seat, walked to the back of his vehicle, and quickly unscrewed the license plate. Next, he crept up behind the other minivan. With one eye on the people inside the gas station, he swapped out the license plates on the two vehicles.

Zac figured the original minivan owners would call the police first thing in the morning as soon as they realized the vehicle was gone. However, the owner of the van he swapped plates with would have no clue. The police would look for a red minivan with a specific plate number. No one would look for the minivan with the other plates. It would take them a couple of days to figure it all out, and by that time, he and the others would be long gone.

Plates swapped, he slipped back behind the steering wheel and drove back to the others.

For the first time all night, Zac felt upbeat; things were going well. He rolled down the window and breathed in the fresh, desert air, reveling in the feel of it flowing through his hair. His mood light, he turned on the radio and flipped through the stations, searching for the perfect song. Music blaring, windows down, and singing on the top of his lungs, Zac drove through the quiet, desert hills.

At the end of the driveway, he turned off the music. The trailer sat dark and silent, mostly hidden from the road. He stepped out and circled the minivan to admire his handy work. Not bad at all.

"Finn, stop!" Teague shouted inside the trailer. The sound and tone made Zac's hair stand on end. He bolted through the front door.

Chaos greeted him as soon as he stepped inside. Cash was unconscious in the living room. Beth huddled in the corner, sobbing uncontrollably while River struggled to get to her feet. In the center of it all, Finn sat atop Teague, pummeling him with his fist. Over and over again, punch after punch. Teague was not moving; he didn't even lift his hands to shield his face.

Zac stormed across the room, seized hold of Finn by the back of his jeans and the collar of his shirt, and hurled him away. "What the hell did you do?" he demanded.

Finn moved to get to his feet.

"Stay down!" boomed Zac. He spun around and leaned over Teague. River was already by his side, lifting his bloody head on her lap. Unable to comprehend what exactly he just walked into, Zac raked both hands through his hair.

"Zac! Stop him!" shouted River, pointing.

He spun around just in time to see Finn take off through the door. Zac took off after him. By the time he cleared the front porch, Finn was already halfway down the driveway. Zac followed, running as fast as possible.

Turning out of the driveway, Finn nearly crashed into D.B. He skidded to the side, slowing down ever so slightly.

"Stop him!" shouted Zac. "Don't let him get away."

D.B. handed spider off to Bells and tried to run interference on Finn, who skirted past, taking off down the road with D.B. hot on his heels.

"Go inside and help the others!" shouted Zac, as he ran past Bells and Max.

He pumped his legs as fast as they would go.

Up ahead, D.B. ran hard, nearly catching up with Finn, but every time he reached out for him, Finn pivoted just in time to get away.

They ran for what felt like several miles, but in reality, it was probably more like two and a half. Zac's lungs were on fire, his legs were numb. Up ahead, a train whistle blew; they were getting near the tracks. Zac's heart sank—he ran faster.

The alarm rang out as the guard arm came down across the road; a moment later, the train rolled by.

Finn cut a sharp right, running alongside the train.

"No!" shouted Zac.

D.B. kept pace with Finn.

Once again, Finn evaded him. He grabbed hold of the ladder and clambered up into a gondola.

"Don't do it!" shouted Zac, his voice breaking. "Finn! No!" was all he could shout, as he watched Finn disappear over the rim of the car.

Zac stopped running. "Finn!" he cried. "This isn't happening," he said aloud. Hands on the top of his head, he paced in a circle, trying to catch his breath. Tears streamed down his face.

Finn, what the hell did you do?

Chapter 39

"Where is he?" demanded Teague. He already knew the answer; it was painfully clear when he saw the way Zac and D.B. walked up the drive. Shoulders hunched, their pace slow; they had no good news.

Fighting back tears, he squeezed his eyes shut, wincing from the pain. His face was a mass of welts and bruises, with one eye completely sealed shut and the other only able to open halfway. As painful as that was, it scarcely held a candle to the soul-crushing pain in his heart at that moment.

Zac's lips moved as though he were trying to say something, but the words were not forthcoming; all he could do was shake his head.

"What the hell does that mean?" Teague stared at Zac, who only looked down at the ground. He seemed unable to look Teague in the eye. "Zac, what the fuck happened?"

"He ain't comin' back," responded Zac, his voice breaking mid-sentence.

"Bullshit!" shouted Teague. "He's probably hiding by the tracks. I'll go get him." He walked down the driveway.

Zac jogged up alongside. "Stop."

Teague continued to walk, ignoring him completely.

"Teague, stop." Zac grabbed hold of his arm, but Teague wrenched it away and went on walking.

"Goddammit, Teague, stop!" shouted Zac, his voice punctuating the dark silence surrounding them.

Teague spun around, glaring through his half-lidded eye.

Zac shook his head. "I'm telling you, he hopped a train. He ain't coming back."

"Bullshit!"

"He's gone."

"The fuck he is! We gotta go down to those tracks. He probably got off a little up the rail."

Zac shook his head. "He didn't get off." He sighed. "We thought he might too, which is why we waited before heading back." He shook his head. "He didn't show up."

Like a cord stretched too thin, something snapped inside Teague. In his mind, he could hear the moment it broke. In his soul, he could feel it. The world turned gray. Raising his hands to his head, Teague collapsed on his knees. Rocking back and forth, he moaned, "This isn't happening. This isn't happening—"

Zac sat in the dirt beside him.

Teague stopped mumbling and sat still, staring at the ground. He tried to gather his thoughts, but there were none to gather. His mind refused to function; it was as though someone had gone into his brain and pulled the plug. He was numb.

"We gotta get going," said Zac cautiously, his voice sounding as though it were floating down a long tunnel.

Zac tried again, louder this time, "Teague, I realize you've got a lot to process. But time is ticking, my brother. Every minute we spend here dealing with what just happened is a minute we'll never get back."

Teague could feel his eyes on him, waiting, hoping.

"It's a matter of life and death for Cash," continued Zac. "We have to get going."

Life and death for Cash. Yes, Teague was well aware of that. He knew full well that they had to get Cash to the doctor. His mind ordered him to get up and move. But his body refused to comply. It was as though all ties to reality had been severed and all he could do was float, aimless.

"Teague!" Zac snapped his fingers in front of Teague's face. "Come on, man, I need you to snap out of it. I need your help right now."

And I need you to fuck off!

Teague imagined a tiny version of himself alone at a console, frantically flipping switches and pressing buttons, feebly attempting to make his body move.

Zac continued to plead with him, though Teague no longer heard anything he said. He sifted through the tiny bubbles of thought that floated around his mind.

An idea materialized. At the moment, it made the most sense. Like an engine roaring to life, energy surged throughout Teague's body. "We gotta contact Porter." He shot to his feet and headed back to the trailer. "We gotta reach out to Porter." He rattled on as though he were ticking items off a list to prepare for a grand party. "My phone's inside." The numbness subsided, leaving behind in its place a sense of untethered frenzy. "He'll know where that train went. We can catch another one and catch up with him."

River stopped Teague at the door. "We can't do that, baby. We have to get Cash to the doctor." She reached out to wrap her arm around him, but he shrugged her off and stepped back.

"Then I'll go alone," he stated flatly.

Zac stepped up to look Teague in the eye. "I need you to snap out of it, brother. I need your help more than I've ever needed it before."

Teague stared back. The look of sadness on Zac's face—of loss and confusion, mirrored his own deep misery.

Tears burst from his one good eye as the world tumbled down around him. "He ain't right," he cried, tapping his temple between each word. "His head's not right. I can't just leave him out there."

"You ain't leaving him anywhere," replied Zac. "He's the one who left."

Teague shook his head. "He's coming back," he moaned. "I have to be here when he does; otherwise, he's gonna think I deserted him." His voice breaking with each word, Teague collapsed on the floor and leaned against the wall.

River sat beside him, tears streaming down her face. She wrapped her arms around him. "It's gonna be okay," she whispered.

Teague collapsed against her and sobbed. "He ain't right. He's gonna do something stupid."

Zac placed a hand on Teague's shoulder.

"What happens if he comes back and we're gone?" asked Teague.

Max knelt down in front of him. "Look buddy, Bells, D.B. and I decided we're gonna stay right here and wait for him, so you don't have to. You go help Zac take care of Cash. He needs you. Get our boy to the doctor." He smiled. "Get yourself seen, too. We'll stay here as long as we can. If he comes back, we'll take care of him."

No more fight left in him; Teague cupped his face with his hands and bawled.

Less than an hour later, all the gear was loaded into the minivan. No more tears left; Teague sat leaning against the wall, staring off into space, fidgeting with his leather bracelet.

"Come on, buddy, time to go," said Zac, holding out a hand.

Teague didn't move. His mind was at war with his emotions, leaving him paralyzed until a winner emerged.

Zac took a knee in front of Teague. "I can't do this without you, man. I'm all alone here. Beth is useless, Cash is in a bad way, and River," he sighed, "there's only so much she can do to help. I need you —we all need you."

The war raged on.

"I'll make you a solemn promise right now," said Zac. "Help me get Cash to the doctor. We get him taken care of. Once that's done, you and I will head out and find Finn. Is that fair?"

Teague stared back at Zac. The war was waning.

"I swear on my momma's grave." Zac held a hand to his heart. "We will find Finn."

"What if we can't?" asked Teague.

"One way or another, we're gonna find him," swore Zac.

"You've got a lot more confidence than I do. What makes you so sure?"

Zac stared at Teague. "I'll find him. And when I do, I'm gonna beat his ass."

Teague scoffed. "You know you can't beat sense into people."

"Maybe so," agreed Zac, "I might not be able to beat sense into them." He grinned. "But I for sure can make it hurt so bad, they think twice before pullin' any bullshit again."

Teague smiled and chuckled. It felt foreign but good. His phone buzzed in his pocket. Thinking it might be Finn, he fumbled, pulling it out, only to see Gunner's name on the screen. He lifted it to his ear.

"How are you doin', son?" asked Gunner, his tone sympathetic.

The sound of Gunner's voice triggered a new rush of heartache and despair. Teague broke down into a fit of uncontrollable sobs.

Chapter 40

AFTER A BRIEF GOODBYE, ZAC CLIMBED BEHIND THE STEERING WHEEL and backed down the driveway.

Beth sat solemn and distant in the passenger seat. River and Cash were in the back, him sleeping with his head on her lap while she played with his hair absentmindedly.

Alone, lost, and broken, Teague sat in the center, staring out the window. He hadn't said more than a few words for a long time. It was as though something broke deep inside him the moment he realized Finn was gone. The person sitting behind Zac looked like Teague, but something was missing; his body was there, but his soul was elsewhere.

The drive was long, sullen, and bleak. The only positive thing was that there was no traffic for Zac to contend with. Even the truckers had packed it in for the night, leaving the highway wide open.

Zac glanced over at Beth. "How are you doing?"

She shifted her head from side to side, never taking her eyes off the road. "As good as anyone, I suppose."

It wasn't much, but at least it was an answer. Zac would consider anything an improvement over the present, silent situation. "Do you wanna help me out?" he asked her.

Beth shrugged. "Not sure what I can do."

"Navigate. If you could do that, it would help me out a lot," said Zac.

"Now that is something I can do," she replied. At the mere mention of her phone, Beth's countenance underwent a dramatic shift. She pulled the device from her pocket and opened the map.

The cold, blue light cast an eerie glow across her face. As she pulled and pinched the tiny screen, her mood shifted from sullen to animated. The longer she interacted with her phone, the more she came back to life.

"Do you have the address?" she asked.

"It's in the group chat. Stoney gave us coordinates."

Beth smiled; for the first time in hours. "I'm on it."

Cash moaned in the back seat.

"How's he doin'?" asked Zac.

"He's hangin' in there," replied River. "How are we doing on time?"

"We've got at least another couple of hours," responded Beth.

River whispered something to Cash.

From his vantage point in the front seat, Zac couldn't hear what she said, but he heard Cash mutter a reply. At least Cash was still somewhat responsive. He peered through the mirror at Teague, who hadn't moved at all.

The rest of the drive was made in silence, sprinkled periodically with Beth calling out directions for Zac. After what seemed to be forever, they rolled past a "Welcome to Las Cruces" sign. Zac sighed in relief. They were on the home stretch.

Following Beth's guidance, Zac rolled up to a narrow pullout along a set of train tracks. Tucked away from the road, he parked the minivan and turned off the engine.

"You sure this is the place?" he asked Beth.

She nodded and showed him her screen. "Yep, this is it."

Zac glanced around. On one side, a set of train tracks, on the other, a cluster of trees. He had to hand it to Stoney; this was a well-concealed spot. For the first time since leaving the mobile home, Zac's nerves were wearing thin. Where the hell is Stoney? He should have been here by now. Random, negative thoughts churned around in his mind. Did they find the right spot? What if something happened to Stoney on the way? What if Stoney couldn't make it, and they came all this way only to lose Cash because everything went to shit?

Zac shook his head. If Stoney couldn't make it for whatever reason, he would have posted something in the group chat. As for the location, he double-checked the coordinates himself—they were right where they needed to be.

"Beth, can you check the group chats to see if Stoney left a message?" he asked.

Her face altered upon opening the chat. "I can't," she replied. "There's not enough service out here to run the app."

Zac stepped out of the van and pulled his phone from his pocket. One bar. Barely enough to run the map, not sufficient to access the group chat. He leaned into the window. "I'm gonna walk up a ways and see if I can't get some service."

"What if Stoney gets here while you're gone?" asked Beth.

"It's dark out here, and no one is around. If a car comes along, I'll see it," he replied.

Beth nodded.

"Think you can take care of everybody while I'm gone?"

She perked up and smiled. "I got this."

Zac tapped his hand against the door then strolled down the road, his phone held high, searching for service. He walked for at least a mile, alone in the quiet night; the only sound was that of his own foot-steps crunching in the gravel. With each passing yard, his anxiety increased.

Suddenly his phone lit up; he was in range. Several messages loaded at once, all of them from Stoney. He was close and should be there in a few minutes. Zac turned around and jogged back to the vehicle.

He arrived to find the doors to the minivan open; Beth leaned against the rear bumper while Cash leaned up against the door frame; River hovering close by.

"Stoney's gonna be here soon," said Zac.

Beth and River sighed in relief. Cash, looking pale and fragile, could barely nod.

Zac looked inside the vehicle; Teague was not there. "Where's Teague?" he asked, doing his best to conceal his rising panic.

"He walked off that way," said Beth, pointing along the tracks.

"I asked him where he was going," said River. "He said he needed to take a piss."

"How long ago was that?" asked Zac, staring out along the tracks.

River shrugged. "Maybe five minutes ago."

Zac's anxiety exploded. A sudden jolt of energy coursed throughout his body. "I'll be right back," he declared. Then he jogged along the tracks in search of Teague.

A train whistle exploded in the night, startling Zac. Up ahead, he heard the telltale sound of a crossing alarm chiming its warning. Zac's anxiety segued into a full-blown panic; he picked up his pace. The train was getting closer. The familiar scent of oil and metal filled the air.

A red glow shone through the trees, the crossing alarm chimed loudly; up ahead, Zac could see Teague standing close to the tracks. Something about his posture was deeply unnerving; Zac broke into a full run.

The whistle blasted.

Teague stepped closer to the tracks.

Zac ran with every ounce of energy he could muster.

The train was close. Zac could sense the vibrations through his feet. His heart felt as though it would beat itself right out of his chest. A few feet away from Teague, Zac launched into the air and tackled him to the ground. The train thundered by, sending a blast of warm air whirling around them, kicking up soot and tiny bits of gravel.

The last cars passed, the wind died down, and the crossing arm lifted, leaving the duo lying on the ground.

"Zac," said Teague. "What the fuck?" He sat up and gently wiped the blood from his nose.

"I thought—" Zac rubbed his head, afraid to say the rest aloud.

"You thought what?" prodded Teague.

"I thought you were gonna jump," replied Zac.

Teague scoffed. "What the hell would give you that idea?"

Zac sighed. "It's been a shit night."

"That it has," agreed Teague.

"You weren't, were you?"

"What?" asked Teague. "Jump?"

Zac nodded.

Teague shook his head. "Couillion." He peered down along the tracks, deep in thought. "I ain't there yet." His response was flat and matter of fact.

It wasn't the denial Zac had hoped for, but at least it was honest. They sat on the ground for a little while longer, then walked back to the others. When they arrived, Stoney was already there, loading Cash in a big, silver van.

Once everyone was set, Zac siphoned some of the gas from the minivan and splashed it around inside. He then lit a match and tossed it onto the back seat. Flames shot into the air, licking at the van's roof, devouring everything inside.

Not long after, they pulled up outside a small, rural clinic. The sterile-looking building was out of place, sitting in the middle of nowhere, surrounded by trees and shrubs on all sides. Were it not for the black, panel van sitting in the parking lot, one would assume the place was abandoned.

The doors whooshed open before them. Bright lights illuminated the off-white interior, giving everything a sterile feel. Zac and Stoney carried Cash over to a gurney and placed him down. The institutional light gave his pallor an even more ashen appearance. At least in the dark, Zac could pretend Cash was doing fine; the bright lights of the hospital destroyed that fantasy.

"Yo, Doc!" shouted Stoney, his voice reverberating off the sterile walls.

At the counter stood a large man wearing jeans, boots, and a black, leather, coat, his short, blond hair riddled throughout with white, his face a roadmap of life. Startled by Stoney's shout, he spun around, took one look at Cash, then hurried down the hall, stopping at a closed door. He banged three times, then leaned his head inside.

Zac couldn't hear what they said, but he could make out there were a few people inside that room. A moment later, a portly man wearing a white lab coat emerged, followed by a tall, stern-faced woman and another man, rough looking like the blond man.

"I cannot thank you enough for the supplies, Manny," said the doctor. "I owe you, fellas, a lot. Those meds will save a lot of lives."

The dark-haired man smiled. "Just don't ask where it came from. It's best you don't know." He grinned. "We consider it payback. We gotta get into heaven somehow." He winked.

The doctor chuckled. "Tell the big guy I'm sorry I missed him."

"He's dealing with some family shit right now, but I'll tell him," replied the dark-haired man. "Come on Pillar, let's leave the Doc to his work." He glanced over at the motley group of youngsters.

A moment later, the two men were gone, leaving behind the hum of the overhead lights and the sound of Cash's labored breathing.

The doctor looked over Cash's wound. "He looks a lot worse than he is," he said, peering up at Zac and Stoney. "He's lost a lot of blood, but I think he'll be okay."

Upon hearing those words, an anvil of weight lifted off of Zac's heart. He sighed in relief.

"You folks wait here," instructed the doctor. "Helen and I will take care of your friend, then come back for you," he said, pointing at Teague. "Grab a seat; there are snacks behind the desk."

Leaving on that note, the doctor and his nurse rolled Cash away into an exam room, River by his side the entire time.

Zac collapsed into a chair in the hall. His entire body ached. Exhaustion settled into his bones; he realized he had been going non-stop for just over twenty-four hours.

"Doc's a good man," said Stoney. "If he says Cash'll be fine, then he'll be fine."

Zac nodded. He wanted to believe that more than anything. "How long have you known him?"

Stoney sighed. "I first came into contact with him back when I was still riding. Doc fixed me up after a real, nasty accident. If it wasn't for him, I'd have lost my arm." He rolled up his sleeve, showing off a thick scar just below his elbow. "I've brought folks to him periodically over the years. He's well known among the rabble as an honest man. Does a lot of work for folks who can't pay on both sides of the border."

The doors to the center whooshed open, and a tall, slender, dark-skinned man strolled in.

"Well, goddamn," exclaimed Stoney. "Look what the cat dragged in." He walked up to the man, clasped hands, and hugged him like an old friend.

"What the hell are you doin' all the way out here?" asked Stoney.

"I was in the area," chuckled the stranger.

"Uh, huh," scoffed Stoney. "Last I heard, Fort Worth was nowhere near Las Cruces."

"It isn't?" teased the man. "I've got to consult my maps on that one." The man laughed, flashing a bright, toothy grin. He looked down at Zac, then over at Teague. "I needed to make sure my boys were all okay."

Thoroughly baffled, Zac shot a glance at Teague, who stared back, equally confused.

The stranger chuckled. "I'm sorry, I forget we've never met in person." He reached out a hand. "It's me, Porter."

Shane

Five months earlier; North Texas.

THE TRUCK ROARED THROUGH THE SQUARE, SPEWING A TRAIL OF BLACK smoke as it slowly rolled past the old courthouse. It had been nearly two decades since Shane ventured to Gainesville; not much had changed. He turned onto South Dixon Street and slowed to a crawl. Seeing the stately old homes that lined the street brought back a surge of emotions—many of them terrible.

He didn't want to be there. Shane vowed long ago that he would never return. This town had too many memories for him, too much heartache.

Shane rolled up and parked the old truck across the street from a stately Victorian mansion. After all these years, it was still impressive with its elegant tower, high peaked gables, and stained-glass windows. The old bench swing still hung on the grand front porch, swaying gently in the early, morning breeze. Distant memories of warm, summer evenings sitting on that swing crept to the fore of his mind. So many hours were spent laughing, daydreaming, and cooking up plans for the future; they were so full of hope back then. He closed his eyes and could hear the melodic tone of her laughter.

Melody. Just thinking the name produced a surge of heartache and a flood of memories, he would rather remain buried. There was a brief period in his life when she was his everything. She made the world a beautiful place. Melody was the only person at the time who treated him as her equal, the only person who never made fun of his eyes. She loved him, and he loved her.

"Yo, hey, we goin' in?" asked Manny. "Or are we sitting out here in the truck all day?"

"You know you didn't have to come along," replied Shane, still peering up at the house, trying to hold fast to the good memories.

Manny clucked his tongue. "Now you know as well as I do that wasn't an option."

"It ain't my fault you're afraid of your sister," teased Shane.

"That ain't it."

Shane scoffed.

Manny stared at Shane with dark, brown eyes. "Who's been your best friend since boot camp?" He paused, not waiting for a reply. "That's right, me, motherfucker. That means I know your history." He flashed a wicked smile. "I also know what you do to people who piss you off. I'm here to keep you out of trouble. Because that old man in there." He pointed toward the house. "Has pissed you off more than anyone alive." He shook his head. "Nah, brother, I'm here to keep you from getting into trouble."

"And because your sister told you to."

Manny vigorously shook his head.

"It's okay to admit it," Shane smirked. "Lots of guys are afraid of women. I've seen how you jump when your sister tells you to."

"Don't give me that shit." Manny wagged his finger. "You don't know what it was like growing up with her. She treats you differently. You don't know how mean she can be. One time she beat me with a two by four."

"I know, I know." Shane nodded. "And if I recall, she did that because you told your mom and dad she spent the night with her boyfriend."

Manny grinned and nodded. "Oh yeah, I did do that."

Shane chuckled.

"You laugh," said Manny. "She's the reason I went into the Marines. I had to get away from her."

Shane scoffed. "Bullshit, Manny. You went into the suck for the same reason I did; a judge gave us a choice, and you and I were too pretty for prison."

Manny pulled down the visor and looked at himself in the mirror. "Yeah, you've got a point." He ran his fingers through his dark, brown hair, peppered here and there with strands of silver, and smoothed his perfectly trimmed beard. "We really are all that. I don't know how the ladies can keep their hands off of us."

"That's an easy one," chuckled Shane. "They avoid you because you've already slept with most of them, and I'm married to your sister."

"That's your fault. I tried to warn you."

Shane's phone rang; it was the old man. As he lifted it to his ear, he scanned the front of the house. "Yeah."

Electronic buzz and the sound of artificial air poured through his phone. "You coming inside, or are you planning on sitting out there all day with your boyfriend?" hissed the old man.

God, he sounds awful. I hope he's in a lot of pain. "Yeah," replied Shane. "We're comin' in now."

The old man coughed. "Come around the back, the door's open." There was a click as he hung up the phone, then silence.

"Well, this is it," said Shane. "Let's go see the old man." He pulled a handgun from the glove box and stuffed it into the back of his belt.

For years, Shane hadn't given this North Texas town any thought. He had practically wiped it from his memory. Then, three days ago, he was awakened by his phone ringing. In the early morning light, he squinted to see who the hell would call him that early. Everyone knew better than to wake him unless it was an emergency. Caller ID showed the caller as unidentified. Shane turned off the sound, rolled over, and wrapped his arms around Catalina, pulling her warm body against his, and fell back to sleep.

It wasn't until later that morning when he finally looked at his phone and played the message that he realized who the unidentified caller was. As soon as the recording played, he recognized the voice; a chill shot down his spine. After so many years, even with sickness, the old man still had an effect on Shane. He could never forget the sound of that evil voice. It was a struggle to get through the entire message. Still, Shane listened patiently as the old man wheezed and coughed his way through an explanation. He was dying and wanted to pass on a few last items of Melody's. Things Shane would like to keep. Being the last remaining member of that cursed family, the old man wanted to be sure that his daughter was remembered.

Shane's initial reaction was to erase the message, block the number and forget all about it. It was Catalina who convinced him to go. She insisted he owed it to the memory of Melody, and that it would help him with closure. In the end, Shane reluctantly agreed and, with Manny along for the ride, made the trek from El Paso to Gainesville.

The dawn air was crisp and clean with the slightest hint of moisture, the grass covered with dew; it would be at least two more hours before the sun rose and burned it all away. The entire neighborhood still sleeping; it was easy to pretend the rest of the world no longer existed.

Shane walked with purpose around the back of the house; he was there for one reason, and one reason only. As soon as that was done, he intended to put this place far behind him.

He strolled down the driveway, past the tower, where the decorative trellis once stood. A slight smile spread across Shane's face. He remembered climbing that rickety, wooden ladder to the porch on the second floor, sneaking into Melody's bedroom. Of course, when the old man found out, he had a fit and cut it all down. His wife's prize-winning wisteria and all; she was so angry at him; they fought for weeks.

Of course, taking the trellis down changed nothing. Two days after it all came down, Shane once again, spent the night in Melody's room.

The back door was ajar, so he and Manny entered slowly, finding the old man alone sitting at the kitchen table.

Frail and sallow from sickness, the old curmudgeon was a withered husk of the man he used to be. The Ben Caldwell Shane knew was strong, vibrant, and cruel. What sat before him was a far cry from the robust man who used to strike fear in Shane's heart with the sound of his voice.

An oxygen tank on wheels sat at the old man's feet; a clear tube leading from the tank to his nose. A pile of blood-splattered, snot-filled tissue sat atop the table alongside a nearly empty box. The room stank of the foul odor of impending death.

"I see you've taken to covering them up," said the old man, indicating the brown contact lenses Shane wore.

In his line of business, it was best not to be memorable. Having two different colored eyes was a detail that witnesses could recall—a detail that could lead police right to him. Shane did not answer; he was not there for small talk.

"Take a seat," choked the old man. The sound of oxygen flowing through the tube, filling the gaps between his words.

"I'll stand," replied Shane.

The old man stared up at him, a glint of evil still sparkled in his eyes. "Suit yourself," he replied. He slid a dusty, wooden box across the table, then burst into a round of coughing that ended in him hawking up a giant gob of blood and snot into a tissue.

Shane pulled the box close, then flipped open the lid. The fresh scent of bluebonnets wafted into the air, a welcome reprieve from the sickness all around him. Melody always loved the smell of bluebon-nets. It was her favorite.

Timid, at first, Shane shifted the contents of the box around gently. A senior photo, like the sort taken for a yearbook, stared up at him with dark, brown eyes. Those eyes. He could have drowned in them forever. When they looked up at him, he believed he could do anything. He sat heavy in the chair, placed the photo on the table, and turned his atten-tion back to the box. A lock of her dark, brown, hair, probably clipped when she was a toddler. He rolled it between his fingers. So, soft and wild, Melody's hair had a wave to it that refused to be tamed. A sad smile crossed his face.

He placed that down gently atop the senior photo. Inside the box, there were more photos of Melody as a little girl, including one for every school year. A picture of her and her cousin Tricia from when they were children. Shane twitched his nose and put that picture aside from the others. He had no desire to keep that one, let it burn for all he cared.

Across the table, the old man tried to laugh but only triggered another ragged coughing fit.

Farther into the box, Shane came upon an ultrasound image. He had an identical one back home. Red ink circled the tiny penis with the words written in Melody's handwriting "It's a boy! Just like daddy." He stared at the little baby, one small hand holding an ear, the other in his mouth.

Shane wasn't there the day that image was taken; he was at Parris Island, in the middle of boot camp. Upon graduation, he returned home for two weeks' leave before heading off for infantry school. Melody was so excited, already referring to the little guy as Finn. She was so in love with the baby, Shane fell in love too. He remembered placing his hand atop her belly and feeling the faintest movement of his son for the first time.

Shane stared at his open hand, the memory of that moment still ingrained in his skin. He looked down at the image and traced the outline of the infant, then twitched his nose and moved his attention back to the box.

A dried bluebonnet; saved from their first date and a red rose from her prom bouquet. Shane pulled out a photo of the two of them together, smiling, arms wrapped around one another, taken the day he left for infantry school. It was the last time he saw her.

Shane placed all the items into the box and closed the lid. He glared across the table at the old man. "Thanks for the box; I hope you die soon, old man."

"Doctors said they don't know why I'm still kickin'," said Ben. "Between you and me, I've been ready to go for years now." He coughed up another wad of blood and mucus. "Every night, I go to bed hoping I don't wake up the next day."

"Well, it appears you and I agree on something at last," replied Shane.

"I can see that the years have only made you more trash than you were years ago," said the old man.

Shane was done. He slid the chair back and rose to his feet. "As much as I'd love to sit here and pass barbs around with you, I got a life to live." He turned and headed toward the door.

"Don't you wanna know the truth?" shouted Ben.

Shane stopped in his tracks. "The truth about what?"

"The truth about your son." A warped smile flitted across the old man's face.

"Look, old man," said Shane. "I know he's buried next to my wife; your daughter, that's all I need to know."

Ben chuckled, then broke out into another fit.

Manny opened the door, and Shane turned to leave.

"He isn't dead."

Shane froze. He locked eyes with Manny, who slowly closed the door.

"That's right," continued Ben. "The boy didn't die that night."

"You got exactly one second to start spitting out details before I rip your heart out," warned Shane.

The old man laughed and pulled a stack of papers from under his chair. He leaned his bony elbows atop the pile and folded his hands.

"That night, I lost the most precious thing in my life; my baby girl. I hated you—still do." He smirked. "I wanted you to feel the same heartache. I wanted to punish you. But when I held that little boy in my arms, I saw her." He paused, letting his mind wander through the memory. "Like her, he too was an old soul; he just stared up at me, calm; studying. His face was hers, but he had your eyes. He was a beautiful kid."

A fuse of white-hot rage ignited deep inside Shane, slowly gaining momentum. When the old man descended into yet another fit of gagging and coughing, it took every ounce of restraint Shane could muster to hold back from strangling the geezer.

Ben slid the papers across the table. "I knew at that moment that there was no way I was going to let you have your son. Not when you stole my daughter from me." He glared up at Shane.

"I pulled some strings and called in some favors. Next thing ya know, we had a death certificate and all."

"Where is he?" growled Shane.

"It's all right there in the papers." Ben pointed his chin toward the stack on the table. "We forged a new birth certificate. I had a friend of mine who was a county judge make it all official."

Shane's entire body trembled. He's alive! Almost twenty years. He's been alive this whole time! He pulled the papers close and leafed through them; one name jumped off the page. Tricia Caldwell. Shane hurled the table across the room and grabbed the old man by his shirt collar, lifting him off his feet. "You gave my son to that bitch?" he roared.

Ben let out a weak chuckle and nodded. "Icing on the cake, wouldn't you say?"

Shane tossed the old man across the kitchen and into the living room like a rag doll, where he crumpled on the floor limp and lifeless. Had it not been for another coughing fit, Shane might have thought he was dead.

Manny stepped in front of Shane. "Hold up, hold up, man."

"No, Manny!" he shouted. "You are not gonna stop me from killing this old son of a bitch."

Manny shook his head. "Nah, man, I'm not saying no. Hell, after what we just heard, if you don't kill this bastard right now, I'm gonna do it." He grinned. "All I'm saying is we need to be smart about it." Manny nodded toward the open windows. "Give me five seconds to make sure the house is clear, okay?"

Shane nodded in agreement. While he waited for Manny, he loomed over the old man, still balled up on the floor.

"All right, all clear," said Manny, as he strolled back into the room. "How we doin' this?"

"As painfully as possible," replied Shane. He kicked the old man two times for good measure, then lifted the limp body, surprised at how light it was. He carried him back into the kitchen and placed him in a chair.

The old man didn't fight back; he merely stared at Shane, wheezing and gasping for air.

Manny lit two candles on opposite sides of the room. He blew out the pilot light on the stove and turned on all four burners, as well as the oven. Gas poured into the room.

The old man slumped face-first onto the table, his chest heaving as he struggled to breathe.

Shane collected the papers and box, then walked out and stood on the back porch with Manny, looking back at the tired, weak old man at the table. He couldn't believe there was ever a time when he feared that man. He closed the door, and the two men left through the backyard and around the corner.

They were almost at the end of the street when a loud boom reverberated through the neighborhood, shattering windows and setting off car alarms. As Manny drove, Shane watched through the side-view mirror as bright, red flames devoured the grand, old Victorian.

"You know he wanted you to kill him," said Manny. He leaned against a giant oak tree and lit a cigarette.

Shane sat on the ground in the old cemetery, staring at two, neatly maintained tombstones, one big and one small. He took a sip from a flask of whiskey.

Manny continued, "He said himself, he wished every night he would die."

Shane was silent.

Manny took a drag from his cigarette and exhaled. "That was one sick motherfucker, man. To do that shit, that's fucked up."

The warm breeze rustled the leaves in the tree. Carrion birds circled overhead; something was dead nearby. Shane ran his hand over the grass, remembering the dog tag he buried there to symbolize the part of him that died along with his wife and son.

My son's alive.

Shane climbed to his feet and brushed the grass away from his jeans. He took a drag from Manny's smoke, then a swig from the flask. Rage burned like fire through his entire body; he let out a mighty roar and kicked the small tombstone over.

"Let's go," he said, as he headed for the truck.

"Home?" asked Manny.

Shane slid behind the steering wheel and nodded. "Then I'm gonna find my son."

THE END

HOBO CODE KEY

YOU'LL GET
CURSED OUT
HERE

YOU CAN SLEEP
IN THE LOFT

WORTH ROBBING

UNSAFE PLACE

WEALTHY

UNSAFE AREA

TURN RIGHT
HERE

TROLLEY

TURN LEFT
HERE

TOWN ALLOWS
ALCOHOL

TRAMPS HERE

TALK RELIGION
GET FOOD

TELL PITIFUL
STORY

STOP

STRAIGHT AHEAD

SAFE CAMP

RAILROAD

POOR MAN

OFFICER

NO ALCOHOL TOWN

HOBO CODE KEY

HOBO CODE KEY

EASY MARK

DON'T GIVE UP

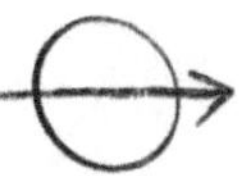

DON'T GO THIS WAY

DOCTOR NO CHARGE

DOCTOR

DISHONEST MAN

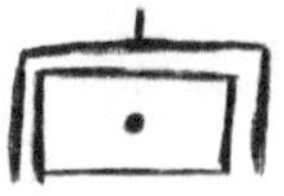

DANGEROUS NEIGHBORHOOD

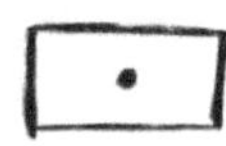

DANGER

COWARDS! WILL PAY TO GET RID OF YOU

COURTHOUSE OR POLICE STATION

CHAIN GANG

CATCH OUT HERE

CAMP HERE

BE READY TO DEFEND YOURSELF

BEWARE! 4 DOGS

BE QUIET

BAD WATER

AT CROSSROAD GO THIS WAY

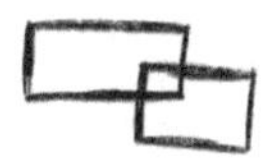

AFRAID

ALRIGHT (OK)

Acknowledgments

Two books in. I hope you're enjoying this as much as I am.

I want to take a moment to thank the people who have encouraged me along this journey. First, there's Meagan. She read the first snippet I wrote; it was more of a short story. Her enthusiasm for the characters encouraged me to write more. She's also the artist who designed and created the covers for both book so far.

Sam McLaughlin for reading the first written manuscript. Let's just say it had serious issues.

Samantha Dayton, Vic Willette, Jackie Lowry, Connor, Rory, and Shannon, all of these beautiful people, gave input and read various revisions along the way. Their feedback and critique helped the book take its ultimate form.

Brenna McLaughlin, her artwork is irreplaceable. From the first compass design to the portrait of Finn. She brought my vision to life and I couldn't be happier.

And of course, we cannot forget, Robert McLaughlin, my partner —my rock. He listens to my rants and ravings, all the while, offering input whenever he can. He is my road trip partner—my sounding board —my anchor. He will always be the love of my life.

A Word from Nancy

Thank you for reading American Nomads. If you enjoyed the ride so far, please take a moment and leave a review, it would be greatly appreciated. We Indie authors need reviews from people who had read and enjoyed our work. All reviews are greatly appreciated.

Want more Nomad stories? There are various origin stories of the characters available to read now FREE on my website. Scan the QR code below with your phone and it will take you right there. While you're there, be sure to sign up for my newsletter. That way, you'll know about upcoming releases and any free content as it comes available.

Or simply follow the link to my website below…

https://www.nancylmclaughlin.com/

I am currently finishing up work on book three of this series, tentatively titled; Imaginary Dragons. It should be ready to publish by fall of this year (2022) After that, we're on to the final book in the series. I hope you will stick around to see how it all ends. I promise it's gonna be a wild ride.

Cash

AN AMERICAN NOMADS ORIGIN STORY

"Number five in the corner pocket." Cash casually tapped his stick on the edge of the pool table. Smirking, he chalked up his cue as his opponent looked on in dismay.

Two more shots and the pile of money on the table would be his. Victory was so close, he could taste it. He could hardly wait to tell his boys all about how he played this big, old dude and took all his money.

The neon sign on the wall cast a red hue upon the clock below; it was two-thirty. Cash should be sitting in biology, bored out of his mind, listening to the teacher drone on and on. High School was a waste of time. Who needed to know most of that stuff anyway? Algebra? When was he ever going to use that in real life? And grammar, what a total waste of time. He had no intention of ever writing a book, so why bother struggling to learn that garbage. Who even needs to know what a dangling participle is anyway? Life was short. Having fun was a far better pursuit than good grades. He was willing to bet the pile of money on the edge of the pool table that no one on their death bed ever fondly recalled the time they got an "A" on an algebra test.

Just sitting in class—any class was enough to make him want to scream. The buzz of the fluorescent lights. The warm recirculated air. The squeaky sound of sneakers on worn-out linoleum floors. The smell of the daily lunch special emanating off of his classmates. That was probably the worst, especially on spaghetti day. The nauseating scent of sour tomato sauce mixed with the cheap perfume that all the girls loved. Why did they wear that crap? Couldn't they smell it? The whole experience was suffocating, almost maddening. There were not enough words for how much he hated the entirety of going to school. Which is why two hours ago, he slipped out a side door near the gymnasium, and rode his skateboard downtown.

When he first arrived at the pool hall, the dank light of the place was a sharp contrast to the bright afternoon sun. He stood in the doorway for a moment, allowing his eyes to adjust. The steady murmur from a dozen different conversations buzzed beneath the heavy beat of some old rock and roll song from a band too old for Cash to know. The smell of cigarette smoke and spilled alcohol hung heavy in the air. He loved every bit of it. He inhaled deeply, taking it all in. Ah, the smell of fun.

Doing his best to fit in and not look like a seventeen-year-old kid who was skipping school, he quickly made his way to the pool tables in the far corner, taking care to stay out of the bartender's view. Cash took up a seat and watched. Only one pool table was in use, typical for the mid-workday.

Two grizzly-looking men with thick beards and lots of tattoos were playing a game of eight-ball. They teased one another between sips of whiskey and took shots at the balls on the table. Their clothing—worn jeans, old t-shirts, and scuffed boots, didn't scream "money." That assumption was shattered when the big guy with the gray beard pulled out a wad of bills to pay the waitress who came by with fresh drinks.

Cash watched in silence, scrutinizing their every move. While reasonably decent at playing, neither man looked like a considerable pro. This would be easy money. All he had to do was find an opening, and he would be home free. These two guys wouldn't know what happened. And he would have plenty of money to pay for festival tickets. He'd have more than enough money left over to waste on all the junk food and weed he wanted.

. . .

Nearly two hours later, he had lost enough rounds to convince the burly men that Cash was a dumb kid with mediocre skills. The stage was set, and the money was his for the taking. All he had to do was sink two more shots. Cash leaned forward and lined up the cue.

"What the fuck are you doing here?" The familiar voice cut through the music, and all the noise of the bar, shattering Cash's concentration. Heart racing, he exhaled and turned around to face his father, doing his best to hide the fact he was trembling.

"It's the middle of the goddamn day. Why the hell aren't you in school?" Demanded his father.

Cold sweat seeped from every pore. His entire body buzzed with anxiety. The anger on the old man's face was plainly visible. This was bad. Cash knew that a cocky response was not a good idea at the moment, yet—

"I could ask the same question of you," replied Cash, his voice cracking. He swallowed hard. "Shouldn't you be at work or something?" His body trembled with a mixture of fear and anger. *Why did I just say that?* It was too late. The words were already out there, bouncing around the dive bar for everyone to hear. He steeled himself for the inevitable response.

Paul Wright wasn't known for his patience and calm demeanor. A mechanic by trade, he was no stranger to hard work and struggling to get by. Though not prone to violence, the old man was never one to walk away from a fight. Of course, he preferred to handle things more diplomatically—well, his version of diplomacy. In the words of Cash's older brother Scott, "Dad's the type of man who will shout the sense back into you. If that doesn't work, he'll kick your ass."

Cash waited for his old man to knock him cold. Time froze; everyone around the pool table stood still, watching, waiting. For the first time in his life, Cash understood the meaning of the term "you could hear a pin drop." A cold shiver ran down his spine; he was heading into unchartered territory. Never before had Cash ever stood up to the old man like this. He was positive he was about to be knocked unconscious. Instead, his father stood inches from him, silently staring directly into his eyes. The anger was there; Cash could see it roiling like violent thunder clouds just below the surface.

Without warning, Paul flashed a malevolent grin. He turned on his heels and grabbed Cash's belongings from the table and shoved them into Cash's arms. He then took hold of his son by his jacket collar and dragged him through the bar and out onto the sidewalk.

He slammed Cash against the brick wall, his skateboard clattering to the ground. "Okay, smartass, do you know who those guys were in there?"

"Yeah, two fools who were about to give me all their money."

Paul released his son and sighed. "You're an idiot. They were members of the local biker club. Didn't you see their cuts hanging on the back of the chairs? Guys like them eat smartass kids like you for lunch and use the leftover bones to pick their teeth. Do you seriously believe they were gonna let you walk out of there with their money?"

Cash shrugged indignantly. He didn't want to admit it, but hearing those two were bikers did change his view of things. *Damnit!* The old man was right. There was no way he would admit that; he would not give his father the satisfaction of being told he was right.

"Real life is not a game," his father shouted. "It's high time you grew the hell up and realized that if you keep playing your games and pulling your hustles, you're never gonna amount to anything in this life. I did not work my whole life so my son could end up a hustler or in prison."

Oh boy, here we go. The I busted my ass speech. Cash rolled his eyes.

The old man's voice bounced off the brick walls of the buildings. "I busted my ass for you and your brother. Gave up everything so you two could have a chance at something better. What the hell is wrong with you? Cash, why are you so damn stupid sometimes?"

"Fuck you!" Cash responded. His voice cracking yet again, much to his dismay. He could feel the heat rising up from his neck to his face. He grabbed his skateboard, and without another word, skated off.

"Get your ass back here!" Paul called behind him. "We're not done!"

Yes, we are! Cash did not stop, nor did he look back. He raised his hand in the air and flashed his middle finger.

As he rounded the corner, he came within inches of crashing into a delivery truck idling in the middle of the street. He cut a hard right and lost control of his skateboard, sending his body slamming into the stone façade of the nearest building while his board rolled into oncoming traffic.

Drivers hit their horns as they swerved to avoid hitting the wooden projectile. "Stay out of the damn road!" shouted one.

"Hey, you should watch where you're going," warned the delivery truck driver.

His arm scraped, his pride injured; Cash didn't respond to the man. Instead, he walked across the street and picked up his board, glancing at the corner, hoping that his father didn't see what just happened, then he dropped his wheels on the pavement and kicked off again.

He rolled into Riverfront Park, found a secluded bench, and plopped himself down. The first order of business was to inspect his board. He flipped it over in his hands, examining the deck. No cracks or chips. Satisfied, he leaned it against the bench. His arm was a different story. An angry red rash ran from his wrist to his elbow. It stung, but the pain wasn't too bad. *I've had worse.* He brushed away the tiny bits of rock dust from the deeper scratches.

Across the park, children giggled and squealed as they splashed at a nearby fountain while tourists took pictures along the river's edge. He envied them all. The tourists because they were doing the one thing he wanted to do most; travel. As for the kids, well, they had the perfect existence, no responsibilities, no concerns about the future. No adults breathing down their necks insisting they "start acting like an adult." There was no inner clock ticking away, growing louder with each passing day, letting them know that soon they would have to join the ranks of the miserable masses. "Better figure out what you're gonna do; after graduation, the free ride's over." He had heard that from his old man too many times to count.

He pulled a crushed pack of cigarettes from his jeans and lit the last smoke. The sound of the flowing water coupled with the children's laughter lulled him into a sense of calm. He lay back on the bench, staring up at the clear blue sky, and watched the fluffy white clouds roll by. If only he could figure out a way to travel all the time.

The clock tower chimed, waking Cash from a light nap; it was six o'clock. He sat up and raked his fingers through his hair. The sun was a red orb sitting on the horizon; the day was coming to an end. His stomach growled. He reached for his wallet, then remembered that he had left all his money on the pool table. *Dammit!* No money, no smokes, and no food. He needed to figure out a way to correct at least one of those problems. It didn't take him long to come up with a solution. *Kayla!*

Cash rolled up on the sandwich shop and peered through the plate glass window. Just as he hoped, Kayla was working behind the counter, her long dark hair pulled up in a neat bun atop her head. She glanced up, seeing him outside, and turned away, ignoring him. Ordinarily, if someone gave him that type of shade, Cash would leave. But he was hungry, and Kayla was his best chance at getting something to eat; the only other choice he had was to go home. And after the run-in with his father earlier, that was not an option. He kicked his board up into his hand and walked inside.

The enticing aroma of fresh-baked bread and deli meat made his mouth water. He walked toward the counter, keeping his eyes on Kayla, who still refused to even look up at him.

"Hey," he said, flashing his best smile.

Kayla didn't answer; she continued wiping the counter as though he was invisible.

"Come on, Kayla," he pleaded, "Don't ignore me. I came all this way to see what you were up to."

She stopped wiping and glared up at him with her dark brown eyes. "You could've saved yourself a trip if you had checked your messages." She tossed the rag on the counter and stalked away.

Messages? Cash pulled out his phone and found several messages waiting for him, five from Kayla. He stuffed the device back in his pocket and followed her across the store.

"I'm sorry, I missed your messages. I had a run-in with my old man, and I lost track of time." He held up his arm to show off his wound, hoping that it would make her feel sorry for him.

Her face softened. "Why does it always seem like I'm only important to you when you want something from me?" she folded her arms.

He was winning her over. He flashed a crooked smile and gently touched her arm. "Come on, it's not like that. I think about you a lot; I just had a rough day." He leaned close and kissed her on the cheek.

Her posture relaxed, and she uncrossed her arms. She smiled. "I get off at nine if you wanna hang out."

"Sure," he replied. "I gotta hook up with the guys at the skate park, but after that, I can come by and get you. We can go hang out at your place."

Her smile lit up her face. "Great, let's do that," she said, almost giddy. "We can watch that movie I told you about."

Cash won her over, now to get what he came for in the first place. "Great!" He kissed her on the forehead. "It's a date then." He moved as though he were heading for the door. "In the meantime, I'm gonna go find something to eat." He patted his belly, making sure to wince, ever so slightly, from the pain in his arm. "I'm starving."

"I can make you a sandwich if you want," blurted Kayla.

"You sure?" He offered his most innocent facial expressions. "I don't have any money, sort of lost it all playing pool."

"It'll be on me." She kissed him on the cheek. "you can make it up to me later."

He grinned. "Absolutely."

Kayla walked behind the counter. "You're always losing your money gambling. One of these days, you're gonna have to stop. If you're gonna move out, you'll need a job so you can pay rent."

I don't always lose, and no, I'm not getting a job. Cash ignored the rest of Kayla's "adulting" speech as he waited patiently for her to finish making his sandwich. Irritation simmered just below the surface held in check by his hunger.

She set him up with his meal in a corner booth, tussling his hair as if he were a child, before going back to work behind the counter.

His mouth watered. The tantalizing aroma of the sandwich

reminded Cash that he hadn't eaten anything since early morning. Without another thought about how annoyed he was with Kayla, Cash dove right in, savoring every bite. Meanwhile, a steady stream of customers came and went, keeping Kayla too busy to spend time bothering Cash with any more of her words of wisdom. As soon as his belly was full, he rushed to leave, shouting a promise over his shoulder to be back by nine. He didn't stick around long enough to hear her response.

Outside, on the streets, people in business clothes carrying briefcases gave way to people dressed in casual, more colorful attire. The sound of cars and delivery vehicles became the soft sound of laughter fused with muted music and tinkling glasses.

From a corner, waiting for the light to change, Cash watched a man, seated at an outdoor patio, stuff several bills inside a small black folder. The man wiped his mouth with his cloth napkin one last time, then stood and helped his date from her chair.

The light changed. Surrounded by a small cluster of men and women, Cash rolled closer, scanning the patio for the server. With one eye on the folder, he kicked hard to gain speed. As he flew past the table, he reached out and swiped the folder, then took off down the street, far away from the restaurant.

Back at the park, he was finally able to inspect the contents of the binder. A crisp one-hundred-dollar bill and a twenty. *Sweet! That'll make up for the money lost earlier.* He tossed the folder into the trash and pocketed the bills. The evening was beginning to look up.

The clock tower chimed eight; time to meet up with the boys. Feeling more optimistic than he had all day, Cash skated across the park to the skate area.

"Hey Cash, where ya been all day?" Kyle placed a cigarette in his mouth and leaned toward the lighter. The flame cast an orange-red glow, highlighting the millions of freckles all over his pale face. He took a long drag then handed the smoke to Cash.

"Where's Chris?" asked Cash as he scanned the park, searching for his friend's telltale neon-green hair.

"He went to the store with a couple of drifters we ran into."

"Couple of drifters, huh, anyone we met before?"

Kyle shook his head as he exhaled. "Nah, at least I've never seen them before. They're cool, not weird like some of them can be, ya know?"

Cash took one more drag from the cigarette then exhaled and handed it back to Kyle. Without another word, he hopped on his board and dropped into the nearest bowl.

The flutter of butterflies in his belly on the initial drop always got his adrenaline pumping. He loved the rush of air and the sense of gliding effortlessly; he could do without the smell of urine at the bottom of the bowl. Luckily, he didn't spend a whole lot of time down there. He came up to the opposite side of the bowl and pulled off a perfect blunt to fakie, then dropped in again, this time pumping his feet to gain more speed so he could pop an ollie at the other end of the bowl.

The adrenaline, the rush of landing perfectly, the sense of freedom, these things were all that mattered. He needed to find a way to do nothing but skate for the rest of his life.

Several minutes later, Cash decided to head back over to Kyle and see what was up. Chris was back, sitting with Kyle and the two strangers. Cash took in the new duo.

Both wore the telltale worn and dirty clothes of train riders. Aside from that, they were very different from one another. One was tall and thin with shoulder-length blond hair and multiple tattoos, including several on his face. The other had more of an athletic build and short dark hair, he could pass for any average high school lacrosse player.

"Cash, my man," said Chris as he reached out in greeting. He turned to the strangers. "This here is Sam," he said, indicating the blond man, "and this is Tripp." He gestured toward the man with dark hair.

The duo nodded in greeting.

"Where ya from?" asked Cash as he took a cigarette from Chris.

Tripp smirked. "Everywhere."

Cash nodded and exhaled. *So, cliché.* He'd expected an answer like that; he just didn't believe anyone would really do it. It took a great deal of restraint to hold back a laugh.

"Uh-huh." He smirked. "So, other than drifting, where're you from originally?"

"Grew up all over the U.S.," replied Sam, "but I guess you could say I started out in Sioux Falls."

It was apparent that Sam was the more down-to-earth of the two. With his genuine smile and casual air, he came across as someone who had nothing to prove. Cash liked that about him. On the other hand, Tripp seemed the sort who played games and wanted to win. Oddly enough, Cash liked that a great deal, probably a lot more than authenticity.

"Georgia," replied Tripp. "Athens."

"That's a little bit of a distance from here. Trains?"

Tripp nodded. "More often than not. Other times, we hitch a ride from anyone who'll give us one."

"That happen often?"

Tripp flashed a knowing grin. "It happens a lot with the college female set."

Sam chuckled.

Tripp handed Cash a small metal flask. He unscrewed the cap and sniffed the contents, bourbon. He wasn't much of a bourbon drinker; come to think of it, he could only recall ever drinking it twice before. *Oh well, I guess this is time number three.* The liquor coursed its way down his throat and into his belly, creating a warm sensation throughout his body. *Not bad.* He passed the bottle back to Tripp, who took a long pull then handed it off to Sam.

Cash found Tripp and Sam intriguing. He wanted to know more about their lifestyle. Where they've been, how they get around. Did they go to a lot of parties? What were the women like? Cash had grown up seeing drifters—he had a basic understanding of their lifestyle. He never met any he genuinely liked before and he intended to make the most of this chance encounter.

He already liked Sam, and he realized right away that he had a lot in common with Tripp. Cash had a powerful feeling that fate had played a role in bringing these two into his life at that moment. This could be the ticket out of a dead-end life he was looking for.

"So, how long you been doing this?" asked Cash.

Sam shrugged. "I don't know, man. I kinda lost track of time."

"You were out for at least a year when I met you," replied Tripp.

"Right, right," agreed Sam.

Cash took another hit from the flask. "So, what made you want to do it?"

"Opportunity presented itself, and I took it," replied Sam.

"I met this girl who rode off and on," said Tripp. "She was hot and liked to have fun." He winked. "She showed me the ropes, then went her own way. I couldn't imagine ever going back to my old life after that, so I kept on riding. Not long after, I met up with Sam."

Tripp took a swig from the flask. "You ever hopped?"

Cash shook his head.

"Ever think about doin' it?" asked Tripp.

"I am now," replied Cash.

A mischievous grin spread across Tripp's face. "Well, my friend, you're in the right company."

The hours slipped by, Cash lost all track of time as Tripp and Sam regaled him with stories of their travels, hardships, and triumphs. They told him about the parties, the drugs, the alcohol, and the women; they also told him about the near catastrophes, the lousy weather, the bugs, and the occasional hunger. Hardships aside, all of it sounded amazing to Cash. He wanted to live it so bad; he could taste the oil and metal already.

"Yo, Cash," said Chris. "It's nearly midnight. Kyle and I are gonna head home. You comin'?"

"If you really want to check it out," offered Tripp. "There's a camp not far from here. Lots of riders there waiting to catch on. You can come with us and see what it's like."

"Yes," blurted Cash. He didn't even need to think it over. He couldn't think of a single thing he wanted to do more.

As his friends headed home, Cash followed Tripp and Sam to the train yard.

Anticipation vibrated throughout his body, his mouth barely able to keep up with his mind as he rattled question after question. To their credit, Tripp and Sam took their time and answered all of them.

They arrived at the train yard and continued past to an area filled with dense forest-like overgrowth. Cash followed as they cut into the densely-packed thicket and trudged for at least a half-mile until he caught the scent of fire. A soft glow emanated ahead—a beacon in the darkness. Music and laughter floated through the night. It was as though they had stumbled upon a hidden village, a place only a precious few were allowed to see.

They stepped into the clearing to the sight of a small bonfire; the skunky smell of cheap weed wafted through the air. Cash was unable to make out how many people were there; it seemed like nearly a dozen. What he could see, though, was a group of young people, many close to his age range or slightly older, laughing and dancing by the light of the fire.

"Tripp, Sam, you brought us a guest," said a young woman as she sauntered close.

Short dark hair, wearing a crop top and torn jeans, she stopped in front of Cash and smiled one of the prettiest smiles Cash had ever seen. Or maybe it was the bourbon—he couldn't tell.

"I'm Tamera. You can call me Tam or whatever." She shrugged and winked.

"Cash," he replied, his throat dry and tense. He thought he heard his voice crack, but again, he was too buzzed to really care.

Tam reached out, wrapped her arms around his neck, and pulled him close. "Well, Cash, you're welcome to come and sit with us. Would you like that?"

She stared up at him with crystal blue eyes; the scent of fire and earth emanated from her body. Her fingers played casually with his hair sending a warm tingle up his spine. Time froze, his heart pounded in his chest, his whole body was on fire.

"Yo, Tripp, got that twenty you owe me?"

Cash glanced over as a blond man with messy hair and a scruffy beard approached, wearing a worn-out backpack.

"Mags," said Tripp as he hugged the man. "Great to see you. And, yes, I got your twenty."

A train whistle blew. Around the fire, several people howled in response to the whistle.

"That's our ride," said Mags as he stuffed the money into the pocket of his dirty denim jacket. "D.B. gear up," he called over his shoulder. He turned back to Tripp and Sam. "These Greenies." He shook his head. "You always gotta tell 'em what to do." He clasped hands with Tripp. "Catch ya later. We're off to Salt Lake." He reached his hand out to Cash. "Nice to meet you." He leaned closer with a questioning look on his face.

"Cash."

Mags smiled and nodded as he shook hands. "As I said, nice to meet ya, Cash. Hopefully, when we run into each other next time, we'll be able to hang for a bit."

The whistle blew once more; it was much closer. Around the fire, the pack howled in response. A dark-haired, gangly teen carrying a holey backpack materialized from a glowing cloud of red-orange smoke.

He stepped up and nodded at Cash, then leaned close to Tam. "I'll catch ya later," he said.

Tam released Cash and hugged D.B. goodbye.

"Well, we'd love to stick around and shoot the shit with y'all, but we got better things to do," teased Mags. He slapped D.B. on the arm. "Let's go."

With a final farewell, they disappeared into the dark brush.

Tam took hold of Cash's hand. "Come on," she said, leading him over to the fire.

She took the time to introduce him to everyone, he did his best to pay attention to all the names, but the only thing he could think of was the feeling of her hand in his. She pulled him gently over to an open space where they took a seat. Like magic, another flask materialized; he sniffed the contents; it was not bourbon this time. Steeling himself, he tilted his head back and took a large swig. Hot fire poured down his throat, cascading into his stomach where it churned like molten lava.

As he gasped for air, he made a mental note to avoid that flask the next time it came around.

Sam took a seat on the other side of the fire with a guitar in his hands. "Give me some requests," he said to the group.

A round of shouts erupted, calling out songs from every genre.

Sam smiled and began to play.

Cash felt more at home than he could ever recall feeling in his life. The music, the people, the scent of fire—the raw energy; this is where he was meant to be. These were his people. This was the life he had been looking for.

Sometime during the night, Tripp and Sam offered to take him along with them to Seattle—and he jumped at the chance. A life of travel and adventure beat out another day in Geometry class any day. With the sun peeking out above the trees, Cash made his way back home. Excited and still feeling buzzed, he made a list of the items he would need to bring with him as he walked the familiar route home.

Sleeping bag, blanket, coat, and gloves. Did he still have that small camping stove? He would need at least a couple changes of clothes, not too much; he had limited space in his backpack.

Still very much in his own head, excited over the prospect of getting away, he didn't even notice his dad in the living room chair by the front door.

"Where the hell have you been?"

Cash's euphoria dispersed like a fine mist in a warm breeze. A deep dread settled in its place.

Paul got out of the chair and stood face to face with Cash. His clothes rumpled, his hair a mess. He looked exhausted, as though he hadn't slept all night. The anger on his face was impossible to ignore.

"Answer me. Where the hell have you been all goddamn night?"

Cash shrugged.

"You think you can just saunter in here whenever? What is this a hotel or something?"

Still no response. All Cash wanted to do was get his things and leave. He shoved past the old man and walked down the hall toward his bedroom. His dad followed close behind, emanating waves of growing rage.

"Don't just walk past me. You're in my house—show some respect."

Cash spun around and glared at his father. What stared back at him was a complete surprise. It was not the face of a man who had both inspired and terrified Cash as a child; it was the soft, aging face of a defeated man. For the first time in Cash's life, a veil had been lifted, and he realized how unintimidating his father really was—how sorrowful and broken.

Unable to look into that face any longer, Cash turned away. "I'm leaving," he said without venom, anger, nor remorse.

Paul's face paled, and his eyes grew wide. "What the hell do you mean, leaving? Where exactly do you think you're going?"

Cash walked into his room and pulled out his pack. "I'm heading out with some friends."

"The hell you are!"

"How are you gonna stop me?" asked Cash as he stuffed items into his pack. "It's done. I'm leaving."

"Yeah?" Demanded Paul, "And how are you gonna get around, big guy?"

"Trains."

"Come again?" Paul shook his head and raised his eyebrows.

"Trains, we're riding trains."

Paul stepped back and crossed his arms. "Let me get this straight; you're gonna leave here to become a friggin' hobo? Is that what you're telling me?"

Cash did not respond. He stuffed nearly every t-shirt he owned in his pack, followed by a couple extra pairs of jeans. At the bottom of the drawer be found an old wooden cigar box. He remembered when his grandfather gave that to him; he thought the box was the most fantastic box he had ever seen. A wry smile spread from the corners of his mouth. Kids believe all sorts of shit is impressive when it's really just so dumb. He flipped the lid open to view the contents one more time. A fifty-cent piece. A cheap necklace that was given to him on his fourteenth birthday by his first girlfriend, Melissa. A purple rabbit's foot and an old, child-size pocket knife. Junk. Nothing but junk. He closed the lid, shoved the box under the remaining clothes, and slammed the drawer shut.

His father continued from the door, "Are you stupid? What the hell is wrong with you? Are you stoned?"

His gear all packed, Cash glanced one more time around the room, making sure he didn't forget anything. It was hard to think with the old man going on and on in the background. He ran through the list of what he needed; he was pretty sure he got it all. As Cash moved to walk out of the room, Paul blocked him.

"You're not going anywhere. Put your shit back now."

Cash did not move. He stared directly into his father's eyes, realizing at that moment that it wasn't his family he hated; it was their life. He couldn't imagine a worse fate than to end up like his parents, middle-aged with nothing but calloused hands, a sad little run-down house, and a mountain of bills. Who in their right mind would even think that an endless nine to five grind was a good idea. Add the house and the kids, and you could forget all about ever doing anything remotely enjoyable again. No, he felt no hatred. He really felt cold, paralyzing fear that he would one day be exactly like his father if he stayed. Lost, broken, hopeless, and sad.

Cash stepped forward, staring down at his father, unblinking. He was leaving this dead-end life behind. If he had to fight through the old man to do it, so be it.

Paul blinked; the look of defeat swept across his face. He looked down at the floor and stepped aside.

Cash brushed past him and headed for the door.

"This is gonna kill your mother, ya know," Paul said, his voice quivering. "You're not even gonna wait 'till she gets home from work to say goodbye?"

His mom. Cash paused in the middle of the living room. He had forgotten about her. He didn't want to hurt his mom, but he had to leave. He finally had a chance to escape the endless nightmare of barely getting by. Life was about adventure and happiness. She, of all people, would know that. She'll understand, he told himself.

"Son," the voice was sad. "Son, look, I'm not good at saying the right words." his voice trailed off. He merely stood, staring at Cash, silently pleading.

Cash spun around at the threshold of the front door. "Goodbye, Dad," was all he said, then he turned and walked out the door.

The early morning air had an electric charge to it, or maybe that was coming from Cash. His body hummed with excitement, his mind reeled with all the possibilities. Walking with purpose, he left his old neighborhood, past the high school, through the city streets he spent his childhood exploring, and out to the campsite.

When he arrived, Tripp and Sam were the only ones still there. The fire was nothing more than a pile of charred wood and ash.

"You owe me a ten," Tripp declared.

Sam chuckled and pulled out his wallet.

"What's this?" asked Cash as he dropped his pack on the ground.

"Just a little wager," replied Tripp, "Sam here was sure you weren't gonna come back. I told him there was no way in hell you were gonna stay. Turns out, I was right." He chuckled and stuffed the bill into his pocket.

The next train whistled its approach.

"That's our ride." Tripp clasped a hand on Cash's shoulder. "You ready, Greenie?"

"More ready than I've ever been."

"Good, good." Tripp smiled. "Remember that when you're hungry and freezing your ass off somewhere in the middle of nowhere."

The whistle blew again, beckoning.

Sam pushed past them, breaking into a jog. "Let's go!"

Cash looked around one last time, above the trees and to the buildings beyond. He had only ever known this city. He could hardly wait to see others. All of them. The energy of new possibilities coursed through his body. He turned on his heels and followed Tripp and Sam into the thicket.

"To Seattle! And wherever the hell else we decide to go after that," he shouted.

As if on cue, the whistle blew.

The trio howled in response.

THE END